Scai is not a witch

In one day Scai has gone from being considered just unusual by the people of her little Welsh village to an outcast fleeing for her life. Left on the church steps as a baby, she knows nothing of her history—or her abilities. Did she really stop the rain just by wishing it to stop? But she is determined to learn all she can. Travelling alone to find her family seems to be the only way she's going to find the answers she seeks.

Her journey leads her to the comical old knight Sir Dagonet, who tells her that she is one of a magical people called the Vallen. Together they continue on, joined by the handsome Dylan and the fiery Bridget on a new quest—to find the fabled Merlin's Chalice, said to hold all the power of the entrapped wizard. Together, Scai, Dylan and Bridget discover that they are the long awaited Children of Avalon, destined to save the world from power-hungry Lady Nimuë—unless she kills them first.

Along the way, Scai finds magic—both in the wind and air that she can control at will, and in the sweet ache of a first love that she cannot.

Other books by Meredith Bond

The Merry Men Quartet:
An Exotic Heir
(originally published as Love of My Life)
A Merry Marquis
(originally published as Miss Seton's Sonata. Look for it in 2014)
A Rake's Reward
(originally published as Wooing Miss Whatley. Look for it in 2014)
A Dandy in Disguise
(originally published as Dame Fortune)

The Vallen Series:
Storm on the Horizon, a historical paranormal novella
Magic in the Storm, a Regency–set paranormal romance

"***In A Beginning***", a short story featuring Lilith

Chapter One: A Fast Fun Way to Write Fiction

Air:
Merlin's Chalice

Children of Avalon, Book One

Meredith Bond

Cover art by Nina Banerji
Editing by Alicia Street at iproofreadandmore.com
Formatting by Anessa Books
ISBN-13: 978-1495963834
ISBN-10: 1495963837

Merlin's Prophecy

Ten score years shall darkness helm
The vessel of King Arthur's realm,
Wending through time's storm—tossed sea
To ground upon this prophecy.

This shadowed epoch shall conclude
By the might of the seventh brood.
Of Avalon, the children three
Will restore right and harmony.

Hark ye to the Lady's line!
The sixth of seventh will assign
Herself to perish with the wind,
Helping to save all mankind.

Seven of seven will blaze
A path through time's dark'ning haze.
Her heirs will be the ones to heal,
And renew sorcery's appeal.

The seventh from my own blood
Will ride the crest of magic flood.
Blending with the powers' peak,
He will bring the peace we seek.

But the mightiest in the land
Will be She — who by her hand
Condemned me to my earthen tomb.
She will see her talents bloom.

Her growing might will presage
The dawning of the golden age.
Unmatched power shall wield she —
Unprecedented sorcery.

But Avalon's child will not fail
To discover my stony grail.
Then one, wielding the power of three,
The greatest earthly force will be.

My power will render her accursed,
Unless the trio all die first.
Or she will be, I prophesy,
Destroyed by one and children three.

Chapter One

Tallent, Wales, 899 AD

I *couldn't stop shaking. I was cold. So cold—and soaked through.*

"It's okay. You're safe." Dylan's soothing voice warmed my ear.

Relief eased through my body, relaxing my tensed muscles, letting me breathe, finally. But I still couldn't stop the tears from coming. I hated to cry, but I'd been so terrified. I'd been so certain I would drown. That I'd never see Dylan again. Never... It had been too close. If he hadn't.... But he had. He'd come back and saved me.

I rolled over, snuggling closer into his arms, letting his soothing words calm me. He was warm and he held me tightly.

He smelled of the water—ever so slightly fishy, but clean and fresh. I loved his smell, and right now there was nothing so comforting. I rubbed my cheek against his soft skin, against the strong muscles of his chest.

"I didn't think you would come," I said, trying to stop the sobs that were still shuddering through my body.

"I will always be there for you. You know that," he murmured into my wet hair.

Dylan's arms were tight around me, his body so warm. But I couldn't stop shaking...

I was wet. Soaked through.

Why was I wet? I took a deep breath. I couldn't smell him anymore. What *was* that smell? Wet feathers? That wasn't right.

I opened my eyes. Bound in my blanket, I could hardly move. But I was still soaking wet, still shivering with cold. I blinked, trying to clutch on to my dream as it began to fade away. My tiny attic room was the same as ever. My wardrobe stood on one side of the door, the table with its basin on the other. What was the dripping...? Oh.

I looked up. Through the thatch of the roof came a near steady stream of water, falling directly onto my bed. After two weeks of nonstop rain, the water had finally found its way through the roof.

I groaned. Whoever that man in my dream had been, he'd felt so good, and now he was gone and fading from my memory faster than I could stop it. I could no longer even recall his name. I'd known it in my dream, but now all I could pull up in my memory were his dark curls and how nice it had been to snuggle up to him. Now I was cold and had to get up before I got deathly ill from lying in a puddle of water. And there was the prayer meeting to prepare for. I sighed.

I unbound myself from my blanket, rubbed myself dry and threw on a woolen dress. I didn't care that it was still summer. The autumn was coming, and the mornings had become too cold to run about in thin cotton anymore—and the rain wasn't helping.

Chapter Two

"Hallelujah," Tomos exclaimed, dropping to his knees. The careworn farmer rocked fervently back and forth. "Hallelujah!"

Looking from Tomos, to my guardian, Father Llewellyn, around to the other men and women standing in the prayer circle with me, and back to old Tomos next to me, I was ready to drop to my knees as well. I was suddenly weak and tired, almost out of breath, and my fingers were tingling.

It must have been all that praying. It was the only explanation for why I felt as if I had just run the length of the town and back.

But then I stopped and listened.

Something wasn't right. The room was absolutely silent.

I turned and followed the farmer's eyes to look out of the window—and lost my breath again. The sun was shining! There was bright sunlight where just a minute ago there had been driving rain.

I ran to the window to be absolutely certain, but my knees buckled under me and I dropped into Father Llewellyn's chair at the sight of a sky so blue. The brilliant sun was pouring down its light and warmth onto the village green, just as I had imagined it in my mind, not a minute ago.

As the warm humidity seeped over the windowsill and into the room, I took a deep breath and closed my eyes against the brightness of the morning, just smelling the sunshine. A laugh burst out of me and I held my arms out, wishing I could embrace the beauty of the suddenly fine weather.

After so long it was finally, finally clear! Two weeks of rain. Farms had flooded. Crops were ruined. The river had been running wild, overflowing its banks so much that even the mill, which relied on the steady flow of water to turn the wheel and grind the grain, couldn't run properly. Stocks of flour were running low. Tempers were running high.

And now, it was clear. Blue sky. Sunshine.

I couldn't hold it in any longer. Letting out a whoop of excitement, I jumped up and turned back to join Tomos in his calls of thanks. But Father Llewellyn's eyes caught me—I froze in place. Suddenly I didn't feel like celebrating any more. Like a cold breeze, Father's serious expression blew the happiness right out of me.

He was staring, not past me out into the sunny morning, but straight at me. All of my joy crumbled into a dry uneasiness. It was an odd light I saw in Father's eyes. The chill of it brought goose bumps to my arms. I had never seen anything like it before in my guardian's face.

The five other people in the room were also looking at me, although none stared at me in quite the same way as Father. I shrank uncomfortably under his gaze. Had I done something wrong?

"What is it, Father?" I asked, moving away from the window.

Father's eyes shifted for the briefest moment to the other people in the room, but then he softened into his regular repose. He smiled at me, but it wasn't a true smile, no matter how hard he tried to make it so. "Nothing. It is nothing, Scai. I'm just so happy that God has finally answered our prayers." Father stole another quick glance around the room. Giving my arm a pat, he said quietly, "Why don't you go and deliver that basket of food to Ellen now? You'll have a lovely walk in the sunshine."

I wanted to question him more. There was something he wasn't saying. But he had turned back to talk to the others, and I got the feeling that now wasn't the time to probe further. Father would never reprimand me in front of other people, but I didn't know what I had done wrong.

<><><>

I put aside my fears for the time being, determined to be as bright and happy as the brilliant sunshine warranted.

Already the heaviness in the air was dissipating as I walked across the village green. The sun felt wonderful, its warmth beginning to soak into the drenched earth. I almost regretted the woolen dress.

Margaret stepped out of her shop just ahead of me, her face lifted to the sun. The older woman had an expression of such unquenchable joy as she took in a deep breath of sunshine that I couldn't help but laugh and join in with her happiness. But as I did so, she caught sight of me. The woman paused for only a moment, her face losing all of its joy, before she turned and went back into her shop.

I, too, stopped at the woman's abrupt departure. She must have remembered something, I told myself, but a chilly breeze slipped past me as I walked by Margaret's shop.

Taking a step into the bakery just next door, I smiled as my senses were filled with the deep, rich smell of bread so good I could taste it. "Good morning, Nye, isn't it glor..."

"Yes, glorious, Scai. What are you up to today? Not getting your nose into anyone else's business now, are you?" the middle–aged man asked. He narrowed his little eyes at my basket.

I raised it and pulled back the cloth so that he could see inside. "I'm just bringing some food to Ellen to help her— "

"And you want a bread to go in it, I suppose? Don't have much today. With this rain..."

"I would be very grateful. Ellen—"

"Yes, yes. All right. For Ellen, poor thing." He reached past his bulging stomach to hand me a loaf of bread from the nearly empty basket at his side. "Be off with you now, and stay out of trouble."

I paused, hurt at the man's brusque tone and angry that he was still treating me like a child. But the warmth of the sun was on my back as I stood in the shallow shop, so I shoved aside my pride and smiled, giving the baker a small curtsy before continuing on my way.

The sky was a touch duller as I walked toward Ellen's house at the very edge of town. Still, the day was brightened by the shouts of children, finally released by the sunshine from their rainy prisons.

I felt eyes on my back and glanced behind me to see both Nye and Margaret standing outside of their shops watching me.

It wasn't the first time they had stared at me as if they suspected me of doing something. I didn't know why they did this, but I wasn't going to let it bother me. Not today. I pulled the warmth of the sunshine around me and continued on.

The sound of men's voices raised in anger had me lengthening my stride up the hill. Old John, the craggy-faced wheelwright, and the farmer, Dafydd, were standing nose to nose just outside the wheelwright's shop. Dafydd clutched a wheel in his thin, strong hands, grasping and shaking two new spokes. "You call this sturdy? This wheel's got to take the weight of the wagon, the grain, and put up with—"

"The wheel is sound!" Old John curled his hands into fists, ready for them to make his point for him if necessary.

"Good morning," I called out in my most cheerful voice. I narrowed the distance between them in a few quick skips.

The two men turned to look at me, Old John taking a step back from his threatening position in front of Dafydd. "Good morning, Scai, what brings you here?" he asked, narrowing his eyes in my direction.

Dafydd looked at me with a nervousness in his eyes. Lowering the wheel to the ground, he shifted away from me.

I ignored the man's body language, certain that Dafydd would forgive me later. Holding up my basket, I said brightly, "I'm bound for Ellen's." I turned to Old John and asked as gently as I could, "John, you don't need payment for mending Dafydd's wheel immediately, do you?"

"Payment?" Dafydd exclaimed. "I have no intention of paying for such shoddy work!"

"Shoddy work, now, is it?" Old John said, taking another menacing step toward Dafydd.

"Dafydd, you know that Old John's work is as good as ever. Now that the rain has stopped, the river should be back to normal within a few days. Your grain will be ground and sold quickly and then you'll have the money you need to pay for the wheel." I turned back to the wheelwright. "It would be all right if he doesn't pay you until next week, wouldn't it,

John?" I gave him my most charming smile, completely ignoring Dafydd's wide eyes and the fact that his ears and cheeks had turned absolutely scarlet.

Old John's eyes flicked from me to Dafydd and then back again. Dafydd had begun to look madder than an ox with a thorn in his hoof, but he kept his mouth shut in a tight, grim line.

"Is that what it is, then? It's just the rain that has kept you from grinding and selling your barley?"

"And how did you know that, Scai?" said a voice from behind me. I turned and saw Tomos there, along with some of the people from the prayer group, Nye from the bakery, and Margaret as well. Some of them shifted or looked away when I moved toward them. One man turned his head away so I couldn't look into his eyes. But most of them stood their ground, glaring anger and accusations at me.

I didn't know what to say. I didn't know how I knew that Dafydd didn't have the money. It had just been there, in his eyes.

"Well?" Old John prodded.

I turned back to Dafydd. He looked at me, but said nothing—just waited with the rest for my explanation.

I wished I had one to give. "He..." I started.

"I never said a word about not having the money, did I, John?" Dafydd interrupted, turning to the wheelwright.

"No, you never did," the other man concurred.

"And little Michael never said a thing about taking a jar of honey from my shop last week, and yet Scai knew he'd done it. And she wasn't even there when it happened," Margaret said, coming out from between some of the men.

"You made the sun come out today. I could see that Father thought so," Tomos said, coming closer. They all began to surround me. I took a step back, but Dafydd was there, frowning at me.

"I didn't, I couldn't... I can't make the sun come out. That's ridiculous!" I stammered, trying to laugh. My eyes flitted from one person to the next. Surely, they didn't think I had anything to do with the weather?

"You *prayed* for the sun to come out, didn't you, Scai?"

Father Llewellyn asked, as he walked into the crowd surrounding me.

My eyes locked onto those of my guardian. Thank God he was here! Safety and support resonated from his eyes. "Of course I did, Father. We all did."

Father Llewellyn nodded. "We all did," he said, indicating the people who had been there. "We all prayed for the sun, and our prayers were answered."

I looked around at the others, but my momentary feeling of security was gone as soon as I did so. Why didn't they believe me?

"We *all* prayed for the sun," I repeated, hoping to get through to them.

"I still say that you're a witch," Margaret said, glaring at me.

"What? No!" I moved closer to Father Llewellyn. He would protect me. There was nowhere for me to go.

"You're a witch, admit it," Dafydd growled.

I spun around to face my accuser, secure with Father right behind me. "I'm not! Father..."

"Scai is a special young woman," Father said, putting his hand reassuringly on my shoulder, "but to call her a witch after all that she has done to help each and every one of you? She is a kind and caring girl, who helps others whenever and however she can."

A breath of relief escaped from me. They wouldn't hurt me, not with Father there. But that didn't mean that they weren't thinking about it. I could feel them—feel their anger, their fear. They wanted to hurt me. Thoughts of witch burnings slipped through their minds. A woman had been drowned a few weeks ago in a neighboring town, accused of witchcraft. They could do the same to me.

"You all know me," I pleaded with them. I tried to keep my voice calm, but my legs had begun to tremble and feel weak.

"Yes, and we all know that you always know too much," Old John said.

"Witch!" Margaret hissed, taking another step forward.

"No! I just help people," I cried, trying to hold back my

tears. I turned to Father. He would help me. He had to.

"You do help people," he reassured me and the others. "And that is just what you were doing right now, wasn't it Scai? You were taking that basket of food to poor Ellen. Why don't you go and do that?" Father stepped back so that I could move from the circle.

I looked gratefully at Father as I slipped past him. He gave me a reassuring smile, but the look in his eyes told me to get away fast. To run, if necessary.

And I nearly did.

I dared to take one look back but turned right around again. They were all watching me.

Chapter Three

Nimuë's fingers were tingling. It was time. With every sense in her body, she knew it was finally time.

She had been waiting for this for almost two hundred years. It was a rather long time to wait for three children to be born and grow up, but it would be worth it in the end. In the end, she would be the unquestioned ruler of the world of the Vallen—and soon after that, the human world as well. It was only right that the Vallen, a powerful race, rule ordinary humans. Why this was not already so, she couldn't fathom.

And as soon as those children were dead and no longer a threat to her, she would be the most powerful Vallen. It would most certainly be worth such a very, very long wait.

Anticipation sent a luscious shiver through her as she opened her cabinet. Reaching to the very back, she pulled out her fine silver bowl and water skin. The bowl gleamed, reflecting the sun's rays throughout the room, as she unwrapped it and set it on the table. Carefully uncorking the water skin, Nimuë poured the precious liquid into the bowl.

As its scent wafted up to her, her senses were overwhelmed with memories of home. The smell of the flowers and rich earth, the taste of the most delicious fruits and the sweetest vegetables. Her ears rang with laughter and song—everything that spoke of happiness.

It was Avalon. And it was something Nimuë had not experienced for a very long time.

Her eyes stung momentarily with unshed tears, but she blinked them away. This was no time for sentimentality. She had much more important work to do.

Focusing on the sacred water of Avalon, Nimuë willed

the faces of the three children to be shown to her. Despite the distance of seven generations, her connection to them should still be strong enough.

Slowly, the world around her faded away. The pounding from the armorer below, the thumping of horses' hooves on the compacted dirt of the courtyard, even the room around her disappeared from her vision, just as the Isle itself had faded into the mists. The only thing left was her own reflection shimmering in the water before her eyes. Softly, Nimuë blew a ripple across its glossy surface—and through the undulating water, another face appeared, replacing her own reflection.

The face was of a pretty, young woman. She was in her late teens, if not older. Her brilliant blue eyes stared out at Nimuë, laughing, full of love and happiness. Freckles sprinkled across her nose and cheeks. A hand appeared, pushing back bright red curls behind her ears. Seeing the clarity of the image sparked a nagging worry in the back of Nimuë's mind. If they all appeared this clearly in her scrying bowl —could they already be too schooled for her to defeat? No! That could not be. Even though they were adults now, they had not yet discovered who they truly were, nor, even more importantly, found each other. She refocused on the water. And she couldn't have killed them while they were still children. Even she had limits.

The scene behind the girl dissolved into recognizable buildings—Gloucester. A slow smile crept onto Nimuë's face. She had been to St. Peter's Abbey not too long ago. Now, it looked as if she would be paying it another visit.

Nimuë stood back from the water for a moment. The young woman did not look like a killer. She did not look like a powerful Vallen either, but looks could deceive. Nimuë smiled wryly as she reflected: no one would have ever thought that she herself could be so... determined.

But there was something else in this face. Something familiar. Nimuë did not know what it was, and she did not have time right now to try to figure it out.

She blew another gentle breeze over the water and watched as the girl's face dissolved into another. Her own—

no, wait! Not her own, but one so very much like hers it was uncanny.

Her own green eyes stared up at her, set above the same high cheekbones as hers and a nose that, although a bit larger, was very familiar. Even the smile, holding a hint of pain, echoed her own. It was the jaw line, distinctly masculine, that distinguished this face from Nimuë's. This was a young man, who despite his meager years—certainly not much more than twenty—had known sorrow and distress. And yet he smiled at her as if he beheld something very pleasing to his eye. What was it that he was looking at that made him smile in this way?

Nimuë shook such ridiculous musings from her mind. This boy was destined to kill her! Did it matter who he was or what made him smile? No. What mattered was that she find him before he found her.

But where was he? Unremarkable scenery gathered behind him. Green trees made up his surroundings, that and a swiftly flowing stream. There was nothing to mark his location. He could have been anywhere in England or Wales. But this did not deter Nimuë. She would find him; she had no fear of this.

Once again, she blew across the sacred water of Avalon and willed for it to show her its third child. But this image was indistinct, the features hazy and indeterminate. Long, straight blond hair was all that she could make out, and even that was uncertain as it fluttered in a breeze against a brilliant blue sky.

But why was this one so unclear? Did she not know who she was? Of what she was capable? Even at this age—for the girl, like the boy, must be in her early twenties. It must be that. There was no other explanation.

With nothing else to see, Nimuë sat back and closed her eyes in exhaustion. It was not easy seeing into the waters of Avalon, and she was out of practice. One arm dropped uselessly to her side, the other resting on her rapidly rising and falling stomach.

Could she be getting old? The thought made her chuckle. No, thank goodness, she was not old, and if she could help it, she never would be. Just as Merlin had been forever old, Nimuë was determined to stay forever young.

But to do so, she would first have to rid the world of these young people. That they had come to her individually was a good sign. That meant that they had not yet found each other. She still had time to kill them off before they discovered each other and their destiny. But she would have to act fast, of that she was certain. She was nearly too late.

Chapter Four

I walked as fast as I could, keeping my eyes firmly on the ground in front of me. My feet kept time with the pounding of my heart. I watched my shoes appear and disappear out from under the hem of my dress as I strode up the hill toward Ellen's house.

The thin wooden door of the house appeared before me sooner than I anticipated and I almost walked straight into it.

It swung open in front of me. "Oh! Scai, you scared me out of my wits." Ellen took a step back into her house, but then stopped, clearly not moving to invite me in. There was a noticeable lack of cooking smells coming from the house. Ellen should have been well into preparing the evening's meal by now, but the only smell was the stale air from the windows being closed for too long.

I took a small step into the doorway but didn't go any further as Ellen took another step backward as well. Surely Ellen didn't think... no, I wouldn't think about Margaret and Dafydd's accusation. I was not a witch. I was a compassionate person, and I was here to offer my condolences.

Holding out the basket, I said, "I'm sorry, Ellen. I was just about to knock. I brought you a basket of food. I am so sorry about Hugh. He was a good man."

Ellen brushed her hair, now liberally sprinkled with gray, out of her face. "Thank you so much. You are a good girl, Scai." Her eyes swam with tears, but she blinked them away before any could fall into the deep pouches under her eyes.

I handed her the basket with one hand and gave her arm a friendly squeeze. "I know that you'll be all right. You're such a strong woman, Ellen. I can't tell you how much I admire your strength during such a difficult time."

Ellen now truly looked as if she was going to cry, but she held her lips firm.

"And if you ever need any help looking after the little ones, I do hope you will call for me. You know I would be happy to help out in any way that I can," I continued.

"Thank you," Ellen whispered. "Thank you, and God bless you." The woman met my gaze for the briefest moment, before turning away to put the basket inside.

Ellen, too, thought there was something odd about me.

But there wasn't! *I wasn't a witch.*

I clenched my fists and spun away from Ellen's house. How could they think that of me? I loved helping people. I'd never hurt anyone. I'd only ever helped people. Why couldn't they see that?

<><><>

Without a conscious thought, my footsteps started in the direction I needed to go, but by the time I was halfway there my fear broke into tears. I lifted up my skirts and ran the rest of the way.

Aron was hammering away at a horseshoe when I ran into the large empty yard by the river. At twenty–two, only two years older than me, he was the youngest blacksmith the town had ever had. If it hadn't been for Hugh's accident the previous week, he would still be an apprentice. Now, he had all of the town's work to deal with on his own.

I stopped a few yards away from where he stood behind a huge anvil in front of the river. Although I was panting and crying, I knew to keep my distance from where Aron was working. The smoldering fire by his side belched out heat—I could feel the intensity of it even at a distance. As I stopped, he looked up, his hammer paused mid–air.

The hot iron screamed as it was dropped unceremoniously into the pail of water, and within moments I was enveloped in Aron's hot, comforting arms. The worn leather apron he wore was soft against my cheek as I sobbed into his chest.

"Hush. Hush, now." He soothed me, just as he had when we were little and I would come running to him when the other children had taunted and teased me. I couldn't imagine not having Aron in my life to comfort and protect me.

The memory of my dream tugged at me. Warm arms of comfort; a strong, bare chest under my cheek; and a hot kiss turning me into a breath of want and need. The memory of it teased me. It hadn't been Aron in my dream. I'd only kissed him once, and that had felt strange and awkward. Who was it, then? I couldn't remember. I supposed it didn't really matter now. It was just a dream.

My sobs dissolved into soft hiccups as Aron's comfort settled into me. Now that I was with someone I could trust, it would be all right.

"Come inside," he said, taking my hand and guiding me into the barn where he both worked and lived.

Aron rested his hip against his worktable as I hoisted myself up onto it. I took my time, knowing he would wait patiently until I had calmed down enough to tell him everything.

It was much cooler in here, away from the warmth of the late morning sun and the blacksmith's fire. I brushed back strands of my blond hair, so fine they stuck to my face with my drying tears, and concentrated on forming the words in my head that would not sound too stupid or melodramatic. But before I could even complete the thought, the words were out of my mouth, tumbling over themselves like leaves caught in the breeze.

"All of the townspeople think I'm a witch because I know what people are thinking. I know what they've done or haven't done and what they mean to say but don't. Father even thinks I made the sun come out this morning, although he didn't say so. We all prayed for the rain to stop, he himself said we did, but..."

"Hey! Stop." Aron laughed.

My words stopped short. I took a breath and looked up at him. The smile on his face faded as my words settled into him. Grasping my shoulders, he looked me straight in the eye. "Everyone in town thinks you're a witch?"

The disbelief in his voice mirrored my own exactly, and

an air of relief blew through me. I knew he would feel this way. I could always count on Aron.

"I know. It's the most ridiculous thing I've ever heard," I said, beginning to feel better already.

But Aron was no longer laughing, not even a smile graced his handsome face. He was staring at me as if he was really considering whether it could be true.

"Aron!"

"No, Scai, I'm thinking about this." He let go of me and stood back, staring down at the floor for a minute. He began nodding his head. "Yes. It does make sense."

"Aron! No." How could he betray me this way?

"But, Scai, wait. You have to admit that you always know things that others don't. Haven't you ever wondered about it?"

"I'm intuitive," I said, with a lift of my chin.

He shook his head. "No one is *that* intuitive. Do you hear people's voices in your head? Can you read their thoughts? How do you do it?"

I widened my eyes. He really believed that I was a witch! "No. I don't." But then I saw that Aron wasn't looking at me as if he were scared. He looked...well, he looked interested, even curious.

Aron was my friend. He was my *best* friend. Could I not be completely open with him, even if I had never been so with myself?

I closed my eyes and tried to remember the first time I'd been aware that I knew what others were thinking. It had been so long ago I didn't think I could remember. But then a hazy scene flitted through my mind... playing on the village green, the other children moving away from me when I said aloud what each one was thinking. They wouldn't play with me after that.

I had sworn to myself right then that I would only use my gift to help people—and I had. But no one seemed to remember that now. They only remembered that I was odd and knew things that I shouldn't.

So how *did* I know what someone was thinking? I shrugged my shoulders. "I don't know; I see it in their eyes. I just look at them and there it is: whatever they're thinking is in my own mind."

"Do you know what I'm thinking right now?"

I looked up at Aron. A lock of his long brown hair had fallen into his eyes, but they stayed focused on me. "You're...you're fascinated with how I know what someone is thinking. And you wish you could do the same thing. And you need your hair cut."

Aron burst out laughing. "I was not thinking that I needed my hair cut!"

I grinned. I couldn't believe it, but I actually smiled. "No, you weren't thinking that, but you do."

He laughed as he brushed his hair out of his eyes. "But this is incredible, Scai." He lowered his voice and leaned toward me to whisper, "You're a witch!" As if it was the most wonderful thing in the world.

And for a minute, I thought it was, too—until reality caught up to me. Then all the good feelings I had been sharing with Aron blew straight out of me.

"No! I'm intuitive. I see what people are thinking, that's all. It doesn't mean I'm a witch."

"Scai..."

"No. Aron, this is ridiculous."

He shook his head. "Why don't you want to believe this?"

"Because it's wrong."

"Scai..."

"It's wrong, and ridiculous, and..." I blinked away the tears burning in my eyes. How could he? How could he betray me like this? Aron was supposed to laugh at this with me, not take it seriously. *I wasn't a witch!*

"...and it's dangerous and frightening," I finished in a whisper. "Witches are the spawn of the devil. That's what Father Llewellyn taught us, and I believe it."

"But that doesn't mean that you..."

"Oh, no? How do you know?"

"What? You are not the spawn—"

"I don't know what I am. Father Llewellyn found me on the church steps." I jumped down from the table, coming close to landing on Aron's foot, but I didn't care. I wanted to hurt him for even thinking that Margaret and Dafydd might be right.

"I don't know who my parents were. All I do know is that I am not a witch," I whispered furiously, before running out of the shed and heading back to the rectory.

Chapter Five

"Father?" I called as I entered the house. I looked in the drawing room, but it was empty. With a shiver of apprehension, I left the room.

The town had seemed empty on my way back from speaking with Aron. It had been very strange. Usually there was *someone* about. But now there was no one. It was as if they had all gone to hide from me.

And now Father was gone, too. Dafydd and the others hadn't hurt him, had they? I raced through the house, searching, my heart pounding with the sharp stab of fear.

I found my guardian sitting in his study at the back of the house. Relief sent me flying to him. I threw myself at his feet and clutched onto his legs just as I used to do when I was a little girl.

I had spent too many afternoons like this after being teased by the other children for being different, or because my parents hadn't wanted me. Aron had always tried to defend me and had ended up in too many fights because of me. But Father had taught me to turn the other cheek, and so I had always ended up here.

And now, just as he had always done, Father Llewellyn gently stroked my head and murmured words of comfort. When the fear loosened itself from my throat, I whispered, "Father, you don't think..."

"No, I don't think, Scai," he began, and relief rushed through me until he added, "I *know*."

My heart clenched in my chest. "But..."

"No. Hush, my child, hush. I am sorry I've never said anything, but I've known since you were a little girl and able to repeat what was in anyone's mind—even when you clearly didn't understand what it was you were saying."

He gave a little laugh as he remembered. "You were such a funny child. But I could protect you then." He grew sober once again. "I don't know that I can anymore."

Gently, he disengaged my hands from around his legs and dropped down onto his knees in front of me. Holding my hands between his, he said, "Let us pray for God's mercy, child. Let us pray for your safety."

I bowed my head and prayed with all my might. We sat, each lost in our own prayers, until the old priest began to recite the Lord's Prayer. His deep somber voice and the familiar sounds were soothing, even though I couldn't understand the Latin words.

"Amen," I repeated after him. I was shocked to see Father's eyes wet with tears.

<><><>

"Scai. Scai, wake up, my dear." The voice nagged at me. My shoulder was gently being shaken. "Scai, now! You need to be gone." The words were spoken in such a terrified whisper, I dragged my eyelids open.

Father Llewellyn was kneeling next to me on the floor. My bed had still been damp the previous evening, so I'd slept on the floor where it was dry.

Worry creased the old priest's forehead. He turned and looked over his shoulder, as if he expected someone to come through my bedroom door.

"What is it, Father?" I asked, propping myself up on my elbows.

"You must go. Now. They'll be here any minute."

"Who will?"

"The townspeople. Margaret, Dafydd, even old Tomos. I think they must have been up all night. They've built a bonfire in the middle of the square."

"For me?" The words were little more than a squeak—I had no voice, no breath. Sudden terror had knocked it clear of my lungs.

Father nodded, his face a terrifying blank mask.

I was up in a moment, pulling clothing out of my

wardrobe with only one thought in mind—run! Father handed me a bag.

"There's bread, cheese, and a skin of water in this."

I shoved a shift, a dress, and my shawl on the top and then tossed another dress on over my head. Father laced me up faster than I could have done with my trembling fingers.

"Are you packed and ready?" I asked, as he worked.

He paused, looking at me with some confusion in his eyes. "I'm not going with you. You'll have to go on your own, I'm afraid."

"But I can't leave you here. What if they turn on you?" I asked.

He just gave me a little smile. "They won't. I'm a man of God. Besides, I'm old. I would only slow you down."

I didn't know what to say. I prayed he was right. With a breath, I had an idea. "I'll go to England. Perhaps I can find my parents."

A smile lit up Father Llewellyn's face. "Yes! Brilliant. That is what I will tell them when they come looking for you."

I nodded, knowing this was right. "And it is what I will do."

<><>

The sun still hadn't risen when I slipped into the blacksmith's shop to wake Aron. I couldn't leave without saying goodbye.

He protested my calls of his name in his sleep and tried to bat me away with a wave of his hand, burrowing deeper into the straw that made up his bed in one corner of the shed.

"Aron. Aron," I whispered.

With a start he was up, nearly hitting my head with his own as he bolted upright. I backed up. "I'm leaving. I just wanted to say goodbye."

He blinked uncomprehendingly at me for a minute then gasped, as if he remembered what was going on. "What? Where?"

I tried not to laugh at his momentary confusion, while I was sure that on the inside my heart was breaking. I'd never had to do something so difficult as say goodbye to the two people I loved the most.

Father Llewellyn had seen me off, crying so hard that I

hoped never to see a man weep as he had. And now, it was I who was about to embarrass myself with my tears. I blinked them away and forced myself to stay positive. This was a wonderful opportunity.

"I'm going to England. We've always known this day would come." I gave a little shrug and tried for a smile. "I had hoped it wouldn't be so soon, but the townspeople have built a bonfire for me... this is the opportunity I've been waiting for to go and try to find my family."

Aron's eyes widened in shock before he shook his head in wonder. "How do you always turn everything around to see the positive? You're amazing, Scai!"

I swallowed at the lump in my throat and forced out a little laugh.

But Aron turned serious. He reached out and grasped my arm as if he wasn't going to let me go. "Are you going to be all right? England is very far away."

I put my hand over his. "I know. But what choice do I have?"

He couldn't say anything. There was nothing to say.

I moved my hand to his cheek, rough with beard. I did my best to put a reassuring smile on my face. It might have been a feeble attempt, but at least my tears were staying hidden within my heart.

Aron sighed. "There are thieves, Scai. In the forest. I've heard tales of them. They're ruthless and don't think twice about killing those who trespass through their territory. Perhaps I should come with you."

I had to keep myself from laughing. How very typical of Aron to want to protect me. "No. You are needed here. There is no other blacksmith now that Hugh has died. And besides, I'll be fine." I gave his shoulder a loving squeeze. "I'll be as careful as I can and avoid anyone who doesn't seem to be friendly."

Aron didn't seem to be entirely satisfied with this but accepted it as truly the only option. "At least you can use your mind–reading skills to tell if someone means you harm."

Fear clogged my throat for a moment at the mention of my "magic." I didn't want to think about that. I still wasn't ready to accept that I even had this ability. Honestly, I only wanted to put it all behind me.

"Don't talk about my... my skills. Don't even think about them. They're not real. I don't... I'm leaving because I want to find my family. That and because I don't really belong here in Tallent. I never have. And it's long past time that I left."

Aron sighed. "It is true that people have never truly accepted you, but..."

"I'll never forget you, Aron. I... I love you," I said, emotion rushing out of me when my tears could not. I threw my arms around my dearest friend and held on as tightly as I could. Before I was no longer able to contain myself, I got up and ran out.

<><><>

Like a winter storm, my heart heavy but my feet flurrying over the ground, I slipped around the outside edge of the village in silence. There was no need to be so upset, I chided myself. I was going to find my real family—I should be happy and excited.

Instead, I was terrified. I was leaving the only home I'd ever known. My friends, my family—well, my one friend and Father Llewellyn, but they were all I had. My footsteps slowed and very nearly stopped altogether, fear for Father Llewellyn blinding me.

Why in the world was I doing this? I started to turn around but then remembered the alternative. I could go and face unknown dangers—or stay and be burnt at the stake as a witch.

My feet started once again to move forward, this time more decisively. But as I stepped out from the last row of barley into the yawning, empty space between Dafydd's farm and the forest, I stopped short. There, standing in the bright morning sunlight, were three large ravens—their sharp black eyes were staring right at me.

One of them hopped forward to get a better look, cocking its head. I didn't breathe. I couldn't. I knew the meaning of this. Ravens were drawn to magic like a moth to a flame.

They were there for me.

They must have sensed my fear. One jumped into the air flying straight for me. I backed up as quickly as I could without taking my eyes off the huge bird.

With a beautiful, terrifying call, a white hawk appeared from nowhere, plucking at the raven with its sharp talons. The black bird was knocked off course, landing hard on the ground not ten feet from me.

Within moments the other two ravens attacked the hawk.

"No!" I almost screamed. I didn't know why the hawk had saved me, but I couldn't stand for the poor thing to be hurt on my account. I stood there, watching the birds fight—two, and then three on one.

It was a flurry of black and white feathers, sharp beaks jabbing at each other and the hawk's razor–like talons slashing viciously at the ravens. Never had I seen such a fight. I started to step forward, trying to figure out if there was any way to help the hawk, but I had nothing to use as a weapon, and even if I did, the four birds were too close to each other. I wouldn't want to risk hurting the hawk. I could do nothing but watch.

Even three against one, the fight was over much faster than I expected. All three ravens, as if on cue, took off into the air, beating a hasty retreat from the superior strength of the hawk. That left me and the hawk both looking up, watching the black birds disappear into the clear, morning sky.

I felt the hawk's eyes on me before I lowered my own to it. It just stood there, staring at me. Briefly, I wondered if it was contemplating attacking me, but there was no malevolence coming from it.

One small movement from the bird confirmed my suspicions. The hawk bowed its head, acknowledging me. A whoosh of relief escaped from my lips, and I almost laughed with relief.

The bird took a few steps backward then turned toward the forest, as if beckoning me on. I complied, walking across the green. As I took my first few hesitant steps into the dusk of the dense wood, the hawk came up from behind me, gracefully flying around a tree, only to come back and circle around me. It soared up and back to circle me once again, as if encouraging me forward, before spiraling up into the treetops to disappear completely.

I laughed at the bird's antics then watched with a hollow heart as it disappeared from view. Still, I was left with a warm feeling of welcome. And, oddly enough, a feeling that I had a friend somewhere close by. I wasn't entirely alone.

With a brighter step, I headed in the direction the hawk had flown, even though the path had changed to one that was hardly worn at all.

Trees and bushes encroached upon the road, trying to take it over. The farther I walked, the closer the trees became. It felt as if the branches were reaching out for me. As the forest became even denser, the sky was blotted out by the leaves of the trees. Only here and there was a ray of sun able to slip through from between the leaves.

I grew cold in the dark of the forest. My footsteps slowed, and I felt as if I were shrinking under the oppressive, towering trees. A heaviness weighed down on me until I could barely keep placing one foot in front of the other.

And then I stopped. Listening.

Silence surrounded me like a stifling blanket of cool air. A sudden rustle of leaves made me jump, and a small fox ran across my path. Once again the silence descended on me. All I could do was to look up at the trees that hung over me and try to get a glimpse of the sky where the hawk had flown.

I took a deep breath and began to walk forward once more. I would see them again. I would. The sky and the hawk were there just on the other side of this forest, I told myself. But fear still tickled at the back of my neck. There were thieves, wild animals, and goodness only knew what else here in the thick of the forest.

If only I could see the sky.

As my fears increased, my footsteps began to speed up. I moved faster and faster. I had to get through the wood. I had to escape from these oppressive trees, which were always reaching out, ready to grab me at any moment.

I had to find the sky.

I ran as fast as I could for as long as I could. There had

to be an end to this. There had to be a break in the trees somewhere.

Chapter Six

"Hiyah!" Galloping hooves raced toward me from behind. "Hiyah!"

I turned and stood frozen with shock. I knew I should get out of the way. I was about to get run down, but my legs wouldn't move. My mind refused to believe that what I saw was real.

A knight in full, gleaming armor was bearing down on me, his horse coming at me at a full gallop.

I opened my mouth to scream, but nothing came out. I couldn't breathe.

The knight continued to race toward me, his hand raised above his head clutching an enormous sword. He came closer, faster, raising his sword even higher, ready to strike me down.

I was dead. There was no point in moving because I was dead.

I just stood in the middle of the path as my death came closer and closer. At the last second, I closed my eyes and clutched my arms against my body.

The heat and the smell of horse invaded all of my senses. Galloping hooves came within inches of me. My hair flew in the gust of air. And then he was behind me.

He had gone straight past!

I spun around and watched as, with a great war cry, the knight struck his sword into the side of an oak tree. The sword wobbled up and down with the force of the blow as the knight let it go. He continued past until his horse slowed down enough to safely turn about and return.

Ignoring his sword, the knight rode straight up to me.

"You all right? Tell me you aren't hurt, wot?"

"What?"

"What, wot?" replied the knight.

"I...I'm sorry?" I looked past the knight at the tree where his sword was still waving gently.

"I've just saved your life; have you nothing to say?" the knight said, puffing out his chest.

"You have?"

The knight pulled up the visor on his helmet to stare at me.

Behind the shining metal were pale brown eyes crinkled with the lines of one who had spent a great deal of time smiling.

"I...I'm sorry. I didn't...I mean, I hadn't...er, thank you," I said. Remembering my manners, I dipped into a deep curtsey. "Thank you, good knight, for saving my life."

The knight gave me a small bow from atop his horse.

"Er..." I began, glancing back at the sword. "May I ask exactly what you saved me from?"

"What?"

"What was it that you saved me from?"

"Oh. Er, that, er..." The knight gestured randomly toward the tree. "That, er, oak."

"The oak?"

"Yes. It was reaching out toward you and, er, oh, hobnobbit!"

A laugh burst out of me, releasing all the fear I'd pent up just a moment ago. For a minute there, I hadn't been entirely certain that the knight was in his right mind, but clearly even he couldn't keep up the pretense.

There had been *nothing* attacking me.

He laughed in great guffaws, leaning back so far that for a minute I was afraid he would lose his balance and fall off of his horse.

The horse sidled a little, making the knight sit up straight again and pull on the reins to control it.

"Well, now you've found me out, wot?"

"What?"

"I say, you've... oh, never mind." He turned his horse

once again and rode back to the tree. Grasping onto the handle of his sword, he gave a tug. It didn't budge. He pulled hard, and then again, so hard that his horse began to sidestep away.

"Fiddlesticks!" He turned back to me and said, "I say, do you think you could give me a hand, wot?"

"Oh, yes, of course," I said, coming forward. But if this big strong man couldn't pull the sword out, I had no idea what I could do. I reached up and tried tugging at the handle, as the knight had done, but the sword was firmly lodged in the tree.

"No, I didn't mean like that!" The knight laughed. "Of course you can't pull it out like that. Use your mind, girl, use your mind."

I let go of the sword and looked up at the knight. "I'm sorry? I don't understand." But a shiver of apprehension ran over my skin like a cool breeze on a hot summer night.

The knight gestured vaguely. "Oh, I say, you know what I mean. Move it with your mind."

"How could I possibly do that?" It was the most ridiculous thing I'd ever heard. I gave a deliberate laugh, but the knight didn't laugh with me. He wasn't joking.

"You know..." The man dismounted and pulled off his helmet to reveal a shock of silver–white hair above a clean–shaven, grandfatherly face. He put his helmet down on the ground, took a step away from me and the horse, and then just stood staring at me.

For a moment I didn't know what he was doing, but then I noticed that his belt was unbuckling itself. Gently, it came off of his body and lay down on the ground. The tunic he wore over his armor began to lift itself off his body.

I was vaguely aware of my mouth dropping open. I snapped it shut again.

Before the tunic was fully off the man, however, it began to put itself back on again. The knight smiled at me. "That's how."

"But... how did you do that?" My voice was nothing but an awed whisper, but I didn't care. What I'd just seen was... was... well, magic.

He laughed. "I used my mind. I just willed my sword belt

to come off and then my tunic, wot?" His sword belt was still rebuckling itself around his waist as he moved forward again.

I took a step backward, keeping some distance between us. It wasn't that I was scared, precisely. I didn't know what I was beyond confused and perhaps a bit nervous. My skin seemed to be prickling, but I didn't know why.

He didn't seem to notice or mind. He just pointed at his sword and said, "Now, you try."

"I can't..." It was ridiculous.

"Have you tried, then?"

"Well, no. But..." This was more than silly.

"Then you don't know that you can't, do you? If you try it and fail, then, indeed, you can't, but if you try and can then you can't can't, wot?"

I had to stop and think about that for a minute, untying his logic, but I thought it made sense. *Was* it ridiculous? Doubts whispered in my mind. Turning back, I looked up at the sword as it sat lodged firmly in the tree a little higher than eye level.

Could I possibly move it with my mind just by willing it to move? No! That was impossible. A shiver ran through me just at the thought of being able to do such a thing.

"No." I turned away. "I'm very sorry, but..."

"Scared?"

"What? I'm not scared! I just can't, that's all." I didn't even want to think about it any further. The thought alone of doing such a thing was terrifying. The implications!

"But you haven't even tried," the knight persisted.

"No, and I'm not going to. It's ridiculous. I am not a witch. I cannot simply move things with my mind." I crossed my arms in front of me, as if that proved my point.

The knight raised his eyebrows. "No, you're not a witch," he agreed. "But you've never moved anything just by willing it to move?"

"No," I said, stopping myself from even trying to think if I actually ever had.

"Not even, oh, say, a cloud?" he asked, wiggling his eyebrows.

A breath caught in my throat making me cough. I *had*

made the sun come out... no, we'd all prayed for it; we'd all done it together. Father Llewellyn had said so.

"Uh–huh." The knight smiled. "And you've never been able to do anything else that is unusual either, I suppose, wot?"

I bit my lip to keep my mouth from dropping open again. How did he know? Who was this man? Could he read my mind like I could read the mind of others? I caught his smiling eyes with mine, just to check. No. He had no bad intentions. He honestly thought that I was like him.

The knight nodded his head toward the sword. "Give it a try. What can it hurt?"

"Witches are burned at the stake! That can hurt a great deal!" I exclaimed. My throat tightened making it even harder to breathe.

The knight's eyes softened and he nodded his head sadly. "Ah, yes. The stake. Yes, I imagine that would hurt, or at least be awfully uncomfortable, wot?"

I didn't say anything. I couldn't, with my throat so constricted, so I just nodded.

"Well, you don't have to worry about that now. I'm certainly not going to turn you in. And as I said, you're not a witch, even if you can move the sword."

"But then how could I...?" I shook my head. This was all very confusing. "Perhaps you wouldn't tell anyone, but what if someone else..."

The knight looked around at the empty forest that surrounded us. "No one here." He then gave me a little smile. "Come now, just for the fun of it, give it a try."

I looked again at the sword. What *could* it hurt? asked a little voice in the back of my mind. It might be fun being able to move things with just a thought, and it would be good to know what I could and could not do. And, after all, those ravens had sought me out, so I must have some magic in me.

I looked closely at the knight again, but everything he had was on the surface—his gentle laughter and his kind encouragement, "*You can do it, I know you can!*" his body seemed to say although no words were spoken.

I turned and focused my mind on the sword, and tried

to move it. Nothing happened, just as I had expected.

"Oh, come now, try harder. Perhaps if you try it like this." The knight pointed at the sword with his finger. "You can do this," he whispered encouragingly.

Raising my arm, I pointed at the sword as he had done. This wouldn't work. It was silly. But just to humor the old man, I gave it an honest try.

Closing my eyes, I took a deep breath and willed the sword to move. I could feel my fingers grow warm as I imagined it wiggling its way out of the tree and then floating down to rest in the knight's hands.

"That's it! Well done, I say, well done. Wot?"

I opened my eyes and staggered backwards, allowing my hand, which was now pointing at the knight, to drop back down to my side. It felt like someone had attached a bale of hay to it, it was so heavy. Luckily, there was another tree directly behind me. I steadied myself against it, suddenly feeling completely drained. The sword was in the man's hands just as I'd imagined it. A chill ran over me and I pulled my shawl closer around my shoulders.

"I didn't do that! You pulled it out while my eyes were shut."

The knight gasped. "I did nothing of the sort. And I take serious offense at your implications."

"But I didn't..."

"Yes, you most certainly did."

Deep in my mind and in my heart, I knew that I had done it, and a very small part of me was happily amazed. But the rest was absolutely and completely terrified. I felt as if I had just proclaimed my own death.

"Now, I thank you, and I think that you might want to sit down for a moment."

That was definitely the best idea. Already, my legs were buckling under me. I allowed myself to slide down the tree that was supporting me. Had I been walking too much or was it just the excitement of what I'd just done? Whatever it was, my legs were like pudding and my heart was racing.

The knight stood over me with a gentle smile on his face as he formally bowed toward me. "Sir Dagonet at your service," he said, as he slipped his sword back into the scabbard attached to his belt.

I tried to stand up again to curtsy properly, but my legs wouldn't cooperate. Sir Dagonet waved my efforts away with a laugh. "Don't bother to rise, my dear."

Grateful for his understanding, I said, "My name is Scai."

"Scai, eh?" he chuckled. "Appropriate, wot, wot?"

"What?"

"I said...er, never mind." He laughed.

I looked up at Sir Dagonet and couldn't believe what this kindly old knight had encouraged me to do. The words inadvertently spilled from my mouth. "You're a witch?"

He looked horrified at the thought. "No, I most certainly am not! I am Vallen," he said with pride.

"You're what?"

"Vallen. We are a magical people, you and I."

"Me? I'm not Vallen," I said. My mind still hadn't decided if this was all real or just some odd dream.

"You most certainly are. You just did magic, did you not? And you've done so before."

I swallowed hard. What *did* he know? "I'm not a witch!"

"Said you weren't, didn't I?" the old knight shook his head. "Vallen, that's what you are."

"What's the difference?"

"Ah! Excellent question. A witch is someone who deals with herbs and potions and uses the magic created by them. Vallen are magical from within."

"Oh." Oddly enough, that made sense to me.

"Anyone can learn to be a witch. Vallen are born with magic, wot, wot?"

"And you're Vallen?"

He nodded. "And so are you."

"How do you know? Can you tell just by looking at someone?"

The old man laughed. "Oh no. Only the most powerful, and well, I suppose not even them, don't you know?"

"Then how did you know that I was... one?"

"Oh, well... er, ha!" The man began to laugh. "Feeling

better, wot?"

"What?"

"Exactly so!"

My mind was still feeling a bit muddled. I needed to understand this better. "So if you're not a witch..."

"Most certainly not!" the man interjected.

"Then you're not afraid of being burned at the stake or swum?"

"Oh, er, that. Well, no, not really," he admitted.

"Why not? Anyone could easily mistake you for a witch, couldn't they?"

"Yes, yes, they could. But, well, I'm rather old, don't you know. I don't think they'd burn an old man like myself, wot?"

"Oh." I thought about that. It *did* make sense. They wouldn't kill an old man—they'd probably have a hard time believing he was a witch or Vallen or whatever. "I wish I were in the same position."

"What? Being old? It's not all that it's cracked up to be," the knight said, pursing out his lips and huffing a little.

I laughed. This man was funny. But then my very real fears shouldered their way to the front of my mind again. "No. I meant that I wish I didn't have to worry about being burned at the stake."

"Oh! Yes, er, well, I wouldn't worry about it too much, honestly."

"Why shouldn't I?"

"Oh, er, I don't know, really."

Well, at least he was honest, if not entirely reassuring.

"But still," he went on, "you shouldn't worry about it. You just be the best Vallen you can be and you leave all that worrying to... er, well, to others, wot?"

I couldn't help but laugh again. "But I'm not actually Vallen..."

"Not Vallen? I'm sorry? Didn't you see what you just did?" he said, pulling at his sword to remind me that I had just removed it from the tree using only my mind.

My face grew warm. "I... I honestly don't know how I did that. Or, even if I really did do that."

"What?"

"Well, my eyes were closed," I began to explain. I really didn't want to be Vallen or a witch—and not only because I would be burned at the stake if anyone were to find out. Being magical was... different. Frightening.

Sir Dagonet just looked at me with complete disbelief. "Oh, my dear, if you only knew. If you only knew how powerful you were."

A cool wind tugged at my hair. I pulled my shawl closer around my shoulders. "But..."

"No, no. Let's not stand here talking of this anymore. We've got to get moving. What? Oh, yes, get moving! Can't linger here too long."

And with that, he picked up his helmet from the ground and clamped it onto his head. He mounted his horse and then looked down at me. "Well? Coming?"

I didn't know what he expected me to do, so I just looked up at him.

Finally, he reached down his hand and pointed to his foot. "Just put your foot on mine and climb up. Never done this before?"

"N–no." I had never ridden a horse in my life.

"Oh, well, it's easy." He reached his hand out for mine once more.

I followed his directions and swung myself up behind the knight, straddling the horse. It wasn't easy or entirely comfortable. My long skirt bunched up around my knees and I wondered how indecent I looked with a good portion of my legs showing for anyone who cared to see. On the other hand, we were riding through the forest and there weren't very many other people about—none, in fact. So I supposed it was all right.

I nearly fell backwards as the horse began to move forward but saved myself only by grabbing onto Sir Dagonet's shoulders.

"Off we go, wot, wot?" the knight said cheerfully.

Chapter Seven

Father du Lac entered the king's privy chamber. King Edward was leaning over his table studying some papers. His finger traced lines along the page, but clearly he was not happy with what he saw.

"I beg your pardon, your majesty," du Lac said quietly.

The king stood up, his intense concentration shattered.

His startled look dissolved into a welcoming smile when he saw Father du Lac hovering by the door. "Father! Come in, come in. I'm sorry, I didn't hear you. Did you knock?"

"I did, your majesty," du Lac said, bowing low before his king—the sweet, enthusiastic boy he had watched grow from the time he was born to the day when he was crowned king, less than six months ago. It had been, of course, a bittersweet day for du Lac. He had known and loved the king's father, the great King Alfred, unifier of these British Isles. But now it was Edward to whom he owed his allegiance.

"And what can I do for you, Father?" Edward asked, strolling casually forward. "Are you ready for that Bishopric I offered you?"

Father du Lac laughed. "No, Sire, I thank you."

"Ah, then it is land. You have finally come to ask for a piece of land for yourself so that you can enjoy your old age as you should—in comfort."

"No, you are too kind, truly." Du Lac raised his hands to dampen the young king's enthusiasm. He was always trying to get du Lac to take his favors, but honestly, the old priest had no desire for such things, as the king well knew. "I am happy to be in your court, Your Majesty, for as long as you will have me."

The king's eyes crinkled in happiness even as his lips turned down in mock anger. "For as long as I will have you? Why, that would be for as long as you live! I don't know what I would do without you looking out for my soul, Father, and reminding me of the importance of being humble in the eyes of God. You are an inspiration to me and my solace." His voice dropped to barely a whisper. "And to whom else could I confide my deepest fears without concern that they would be broadcast throughout the court?"

Father du Lac spread his hands, welcoming the king's confidence. "I have concern for little else than your eternal happiness."

Edward, always very clever and aware of the smallest nuance, raised his eyebrows. "Concern for *little* else, Father? Then there *is* something else that concerns you? Out with it."

Father du Lac bowed his head and tried to hide his smile at the king's quick—wittedness. But then his true reason for having disturbed his majesty this morning came to the forefront of his mind and all of his amusement drained from him in an instant.

He lifted his head and looked the king directly in the eye. "Sire, I am only concerned about one other thing—it is something I feel is extremely disturbing. Something that needs your immediate attention and, I am afraid, action."

Edward, too, lost his smile. His face became as serious as it had been when Father du Lac had come in and found him poring over the papers that still lay strewn over his table. "What is it, Father?"

"The witches, Sire," the old priest said succinctly, knowing that the king was one who appreciated directness. "They are a serious threat and becoming more so even as we speak."

"Witches?" Edward repeated as if he was certain he hadn't heard correctly.

"Yes, Sire. They are corrupting our youth. They are teaching their devil—worship and spreading their heresies. They must be stopped."

"Witches," the king said again, clearly still trying to make sure that he understood the priest's point.

"Yes. Your father sent out a decree banning all witchcraft and condemning any who practiced it to burn at the stake or be drowned. I would ask that you do the same."

The king drew his eyebrows down, thinking about this. He turned away from du Lac and paced back to his table, where he turned and faced the priest once again. "If my father sent out this decree, then why are there still witches? Why weren't they eradicated?"

That was, indeed, an excellent question and showed that the king was thinking about this seriously. "I am very sorry to say that his order was not followed as it should have been," du Lac admitted. "He did not follow it up with any sort of enforcement. You, Sire, I am certain, will not make the same mistake."

Edward stood looking at du Lac for a moment, but then he abruptly turned and looked back down at his table. "Do you know what these are, Father?" he said, indicating the papers.

"No, Sire."

"They are battle plans," the king told him. "Troop movements. You do realize that we are at war, Father?"

Du Lac began to get a sinking feeling in his stomach. "Yes, Sire."

"The Danes. They are like a disease in the core of Britain. A disease that is spreading, trying to take over everything—trying to kill us." Edward's voice was quite loud by the time he had finished speaking. This was something that upset him immensely. The king had said as much to Father du Lac only the day before when they had met for Edward's daily confession. "And you want me to enforce the killing of witches. Witches!"

"Your Majesty..."

"Father du Lac, you are a good priest and a good friend, but you do not understand statecraft. You cannot possibly comprehend what I am faced with here." Edward indicated the papers once more. "If I were even to suggest to my lords that they send men out to every little village in the country to get rid of the witches there, I would be laughed at. Mocked for my stupidity, my naiveté. I would lose what little respect I have among these men who are only just beginning to think well of me."

He paced back and forth furiously in front of the table. "Father, I am trying to establish myself as a great and powerful king. I am trying to bring my country together to fight this disease that is threatening it. I need my men to follow me into battle against the Danes." He stopped and turned toward du Lac once again. "And you want me to see to the eradication of some witches?"

The mocking tone of his voice stabbed the old priest in his heart and in his hopes. The king did not understand the importance of eliminating these witches. But, clearly, there was no way to convince him of this. Not now. Not when he was so troubled. After all, he was just a boy who had been raised to this great position only a short time ago.

If only there was more time to allow him to grow and consolidate his position. But there was not. This was truly something that should have been taken care of years ago, but King Alfred had had the same problem with the Danes and not the manpower to devote to the extermination of the witches. Father du Lac had let it go then. But he could not afford to do so now.

The priest took a breath, about to muster new argument, but the king forestalled him. "Father, you are concerned about these witches. I understand that, and I respect your opinion that this is something that needs attention."

"Yes, Sire," du Lac said.

Edward strode around the table, thinking. "You say that these witches are corrupting our youths. Teaching them the ways of the devil, right?"

"Yes, that is right."

The words had barely left the priest's mouth when the king continued with, "Then this is a problem concerning the souls of my people—a Christian problem."

"Er..."

He looked up at the priest and spread his hands as if the answer were obvious. "This is clearly an issue that needs to be addressed by the pope."

"But..."

Edward barely let du Lac get in the word. "No, have no fear, Father. You see, you are in luck. The pope's own emissary, Father Bellini, is going to be here to pay us a visit. You may address him at that time. Present the issue to him. I'm certain that he will understand the dilemma and take your petition to his holiness in Rome."

He smiled, so happy to have found a solution to this problem without having to do anything about it himself. "And it will be so much more meaningful, I'm sure, that the decree come from the church. Your problem is solved."

And just like that, the priest was dismissed. The king went back to his papers and his war planning and forgot all about his confessor.

But was this the answer? Father du Lac wondered as he walked thoughtfully back to his chambers. Could this, in fact, be the solution he sought? It was not one that he had thought of before, he had to admit. And the king might be right: the decree might be more meaningful coming from Rome.

Father du Lac was willing to consider this solution—for the time being.

Chapter Eight

Travel was much faster on horseback. I figured that we must have covered the same distance in just a few hours as I had in a day of walking. When I commented on this, Sir Dagonet laughed. "Haven't even pushed the beast too hard. With two of us on his back, I don't want him to get too tired, wot?"

Still, by the late afternoon, it was clear that I wasn't the only one who was feeling tired. The horse had slowed, and I wasn't certain, but I thought Sir Dagonet might have fallen asleep altogether—if it was possible to sleep while sitting upon a horse.

I was very tempted to rest my own head on Sir Dagonet's back, but just as I did so, the trees began to thin. As we entered a small clearing, I breathed a sigh of relief.

My whole body filled with warmth and good feelings in the brilliant sunlight, like a raisin soaked in warm water. All the life seeped back into me and I tilted my head back to bask in the sunlight.

Sir Dagonet, too, perked up—or woke up. "Eh, wot? What?" he said, looking around, a little confused.

"Can we stop here for a little while?" I asked.

The old knight jumped at the sound of my voice, as if he'd even forgotten that I was behind him. "Oh, er, yes, of course. Yes, brilliant idea, brilliant idea." He pulled up on the reins.

I slid off the horse's back and immediately felt all of the aches and pains from sitting in one position for too long. I could hardly walk but forced myself to hobble around the warm grass until the aches began to subside.

Sir Dagonet disappeared into the woods for a minute but

came back looking much more content. That was a good idea. I slipped off to relieve myself as well. When I came back, Sir Dagonet was sitting on the grass nibbling at some bread and dried meat, his helmet on the ground next to him staring blankly at the road beside him.

"Come and have a bite, you'll feel much better for it," he offered.

"Thank you. I'm already feeling much better just being out of that forest."

"Er? Oh, yes, don't like confining spaces, do you?"

"No, not at all," I answered, with a decisive tone that made Sir Dagonet laugh.

We ate in silence for a few minutes, but my curiosity got the better of me and I asked, "What brought you to this part of Wales, sir?"

"Eh? Oh, er, I was in the service of Lord, er, Lord, er...well, of a nobleman. He sent a bunch of us off to deliver a package to King Offa of Wales and, er, I sort of got left behind."

"Left behind?"

He cleared his throat awkwardly. "Yes."

"How?"

"Couldn't quite keep up, don't you know, wot?" He kept his gaze focused on the road, looking back the way we had come. I couldn't tell if he was looking for his lost companions, or he was embarrassed by his admission.

"Oh, how terrible. So they just left you behind?"

"Well, er, yes. But that's all right. I found you, didn't I, wot?"

"Well, yes, but..."

"Shhh!" Sir Dagonet held up his hand to stop me from speaking.

"What?" I turned around to look back into the woods.

"There's a horse approaching," Sir Dagonet whispered. "Quick, hide us."

"What?"

"Hide us! Either this is a thief come to steal all of our worldly goods, or—"

"Someone who could see us burnt as witches?" I

whispered back, feeling the hair stand up along my arms.

Sir Dagonet responded only by raising his eyebrows.

We both stood. I started for the woods, but Sir Dagonet grabbed my arm. "No time for that. Bring down a cloud; we can hide in its mists."

"But..."

"What?"

"I don't know how..."

"And you didn't know how to remove my sword from the tree either." Sir Dagonet just looked at me with a small smile and an expectant look in his eyes.

The sound of hoofbeats were getting closer. I had to try.

I looked up into the sky. A few small, puffy white clouds floated overhead. Pointing up at one, I slowly curled my fingers down toward my palm, pulling the cloud down with them. It wasn't a big gesture, but it worked. And this time my fingers didn't tingle at all. Somehow, pulling a cloud out of the sky was easy compared with removing the sword from the tree.

Still, it was amazing to watch as the cloud obeyed me, descending to the ground. With a giggle, I looked over at Sir Dagonet. The old man beamed with pride.

"Oh, well done! I say, well done, wot?"

Within a moment, we were both enveloped in the cloud, and I couldn't see two feet in front of me. I laughed again, rather thrilled at my own ability, until Sir Dagonet hushed me. The sound of the horse had slowed as it approached the clearing, which was now filled with the white mist of the cloud.

I realized I was trembling. I wished the horseman would just move on.

I wasn't entirely certain whether my sudden chills were due to my fear of the horseman—or the reality that I had just done magic.

I simply could not deny that I was a witch, or, I supposed, a Vallen now. Not to myself, nor to anyone else.

Suddenly, I noticed the cloud thinning rapidly, and a light rain was falling down on us. I could see Sir Dagonet again, and he looked as surprised as I was.

Drops of water clung delicately to him as he turned to look at the rider. I followed his gaze and was met by piercing green eyes—so green that even from this distance they stood out from the man's tanned face. He looked oddly familiar, but I couldn't remember having ever met him.

I took a step backward even as I turned to face the strange, stunningly handsome man. His curly black hair, reached down nearly to his shoulders—his very broad, strong shoulders. There was nothing effeminate in him at all, despite his lovely hair. Indeed, just the opposite. I felt very small and feminine in his presence.

He held his arm out in front of him as if he had pushed aside the cloud. My heart missed a beat as Sir Dagonet strode over to him, saying, "Well met! Well met!"

The man dismounted and bowed politely to Sir Dagonet. Still, he said nothing, just looked from Sir Dagonet to me and back again, his eyes lingering a little longer on me. Perhaps he recognized me as well?

"Well, that was a fine bit of magic, I say, wot?" Sir Dagonet said, pulling the young man's attention back to himself.

The man's eyebrows rose into the curls that hung down over his forehead. He eyed Sir Dagonet warily. "Magic, sir?"

"Yes, of course. Oh, no fear, no fear, we're all Vallen here, I say, wot?" Dagonet said merrily.

The man's shoulders came down an inch as the stress of being discovered seemed to flow away from him. Oddly enough, I couldn't "hear" his thoughts even though I looked directly into his eyes and he looked back at me. I was certain that his were thoughts of relief, though, and I respected him for his caution at being found out.

How odd that the man's mind was absolutely quiet. I looked harder at him and actually concentrated on hearing his thoughts, but there was nothing. I couldn't "hear" him at all. So accustomed was I to being able to know someone's thoughts that this silence made me feel rather uneasy. How was I to know if he was trustworthy or not? There was no way to tell.

Was it him or me? Could I not hear his thoughts because

he was Vallen, or was something blocking my ability?

The man raised his eyebrows at me, but his attention kept going back to Sir Dagonet, as if he wasn't sure who he was supposed to be watching.

I caught Sir Dagonet's eyes for a moment. His thrill at meeting the young man came through loud and clear. So it wasn't me, and it wasn't because he was Vallen.

But then how was it that this stranger's mind was closed to me? And why was he so familiar? I couldn't have met him before—I certainly would have remembered someone whose mind I couldn't read.

There was something odd going on. I knew him, but I didn't know him. I felt I should be comfortable with him, but I was unsure of him because I couldn't read his thoughts. This man completely put me off balance.

"My name is Dylan," the man was saying with a polite smile.

"Sir Dagonet at your service," my new friend said, with an inclination of his head. "And this lovely young lady is Scai."

Dylan bowed to me as I curtseyed to him. "Where are you and your daughter bound, Sir Dagonet?"

"Oh!" Sir Dagonet burst out laughing. "Oh, no. Scai is not my daughter. No, I say, wot?"

Sir Dagonet didn't seem to think there was anything odd or dangerous about Dylan, but then he wouldn't notice his silent mind.

I forcibly pushed aside my worries, determined to give Dylan the benefit of the doubt—at least until I was proved wrong. And, after all, there was something oddly familiar about him. "We only met this morning," I offered, allowing my own smile to shine through.

"Really?"

"Sir Dagonet was kind enough to save me from a threatening tree. After that, it was only fitting that we travel on together." I giggled, inviting Dylan to join in on our joke.

Dylan gave me a confused look, but a small smile played on his lips. "I, er, see, then. Where are you headed?"

"I am going to England. Sir Dagonet has kindly offered to escort me," I answered.

"To protect you from attacking trees?" Dylan asked, finally allowing himself to dissolve into a chuckle.

"Oh, yes, vitally important to protect young ladies from trees. They can be dangerous things, don't you know?" Sir Dagonet laughed with him.

"Well, if you would not mind another to help protect you, Scai, I would be honored to do so," Dylan offered with a bow.

I forced another little giggle. "Never had I thought to have *two* such brave men to protect me on my journey. I am honored indeed." And this way, I could keep an eye on him.

Chapter Nine

I moved with care through the forest. It was dense with enormous oak trees and reaching beeches intertwining with majestic hawthorns. This was an old forest indeed.

Gnarled branches reached outward and then twisted back on themselves, creating a beautiful, intricate knot that twisted this way and that. I ran my hand along the rough bark of a tree, following one branch as it wove in and out of the others. Careful to keep hold of the same branch, I moved toward the center.

The branch split and intertwined with other limbs from other trees, like long, reaching fingers. At last, I came to the heart of the knot, where sat a stone, white goblet. Branches blended with the veins in the stone, as if the cup had grown from them like a leaf. But when I reached out for it, I found that the branches were merely cradling the chalice within their gentle claws.

It took both my hands to lift the large cup from its pedestal of branches. It weighed down my arms, and I had to be careful not to spill the fresh, sweet-smelling water that filled it. I couldn't resist—I tilted the chalice and took a sip.

A burst of sweetness exploded in my mouth, as if I had bitten into the first fruit of summer. I was filled with a heavenly bliss, all of my senses alive to the taste, the smell, the feel of the water in my mouth. Closing my eyes, I let the taste and the feeling of joy wash over me—and suddenly I was flying free, floating in the water, hampered only by the luminescent walls of the goblet all around me. The sides were so far apart I could stretch out my whole body and not reach from one end to the other.

Floating in this blissful chalice, the water gently supporting me, lapping deliciously over my body, I had no fears. All my worries were gone. I was in the right place; I was doing the right thing. I had a purpose, and it was to be here.

I twisted and laughed, joyful beyond anything I had ever felt before. But even as I did so, the water turned freezing cold. Icy fingers poked into my sides, my arms, my legs.

My happiness ripped away as I was engulfed. I cried out but choked on ice-cold water.

I awoke from my dream, coughing and drowning in truth. Tumbling and turning, I flailed my legs and arms, frantically trying to find air. My feet struck something hard—the rocky river bottom. I pushed off with all my might, managing for a moment to get my head above the raging current.

I gasped in a single breath, but didn't have time for another before liquid hands pulled me down once more. The weight of the water sat on my chest, pressing me to the bottom. I tried to move, but it was too much. The water held me fast against the floor of the river.

No, I would not submit!

I fought against the river once more, clawing my way up, twisting and turning to escape. I reached the surface and stole another quick, gasping breath. I had to find a way out, something to grab on to. A rock, a branch, there had to be something. I tried to look around, but the water's strong grip pulled me under again, pressing me down, this time pulling me along as it rushed downstream. I would surely drown if I didn't do something fast. Blackness closed in on me as I ran out of air again. For a moment I shut my eyes and stopped struggling.

No, I would not give up. *Out.* I had to escape from the icy fingers of this water. When my feet touched the bottom, I pushed off again. Rejecting the smothering water, I reached out for the sky with all my might. With all my heart. With all my will.

Once more, I pushed the water down with my arms, reaching up again. I pushed down and then reached up. Again and again, until it was no longer my own arms I saw in front of me but...wings?

I had wings!

And I was no longer in the water. I turned my head to one side and looked down. The raging river was far below me.

I was high in the sky. But the river seemed to be growing bigger, coming closer. I turned my head back up into the air and pumped down once again with my wings. Again, I rose up into the air. I was flying!

I laughed at the wind in my face. Never had I been so light, so free. The air fluttered through my feathers as I stretched out my wings to glide along on the current.

But the river caught my eye once more. Something dark fought against the water. Sir Dagonet! Fear clogged my throat.

I banked my wings and headed straight toward the old man. He was thrashing around in the water, trying to keep his head above the current, just as I had been doing only moments ago. But how could I get him out?

In the dim light of the early morning, I spied a tree just ahead of me that had fallen into the river. Its roots were still firmly attached to the bank while its trunk lay sprawled halfway across the water.

With two strong pumps of my wings, I sped toward it, landing with a bump on my own feet. Straddling the tree trunk and tightening my legs around it with all of my strength, I desperately reached out my arm into the river.

"Sir Dagonet! Sir Dagonet, grab hold of my hand," I called to the knight, who was approaching in the rush of the water.

He surfaced for a moment. I called to him again, gripping the tree even harder with my legs. Just as the man was about to be swept past, I reached out and grabbed his floundering arm. My own arms felt as if they were about to be torn right out of my body, but I held on with all of my strength.

The excitement of flying, which had allowed me to forget my exhaustion, was gone, leaving only leaden limbs in its place. There was no way I was going to manage to save Sir Dagonet by myself. I searched the bank for any sign of Dylan, but he was nowhere to be seen. We must have left him back where we'd fallen into the river, unless he had already succumbed to the pull of the watery hands.

No, there was no one but myself—and my magic!

With my grip on Sir Dagonet's hand as tight as I could

make it, I stared intently at Sir Dagonet and concentrated. Taking a deep breath, I imagined him coming closer to the tree on which I was perched. Closer. Closer.

My arms were ready to fall right off. My hands were losing their grip. I was about to drop from weariness when the weight stopped pulling at me. I blinked a few times. Sir Dagonet was reaching out to grab onto the trunk. His hand slipped once but then found purchase. With a great heave, he pulled himself out of the water.

I grabbed onto his tunic to guide him and to make sure he didn't slip back into the churning river.

He lay panting on his stomach, his legs still dangling into the water. I rested my head on his heaving back.

Slowly the two of us managed to catch our breath, but I didn't think I would ever be able to move again. I was so tired.

As soon as he was able, Sir Dagonet pulled himself the rest of the way out of the water then dragged himself, and me, to the shore.

Dylan ran up to us just as we stepped foot onto dry land. "Are you all right?"

"Yes, thanks to Scai," Sir Dagonet said, still out of breath.

"I...I couldn't believe it. Scai, you turned into a bird and flew straight out of the water," Dylan said. His face was pale, but filled with awe.

My mind was little more than mush from my exhaustion. "I...I was a bird?" I whispered, my teeth beginning to chatter in the cold air of the autumn morning. But even as I said it, I knew that he was right. I had felt myself fly. I had flapped my wings and glided above the surface of the water. It had been incredible!

Even the shivering Sir Dagonet was looking at me now in amazement. He, who was used to magic, looked at me as if I had done something truly extraordinary. I wished I had the energy to ask him why he was looking that way, but I was too far beyond tired. My legs gave out and I sank to the ground, unable to even stand any longer.

"I don't know how I did it. I just..." I paused. "I just needed to get out of the water, and so I did," I explained to the two men with a shrug of my shoulders, even as I curled my knees up against my chest and wrapped my arms around them.

"Well, let's get warm first. Then you can see if you can do it again, wot?" Sir Dagonet gave an encouraging smile.

"I don't know that I can," I said, reluctantly allowing Dylan to pull me to my feet. I could barely move, but if I didn't I would surely die of cold sitting there on the riverbank. Tears threatened me as I realized just how far I was going to have to walk to reach our campfire and my dry clothes.

Now would be an excellent time to turn back into a bird so that I could fly back to the fire, but there wasn't an ounce of energy left in me. I could hardly walk.

Sir Dagonet, too, was pale with exhaustion, but he turned and put his arm around me and supported me all the way back. Resting my head against his shoulder, I forced myself to place one foot in front of the other. Oddly enough, Dylan looked ready to drop as well—even though he didn't have a drop of water on him.

<><><>

"I don't understand how we ended up in the river," I said, dropping to the ground after coming out of the woods where I'd changed into dry clothing. I was still tired. All of my muscles ached, protesting every move I made, but at least my initial exhaustion was beginning to wear off.

"Nor do I. Quite odd, wot? I woke up in the water."

"So did I." I looked over at Dylan, who was seeing to his horse. "And yet Dylan wasn't pulled in at all."

"He was on the far side of the fire, away from the water, don't you know?" Sir Dagonet explained.

I nodded, remembering that that had been the case. Lucky.

Dylan rejoined us. Was it odd that he didn't make eye contact with either me or Sir Dagonet? If only he would look at me I would...ah, no. I remembered that I couldn't hear Dylan's thoughts. If only I knew what he was thinking...

Sir Dagonet was nibbling at a piece of bread. It was a good idea. I was famished. I reached into my bag for the bread I'd brought with me. "I'm still quite tired from the water and,

I suppose, from flying."

Sir Dagonet nodded, a little twinkle lighting up his eyes. "Not surprising. That was a lot of magic you did, wot?"

I stopped as the realization of what I'd done hit me. Whenever I had performed magic it had been intentional, conscious. How had this suddenly become something I just did naturally? It had felt good. Normal. I couldn't help shaking my head in astonishment.

"Doing magic makes you tired?" I asked.

"Oh, yes. Weren't you tired after removing my sword from the tree?"

"Yes, I was."

Sir Dagonet nodded. "Using magic is like using your muscles. It takes strength and energy, but the more you do it, the easier it becomes." He paused to take a drink from his water skin. "I can take off and put on my armor without a thought because I do it every day, but ask me to move something larger or heavier and it would take a great deal out of me, don't you know."

I nodded. "That makes sense. It doesn't take any energy for me to hear what other people are thinking because I do it all the time, but, as you say, I was very tired after moving the sword, and I'm still exhausted from turning into a bird."

"What do you mean, 'hear' what other people are thinking?" Dylan asked, his eyes widening a little.

I gave a guilty little shrug. "When I look into someone's eyes, I...I just know what they are thinking at that moment— except for you. I tried to hear your thoughts yesterday but couldn't for some reason," I admitted rather sheepishly. "Normally I know right away what someone is thinking when I look at them, but from you there was absolute silence."

He nodded, his expression serious. "I keep my mind closed to others. You should, too, if you can."

"You keep your mind closed?" I asked, amazed that such a thing was possible.

"That's handy! How did you learn to do such a thing?" Sir Dagonet asked, clearly as intrigued, and possibly as suspicious, as I was now.

Why would someone always have such protection, like

armor covering their mind, as if they were expecting someone to attack them at any time? It seemed like an unnecessary precaution—unless you had something to hide.

Dylan shrugged. "I just figured it out. My tutor could listen in on the thoughts of others, so I learned to block out her intrusions."

A laugh burst out of me, dispelling some of the tension. "That would be awkward if you hadn't done what you were supposed to. She would know right away, wouldn't she?"

Dylan gave a small smile. "As I say, I learned pretty young to close my mind to others."

"But you can open your mind if you want to?" I asked.

"Oh, yes." He looked at me and, without opening his mouth, said silently, *"But I always keep it closed, just as a precaution. You never know when someone might be listening."*

I gasped. "You projected your voice into my mind!" It was incredible. How did he do that?

Dylan gave me a mischievous smile. "You can probably do it, too, if you try."

A shiver of excitement ran through me. I *could* try it. I was beginning to thoroughly enjoy testing out new magic and trying to find the limits of my abilities.

I was so excited at the prospect of trying out the new magic that I pushed aside my suspicions of Dylan for the moment and reached inside of my own mind. Looking at him, I silently projected the words *"I'm trying. Can you hear me?"* at Dylan.

"Yes, that's right. It was strong and clear. Normally, I can't hear what others are thinking, but I could hear you because you put the words into my mind."

I laughed and clapped my hands. I could feel the effort that it had taken to do that small bit of magic, but it was so little that I could dismiss it easily. If nothing else, I was learning new magic from Dylan. But he was always on his guard... My worries poked at me.

Sir Dagonet heaved himself up off the ground. "We've spent the whole morning here. About time we set off, wot?"

Dylan stood up as well, although much more reluctantly.

"I'm still tired," I admitted, "but not so much that I can't travel on, especially on horseback."

"There's the girl!" Sir Dagonet said with approval. He turned to Dylan, who was gathering up his saddlebag. "And you're getting some of your energy back, too, Dylan?"

Dylan started and jumped back as if Sir Dagonet had just jabbed a knife at him. "Me? I have no lack of energy."

"No? You seemed to be quite worn out after our little adventure in the river." The smile on Sir Dagonet's face didn't quite reach his eyes, but I forced myself to stay out of his thoughts. "Maybe it was just the excitement of the moment or the rushing water, wot?"

I glanced over at the river now. It was as calm as it had been the day before. So how was it that it had turned into such a violent, raging maelstrom earlier that morning? It didn't make any sense.

Dylan turned away to place his saddlebags on his horse's back, but didn't answer Sir Dagonet.

Could *Dylan* have had something to do with the river rising? Was that why he was tired, because he'd used a lot of magic churning up the river? Was it even possible that he could have turned such a placid stream into the raging river I had experienced?

I didn't know enough about magic or the limits of it—but if I could make clouds move, maybe Dylan could affect the movement of the water.

It was rather scary that he could, and would, do something like that—but it wasn't something I could dismiss, not in light of his already suspicious behavior.

Still, the thought terrified me. If it were true, then Dylan had tried to kill me and Sir Dagonet.

Chapter Ten

Nimuë stared into the water of Avalon. After smelling it again after so many years, she found herself going back to it again and again.

She missed her home.

How ridiculous! She was not a child any longer. Yes, she had spent most of her life on that island, but she had not been back for almost two hundred years—not since she had closed the mists in on it. Not since she had trapped Merlin in that tree.

The world had died a little when Merlin had no longer been a part of it. She had felt it. Everyone, even the lay people, had felt it.

But, still, she did not regret it. She did not regret entombing him, not for an instant. "Merlin had simply outlived his usefulness," she murmured to herself.

"Do you really think so?"

The voice caught Nimuë unawares. She started, looking around her room. The bed, wardrobe, trunk—all were as normal. There was no one there.

"Nimuë, tell me you do not miss him. Tell me you do not miss the way things were," the voice said again.

This time Nimuë looked down at the water in front of her. Her sister's visage shimmered in the slightly undulating liquid.

She had hardly changed a bit. But then, time moved very differently on Avalon than it did here in the outside world. Morgan Le Fey's strawberry blond hair had only the slightest touch of silver glittering within it. Perhaps there were a few more lines around her pale blue eyes, but certainly nothing that said that she was well over two hundred years old.

"Sister! What a surprise," Nimuë exclaimed with honest joy.

"You are looking well, Nimuë," Morgan said, cocking her head a little to the side as she looked up at her.

"Of course. My magic is strong. Although I live in this world, I still age as if I were on Avalon." Nimuë chided herself silently for her curt answer. Why could she never speak nicely to Morgan? She had not seen her sister for a long time. She had missed her, but still she could not speak to her in anything other than a churlish voice.

"And yet, the years pass by so much more quickly for you. It does not, however, stop you from remembering, or thinking about your old...alliances, shall we say?" A sly smile crept over Morgan's beautiful face.

"If you are referring to Merlin, you know we had more than just an *alliance*."

"But you never truly loved him. You bore him a child, and yet your heart was left untouched."

Nimuë suppressed a grimace of pain as her sister's words cut straight into her heart. Morgan would never know, never understand the love she'd had for Merlin. "I suppose you loved Arthur with your heart and soul, then?" she said, as always, swapping blow for blow.

Morgan's face lost any trace of a smile. "Yes, I did. And I still do."

"Which is why he still lies there in state."

"And will do so until the time is right."

"Yes, yes, until the world needs him again," Nimuë said with an exaggerated sigh.

"Until they are ready for him." Morgan's words were clipped with anger.

Nimuë sighed for real this time. It was the same old thing. Honestly, her sister never changed.

"Now tell me, sister." Morgan interrupted Nimuë's thoughts. "What is it that makes you think so hard of Avalon and Merlin? What is it that has called me to you once more?"

Nimuë paused. She had not realized that her thoughts would draw her sister to her—she had forgotten. "The prophecy," she answered shortly.

"Ah, the prophecy. Merlin's last. Yes, I remember it well. Has it begun?"

"I have seen two of the three children in the water. They are grown, but the three have not yet met."

"And the chalice?"

Nimuë scowled. "I do not know where it might be."

Morgan nodded, clearly enjoying her sister's ignorance.

"It does not matter. It will not come into play," Nimuë insisted.

"So you will kill the Children of Avalon before they have had a chance to find it?" Morgan asked dispassionately.

Nimuë gave a little shrug. "Of course. He allowed for the possibility that I would do so." She paused. "He knew me well," she said, her voice softened, remembering.

She pushed away her memories—they would not serve her now. She had much more important things that concerned her. "They are no match for me. I will stop them," she added with deadly quiet.

" 'One will gain the power of three...' " her sister quoted.

" 'And the mightiest force in the world will be,' " Nimuë finished. "I assure you, I have not forgotten. I will not kill them right away. Unless there is no other alternative, I will keep them alive until I have gained their powers."

"Capturing them will be much trickier than simply killing them," Morgan pointed out.

"I know. But while they are adults in this world, in ours they are little more than children, after all. It should not be a problem."

Morgan nodded. "Good luck with that." She smiled. An unseen breeze blew across the water and her sister disappeared into the ripples.

Nimuë stood staring into the silver bowl for another few minutes. The vision of the girl, the redhead, came to her mind and suddenly she knew exactly who it was the child had reminded her of. It was her sister! She had the same smile. The same mouth.

Of course! The Lady's line. The prophecy had said that two of the children would be of the Lady's line. Naturally,

Merlin was referring to Morgan. And of his own blood—that would be the boy with her face. Nimuë smiled. He may be of Merlin's blood, but he had her own handsome visage.

After two hundred years, her and Morgan's own descendants were going to try to destroy her. How ironic! Merlin did always enjoy a good joke.

Well, as Morgan had said, good luck with that. Nimuë laughed.

Chapter Eleven

With effort, I pulled my attention away from Dylan, who had now mounted his horse. Sir Dagonet suggested that I ride sitting sideways to accommodate my skirts. I nodded, accepting his hand to help me onto his horse. I didn't feel quite as secure as I had riding astride, but it was certainly more comfortable—and my legs weren't showing indecently as they had been.

As it neared nightfall, Sir Dagonet and Dylan began looking about for a likely place to stop for the night. A sound caught my attention. Dylan seemed to hear it, too, because he turned suddenly and looked at me.

"What is it?" Sir Dagonet asked.

"Someone's in great distress. Can you feel it, Scai?" Dylan asked.

"I can't feel another's emotions, but I hear it," I said, as Dylan dismounted. He took a few hesitant steps toward the woods that clung to the road we were following. A trickle of a stream led from between the trees and emptied into the river to our right.

Tying his horse to a tree, he disappeared into the woods.

I dropped down off of Sir Dagonet's horse and followed him.

I found him squatting next to a woman who was huddled over the stream. The woman was on her knees, rocking back and forth, her face hidden in her hands.

"It's all right, now. It's all right," Dylan murmured.

I noticed that the woman's shoulders were shaking as if she were laughing—or crying. Squatting down on the ground on the other side of her, I gently placed my hand on her shoulder. "Please, let us help you."

The woman looked up at me. Her eyes were filled with tears and despair. She shook head. "You can't. There is nothing that you can do." She buried her face in her hands once again.

"*Her husband has left her*," I projected into Dylan's mind, not wanting to say the harsh words out loud. "*He's gone to serve the local lord, to fight for him. She doesn't know what she's going to do without her husband. She loves him deeply and is afraid he'll be killed.*"

Dylan caught my eyes. "*Thanks, I'll see what I can do now.*"

He turned back to the woman, clearly dismissing me. But I wasn't ready to leave him alone with her. I wasn't certain I trusted him enough, so I stood up and moved away, but stayed within sight.

Dylan settled himself down onto the ground next to the woman, placed his hand gently on her shoulder and began speaking to her in a soothing voice. I couldn't hear what he was saying, he was speaking too softly, but the woman stopped her rocking and turned her tear–stained face to Dylan's, listening to his words.

She then began to speak to him. She told him of her life and her family—four children and her husband's parents. They all lived together in the village not too far from here. But the local lord had come looking for men. He'd offered them a huge amount of money if they would come with him. Her husband couldn't pass up the opportunity, but she desperately wished that he had.

"He's going to return to you," Dylan told the woman.

Her eyes grew wary. "How do you know this?"

But Dylan just shrugged his shoulders. "I just know. Do you believe me?"

The woman thought about it for a moment and then slowly nodded her head.

"Good. Because it's true. He's going to come back to you. It may not be for some time, but eventually, he will be back. Until then, you and your children will be fine." He spoke with absolute certainty, and something else. There was something else in his voice—a touch of magic, perhaps? I couldn't put my finger on it, but there *was* more. There had to be because the woman looked very calm now and almost happy.

"That was a very good thing you did," I said, after the woman had left to return to her home.

Dylan stopped short at my words.

I had waited for him just inside of the woods by the road. I didn't know what to think of him anymore. Only that morning I had believed him capable of intentionally harming, perhaps even killing, myself and Sir Dagonet, and now he had been so kind to this stranger, using his magic and his words to make her feel better and allay her fears. So which was he, good or bad? I couldn't figure it out. It was disturbing.

"You heard me speaking to that woman?" he asked.

I nodded.

Dylan's mouth formed a slash across his face. "How dare you eavesdrop on my conversation with her? You had no right to do that."

My mouth dropped open. "But I told you what was wrong, why she was there crying."

"Yes, but then you should have left. You seem to have no concept of privacy," he said, before turning and walking away from me.

"Why are you so angry?"

Dylan spun back around. "Because you listened in on a conversation that you had no business hearing."

"But...I don't understand why you wouldn't want me to hear your conversation. It wasn't private. And I do know when not to listen," I retorted, stinging from his angry words. "But this didn't seem to be a time when I shouldn't."

"Well, it was," he said. He turned away, but didn't move. Instead, he muttered, "I would appreciate it if you wouldn't tell anyone what I did."

"Why? And who would I tell?"

Dylan turned back around. "I don't know. Sir Dagonet, or anyone. I don't like people to know..." he stopped.

"To know what? That you help others?" I didn't know what to think of this.

"Yes."

"How did you help her, by the way?" I couldn't help

asking. The only thing that I could make out was that he had said a few very kind words, but the woman seemed extraordinarily relieved for just that.

Dylan shrugged and looked off toward the stream. "If I touch someone, I can—I can project feelings into people. I can make them angry or calm. It's a rather powerful ability."

"Yes, it certainly is," I concurred, amazed that anyone could have a power like that. "So, you just made her feel calm and happier?"

"Yes..." Dylan paused and looked me directly in the eye. "You won't tell anyone that I did this," he said firmly.

I heard the words in my mind as well as normally—and then I felt the oddest sensation. It was as if I knew that even if I wanted to tell anyone of Dylan's ability, I wouldn't be able to. The information was locked in my mind.

"What, what did you just...?" I asked, suddenly feeling panicked.

"I'm sorry," he shrugged, not looking at all repentant. "I put a suggestion into your mind."

"A suggestion? What does that mean?"

"Well, although it's called a suggestion, it's really a command. Now, even if you try to tell someone about my ability, you won't be able to."

I nodded. "Yes, I can feel that. Can you remove it?"

"I can. But I don't want to."

I opened my mouth, so angry I barely speak. "What? What do you mean, you don't *want* to? You can't just go around putting locks in people's minds! That's not right."

"I know, but sometimes it's necessary to do that. It ensures that others don't give away your secrets. I don't do it often, I assure you."

"But you should never do it. It's wrong."

"It's necessary."

"No. It's never necessary to impose your will on a person in this way." I was beginning to panic. The magic Dylan had put into my mind was snaking itself down, slowly winding its way around my throat, choking me.

Closing my eyes, I forced myself to calm down. Taking a few deep breaths, I slowed my rapidly beating heart. And then I attacked my problem—this "suggestion" that Dylan had put into my mind. It was like a lock, but like a lock it could be pried open. I did just that, prying the suggestion out of my mind. The lock burst, and in the same shot of energy I projected into Dylan's mind, "*You will never do that to me again!*"

Dylan's mouth dropped open, but I didn't wait to hear what he had to say. I spun around and returned to Sir Dagonet, who sat facing the river a short distance away.

Still furious, I took my bag from where it was strapped to his horse and threw it onto the ground next to where he was sitting.

Sir Dagonet jumped. "Hobnobbit! I lost it."

"Lost what?" I asked, dropping down onto the ground next to my bag.

"The fish. I had nearly lured it onto my hook and now it's gone."

"Oh." I drew my knees to my chest and wrapped my arms around my legs.

Sir Dagonet narrowed his eyes at me. "I say, something's wrong. You're strung tighter than a string on a long bow. What is it that's got you ready to snap?"

I tried not to smile at Sir Dagonet's colorful analogy. I glanced behind me to see if Dylan was there. He wasn't, so I told the knight all that had just passed. I noted with satisfaction that his eyebrows went up a notch when I told him about the "suggestion" Dylan had put into my mind. They went up another notch when I told him that I had broken it.

What I didn't see was Dylan coming up behind me while I talked. I only realized that he was there when Sir Dagonet looked up and said, "Why didn't you want Scai to tell anyone that you'd helped that woman?"

I twisted around and looked up into Dylan's scowling face.

"Because knights aren't supposed to make people *feel* better. I'm sure you know that," he replied, biting out his words in his anger.

Sir Dagonet looked perplexed for a moment. "And who told you that?"

Dylan's eyes widened in surprise. "Why, my foster–brother... when he beat me for comforting a woman from our local village."

Sir Dagonet just shook his head and gave Dylan a sad smile. "Well, he was wrong, don't you know? It's a knight's duty to save the damsels in distress, whether it be physically or emotionally. Did your foster–*father* never tell you that?"

"No," Dylan said. "He left most of my training to his eldest son."

"You weren't raised by your own parents?" I couldn't help but ask. Was he, too, abandoned by his parents? Was that the connection I felt with him?

Dylan and Sir Dagonet turned to look at me, and then Dylan answered, "No. From the time I was seven I lived with a foster family whose duty it was to train me to be a knight."

Oh. A slight feeling of disappointment wafted through me. I brushed it out immediately, knowing it was wrong.

Sir Dagonet nodded in agreement with Dylan. "That's right. Boys from noble families are sent to another nobleman's home to be trained, don't you know. Weaponry, horsemanship, how to care for armor, all that a knight needs to know, wot? In return, the boy works as a page for his foster family—only fair. At thirteen, he becomes a squire to a knight in the household and completes his training until eighteen or so when he is knighted himself."

Dylan nodded and then added, "I was also taught to read, write, and work with numbers. My foster–mother taught me how to use my powers."

"Excellent, wot!" Sir Dagonet approved.

"You were *trained* to use your powers?" The words blurted out of my mouth as I was engulfed by jealousy. Not only hadn't he been abandoned by his family, they had made sure he had everything he needed. Everything.

Dylan raised his eyebrows—could he sense how jealous I was? "Yes. My parents deliberately chose my foster family knowing that they would be able to teach me to be both a powerful Vallen and a knight."

"Clever, wot?" Sir Dagonet said, nodding his head in approval.

I shoved my unkind feelings out of my mind. "Have you seen your parents since they sent you to live with this foster family?" I asked, thinking of how lonely I had been growing up without my own parents.

But my question seemed to catch Dylan off guard. He thought about it for a moment and then shrugged. "I've seen my father a few times. He came for visits and to check on my progress."

"Not your mother?" I couldn't help but ask.

"She died at my birth," Dylan said, without a touch of emotion to his voice.

My heart wept for him, but I was relieved that his father had taken some interest. I was sure that I was taking Dylan's experiences too much to heart, so I pushed them out of my mind and asked about the other thing that had sparked my curiosity. "So your father knew that you were a powerful Vallen, even when you were as young as seven?"

"Oh, yes. I think he knew even before I was born that I would be," Dylan said offhandedly.

"What? How?"

Dylan suddenly looked a little wary. "I, er...I don't know."

He was lying! I didn't know how I knew that without being able to see his thoughts, but I was certain of it. I looked to Sir Dagonet to see his response, but his face was set in its usual light smile.

I was certain Dylan wouldn't be so careless as to reveal anything further, so I turned the conversation back to where it had begun. "So you are a knight, then?"

Dylan's scowl returned. "No. I was made squire to my foster–brother, but he's enjoyed my services so much that even after over five years of service as his squire he still seems to be in no hurry to have me made a knight."

"Oh, I say, that's not right," Sir Dagonet exclaimed.

"No. That's why I left his service and have struck out on my own."

Sir Dagonet tsked. "A sad case. Not trained to care and then taken advantage of."

Dylan just shrugged. "I've always had to fight for what I

felt to be my right. Nothing's changed, and I can't imagine it's going to in the future. That's just the way life is."

A small smile tugged up one corner of Sir Dagonet's mouth and his old twinkle shone in his eyes. "In the days of the round table, knights always had to fight for what was right. We fought for ourselves, for others, and naturally, for King Arthur. That's what knights do, don't you know? We fight to protect the weak and make sure the strong don't overpower them and take advantage of their position."

"We? You speak, sir, as if you were one of those Knights of the Round Table," Dylan said, his voice laden with amusement and incredulity.

"Oh!" Sir Dagonet looked flustered for a moment. "No, no." He forced out a laugh. "No, I meant *even today*, we knights have to fight for what is right, wot, wot?"

Dylan looked at the old man with narrowing eyes. "Sir Dagonet."

"Eh?"

"Wasn't there a Sir Dagonet who was one of the original knights of King Arthur's round table?"

"Oh, er..." Sir Dagonet began, his fingers seemed to crawl up the left sleeve of his tunic and play with something there.

"He was the jester, the fool, if I remember correctly."

Sir Dagonet's cheeks turned pink, and his fidgeting fingers fiddled around his left wrist. "Not a fool! I say. I, er, he was as brave and strong as any of them. And, er, quite handsome, too, from what I've heard." He paused to preen a bit. "I was named after him. He's, er, my ancestor, don't you know. Yes, my, er, great–great grandfather or something of the sort."

"Really? That must be thrilling, knowing that you're descended from one of the greatest knights this land has ever seen," I said.

Sir Dagonet's face flushed a deeper shade, but this time with pleasure. "Oh yes. Yes. Quite thrilling."

<><><>

Later that night, I went over the events of the evening again and again in my mind. I just couldn't figure out if Dylan was a good person or not. I could feel that I was attracted to him, but I worried that, perhaps, I should not be. I couldn't help but wonder what Father would make of him. I'd always gone to him for advice on how to deal with people. Now I just missed him immensely.

I was absolutely certain I needed to watch and be wary of Dylan, even after he had been so kind to that woman. Now that I knew he could affect one's emotions, I didn't trust him not to fool with mine. I had to learn to block out other magic—fast.

The following day, the road turned away from the river and the forest closed in on us once more. I was becoming reconciled to my feeling of claustrophobia when Dylan began behaving as skittishly as I felt. Suddenly, his pace picked up and Sir Dagonet's poor horse did all that he could to keep up. Considering that he had two passengers instead of just the one, it seemed a little unfair.

Against my better judgment, I suggested that night that I ride with Dylan to give Sir Dagonet's horse a break for a day or two. What I hadn't realized when I made the suggestion was how different it would be to ride behind a man nearly my own age as compared to the grandfatherly Sir Dagonet. Suddenly, I found all of my worries about my attraction to Dylan turned into a reality.

Dylan's strong, muscled shoulders blocked my view of the road ahead. He was much taller and broader than Sir Dagonet. When I held on to Dylan it wasn't the cool metal of his armor that I felt under his tunic, as he had none. Instead, his shoulders were warm and I could feel the movement of his muscles underneath his clothing as he controlled his horse with skill. It gave me an odd feeling in the pit of my stomach, and I found myself rather tongue–tied. The following day, I was just as happy to return to the easy comfort of Sir Dagonet and didn't even think of riding with Dylan for a second day for fear of allowing my attraction to grow.

On the third day after we had left the side of the river, I began to thirst as if I hadn't seen water in a month. Our water skins were just about empty, and so far we had yet to come across even the smallest trickle of a stream. The forest was nothing but unrelenting trees towering over us and encroaching into the roadway. Even the sun was barred from entry into the forest, except for the occasional shaft of light that forced its way through the thick foliage.

As the third day came to a close, my head was spinning with thirst. My mouth was dry and my lips cracked. I had been unable to eat even a bite of my bread that morning, it just crumbled to dust in my mouth, and now I was ready to drop with fatigue and hunger.

With effort, I kept my head upright, resisting the urge to rest it against Sir Dagonet's broad metal back. He, too, was sagging in his saddle and seemed to be doing almost as poorly as I. Dylan too looked wan but managed to keep his head up and his back straight even through the relentless dryness.

We endured another full day of this, but that night Dylan began to speak of turning back.

"No!" I cried, my voice so parched it was hoarse. "There is nothing that will make me turn back," I continued, moderating my tone just a touch.

I looked to Sir Dagonet for backup. As exhausted and dehydrated as I, he still nodded his head. "We'll go on and hopefully come across some water or a village somewhere up ahead, wot?" His voice was weak, but, thankfully, just as determined as my own.

"You may turn back if you wish," I told Dylan.

"No. If you go on, then I shall as well," he replied with resignation. "But I think it is a mistake."

We drained the last few drops from our water skins the following day, and I nearly cried as we did so. If we didn't find water soon... but, no, I wouldn't even think of it. We *would* find water. It was just up ahead.

I convinced myself of this and did my best to convince the men as well.

It was with a jump and a burst of excitement that I greeted the crack of lightning and roll of thunder that tumbled toward us near the close of that day.

I couldn't resist the urge to throw back my head and open my mouth to catch the first of the fat raindrops that fell from sky. Within moments, I was cleansed of the dust that had caked itself onto every available surface of my body.

Oh, it felt so good! So cool and refreshing.

I opened my arms wide and welcomed the rain. It continued throughout the day and the following night. It rained until the road we were following became a river, treacherous to navigate with its unseen dangers of pit holes and rocks for our horses to stumble over.

As the cold rain drenched us all, I pulled out my shawl, but it was no protection against the water that pelted us constantly.

Sir Dagonet shivered in his suit of armor. The metal did nothing to protect him. The rain worked its way into every nook and gap and soaked him to the skin as thoroughly as Dylan and me. Indeed, he could barely move after a few hours because of the rust that was beginning to stiffen the joints of his armor. Luckily, he wore only the top half, carrying the leg plates strapped to his horse's side. So while his legs were free, his body and arms were becoming stiff as a board.

But there wasn't anything to be done for the old man—not until we reached Gloucester, the first city we would come to across the English border.

Chapter Twelve

Father du Lac moved smoothly through the crowded audience chamber. Many of the richly dressed noblemen stopped and stared; others bowed their heads in greeting. He nodded here and there to acquaintances, men he had known over the years—many of whom had sought out his advice on how to deal with the king or had pleaded with him speak to His Majesty on their behalf. Yes, he held a rather important position in this court and everyone knew it. It was one of du Lac's little pleasures.

"Father, how wonderful to see you!" A voice came from behind him, swiftly followed by a clap on his shoulder.

Father du Lac turned and found Lord Lefevre smiling brightly at him. "My lord," du Lac said, with gentle enthusiasm as he bowed his head in greeting. If there was any nobleman he would have wanted to meet this afternoon, it would have been Lord Lefevre.

"It is quite a crowd today, isn't it? It's because of the pope's emissary, I suppose," Lefevre said. The fellow was tall, but he still had to crane his neck above the crowd to see the dais where the king and the bishop sat side–by–side.

"I hope you and your family are well?" du Lac asked.

"Indeed, thank you, Father," Lord Lefevre said, turning his attention back to the priest.

"And everything in Gloucester?"

"Very well. In fact, I have come to report as much to the king," he said. It was clear his lordship was quite proud of the fact that he was bringing such good news in these difficult times.

"Excellent. I am glad to hear of this, as, I am sure, His

Majesty will be." Du Lac paused for a moment and then added a little more quietly, "I may be traveling to Gloucester some time soon. I am glad to hear that all is well there."

Lefevre's eyes widened in polite surprise. "Really? Well, you do know that you are always welcome in my home."

Ah, that was just what he had been hoping to hear. "Thank you. I will look forward to your wife's excellent cooking."

Lefevre laughed. "I'll warn her that you're coming. Now, if you will excuse me, Father, I will take my turn before my king," Lefevre said, beginning to move away.

"I am just behind you."

That stopped his lordship. He turned back around. "Don't tell me that you need to come to court in order to have a word with the king?" he asked a little incredulously. "Don't you speak with him every day at his confessional?"

Father du Lac gave a slight laugh. "I do. It is Bishop Bellini to whom I need to speak today."

"Ah." Lord Lefevre nodded his head, understanding. "Well, come along then, let's see if we can fight our way to the front."

Father du Lac followed behind Lord Lefevre as the man wended his way through the crowd. It was a daunting task, considering just how many men there were in this relatively small room. Finally, he stopped at the sergeant at arms who announced all petitioners to the king and, today, to the bishop.

"Lord Lefevre of Gloucester!" the man called out, motioning for his lordship to advance toward the dais.

Lefevre bowed low and then stood tall to announce in a voice loud enough for all within the vicinity to hear, "Your Majesty, I am come to offer my compliments, and to inform you that I hereby pledge three thousand men to your efforts to rid our country of the Danes."

"Three thousand men? Lord Lefevre, that is a good number," the king replied. "With your men added to those already pledged, we will have an army nearly ten thousand strong." He smiled at everyone around him, truly thrilled at this turn of events. "With this army we will route those Danes and drive them from our shores!"

A cheer went up from all around room as the news spread.

Silently, du Lac gave his thanks at this good news. He hoped that the bishop would be moved by this good cheer as well. A look into the emissary's serious face didn't inspire very much confidence, however.

As he moved away from the dais, Lord Lefevre was greeted with slaps on the back and words of encouragement. Du Lac was happy to watch this camaraderie, but once the excitement in the room had calmed down a bit, it was his turn to step forward and advance his own petition.

"Father du Lac!" the Sergeant at Arms called out.

Du Lac stepped forward, feeling slightly conspicuous in his plain brown robes, especially when faced with the splendid vestments of the bishop before him. "Your Majesty," du Lac said, bowing low before his king. "Your Excellency," he said, bowing again. "I am come to ask that a petition be sent to his holiness, the pope."

The bishop raised one eyebrow but said nothing.

Not precisely heartened, du Lac continued. "Sir, we have a serious problem in this country with the spread of witchcraft. We have been attempting to fight against it for some time now, but perhaps a papal edict will do what the king's decree could not."

The king shifted in his chair and looked off to the side of the room.

Du Lac continued, a trifle sorry to have had to be so blunt in front of His Majesty, especially when the boy was in such a tenuous position. "I fear for the souls of our people, Your Excellency. And especially for those of the children who are being taught devil–worship by these witches."

"Devil–worship and witches? Is this a widespread problem? I was told that, with very few exceptions, the British people love and support the church."

"We do, sir, but as you just noted, there are exceptions."

"You expect me to tax his holiness with your exceptions? A papal edict to get rid of a few witches?" The bishop sneered. He then paused and looked du Lac over in an exaggerated and demeaning fashion. "And who are you, priest, to even put such a petition before me? Who are you to demand such petition be put before his holiness, the pope?"

Shame pierced painfully through Father du Lac for the briefest of moments, but it was shoved aside by burgeoning anger. How dare the bishop look down his holy nose at him? He was the king's confessor! He was...

But the king had heard the emissary's cutting remarks as well and leaped to Father du Lac's defense. "This man is my confessor. He has been the most esteemed cleric in the court since I was a child. You will, sir, speak to him with respect."

Du Lac bowed his head, keeping his eyes down on the ground before him, lest the pope's emissary see the blazing anger he was struggling hard to control.

From the corner of his eye, du Lac saw the emissary wave a hand negligently. "I don't care who he is, this matter is too insignificant for the pope to be concerned with."

"But the souls of my people..." the king argued.

"They must be looked after by Your Majesty. You are a Christian king, you can deal with this matter, or if it is too insignificant even for you, pass it down to the parishes to deal with." The man shifted in his seat, clearly bored with this topic. "Just send out the word that any witches are to be destroyed, and let them take care of it."

"A royal decree was not heeded," du Lac said, having finally gained control of his emotions. "We need a word from Rome."

The bishop shifted his gaze back to du Lac, looking at him as if he were some sort of insect that had crawled up before him. "It is not the obligation of the pope to be the strong arm of your king. It is a local problem, deal with it."

Father du Lac looked to his king. Surely now he *had* to do something about this, if only to save face.

His Majesty did not look at all happy with this. "Very well. Father, my own royal decree will be sent out to all parishes condemning to death any who are caught engaging in witchcraft." He paused and then added even more grudgingly, "And word will go out to all of the lords and landholders in the kingdom to see that this decree is followed."

It wasn't done with enthusiasm, but it was done. "Thank you, Your Majesty." Du Lac bowed low toward his king, ignoring Bishop Bellini, before turning and walking away.

"Your impudence!" the bishop bellowed from behind him. But Father du Lac just kept walking. He was not going to bow to such a man as Bishop Bellini. He didn't deserve respect.

Chapter Thirteen

Sir Dagonet's shivering didn't abate for three days. The poor old man sat with teeth chattering through the pouring rain. There was nothing I could do. I felt so helpless, but I could barely even see the sky, let alone have any effect on it. Stopping for the night brought no relief. It was impossible to get any rest with the rain constantly falling on us. We were beyond exhaustion as our horses splashed through the water, slowly plodding along all day.

Once again Dylan began to speak of turning back, but there was nothing that was going to make me turn around now. We had to be very close, and it was only in Gloucester that we would be able to get help for poor Sir Dagonet. Dylan scowled at me and grumbled, but there was nothing he could do or say that would convince me to turn back.

The trees began to thin out again, and very soon they disappeared altogether, giving way to stretches of fields. Like a blanket being pulled down from covering my face, my breathing came easier and freer, despite the steady downpour that still drenched us and kept our progress slow.

Hope surged through me. Gloucester had to be close by. Soon this interminable journey would be over. I did my best not to sigh aloud.

I looked up into the endless sky and gazed longingly into the distance ahead of us. And with a sudden shock, I realized that the sky I was seeing was as blue as on a midsummer's day! There were no rain clouds in front of us. There were hardly any overhead, and yet the rain continued to fall. How could this be?

It had to be magic. I was horrified and amazed all at

once. Anger hit me like a gale wind nearly knocking me right off of Sir Dagonet's horse.

Sir Dagonet's head nodded gently in front of me. He was asleep. I reached around the old man and pulled on the reins to stop his horse as I had seen him do many times before. The beast slowed until it came to a standstill. I slid off as Sir Dagonet awoke with a start.

"I say, wot?" he croaked, his voice thick with congestion. He looked around to see where we were. But I didn't pause to enlighten him. Instead, I simply ran ahead to Dylan's horse, which was still plodding along in front of us.

I grabbed at his leg as I ran up next to him, shouting, "How dare you!"

Dylan pulled his horse to a stop and looked down at me in confusion.

"This"—I gestured to the rain—"this is all your doing, isn't it?" I glared up at the sky. The few clouds that were hanging overhead skittered away, leaving only bright sunshine and a cessation of the rain.

Dylan didn't say anything but dismounted from his horse.

"You're tied to the element of water. You made the river rise up and pull me and Sir Dagonet into it, and now you are trying to kill us with this unrelenting rain!" When he didn't say anything, I cried, "I can't believe you would do this!"

He said nothing. Indeed, what could he say? He was guilty; I could see it clearly in his eyes.

I pushed past him with a growl to inform Sir Dagonet of what had been going on. I wasn't three steps away when I was knocked off my feet by a gust of wind hitting me squarely on my back. That was followed by a torrential rain, harder than anything we'd had to endure the past few days.

I could barely manage to stand against the force of the wind and rain that pushed at me. Putting my arm to my forehead to try to shield my eyes from the storm, I saw that Sir Dagonet had dismounted.

"Scai! Dylan!" His words whipped past me. "Come back, quickly!" He turned and began leading his horse toward the forest where they could, hopefully, get some shelter from the storm.

But instead of following him, I turned to Dylan. He, too, was attempting to lead his horse back to the forest, but the harder he pushed forward, the harder the wind, which had whipped around to come from the other direction, pushed him back. Somehow the horse escaped the wind and bolted for the cover of the woods.

I was at Dylan's side in a moment, helped by wind and rain.

"All right! I admit it," he called out above the noise of the storm. "I made it rain. I'm sorry! Now stop this, Scai."

Oh, he was one to throw blame about so easily. "Me? I'm not doing this! You stop it. It's your magic," I called out, using the strength of my anger in my fight to stay upright against the force of the storm.

Dylan caught me with an arm around my waist as I was about to blown away. "What do you mean? This isn't my magic. I'm not doing this!"

Holding on to his arm, I regained my footing, but had to keep my head down against the rain that bit into and through my thin dress. If he wasn't doing this, then who was? Confusion shifted through me. I tried to look up at Dylan, but rain and wind whipped into my face and I was forced to tuck my head down again.

It was all both of us could do to stay on our feet as we clung together. "Scai, you've got to stop this. I can't." Dylan's words flipped past me.

I shot a look up at him. "I can't stop it!"

"Yes, you can. This wind is your domain."

"And the rain is yours. We'll do it together," I said, practically having to scream to be heard above the storm.

Dylan nodded. He shifted himself so that he could grasp both of my hands. As soon as he did so, heat and magic jolted up my arms. I grabbed hold of it with my mind and pushed back with my own.

"Good," Dylan said, nodding approvingly.

I dared to look up at him. Immediately we locked eyes. And just like that, we were bound together, almost as if someone had tied a mental rope from him to me. I was completely connected to him—almost a part of him. Somehow, despite the wind and rain, I felt better than I had in a long time. Warmth and energy coursed through me. Hope and determination followed, giving me a strength I'd never known before.

Dylan gave me a surprised smile—he must have felt it too. But then, as fast as the moment had come, he pushed it aside and called out, "Now, on three we'll put an end to this storm. One..."

"How?" I interrupted.

Dylan looked confused for a moment and gave a little shrug. "You just will it to end. Imagine a blue sky and the sun shining."

That was something I could do. I nodded.

"One, two, three!" Dylan called out.

I formed a picture in my mind's eye of what the field had looked like before the storm had hit. It was hard concentrating with my eyes open, staring into the intense green of Dylan's eyes. There was the wind and rain to contend with, as well. I just wished it would stop so I could form the picture, so I could see the sun. I concentrated harder, seeing the green of the grass in Dylan's eyes, seeing the clear blue sky and the sun reflected in them.

And then I realized I truly was seeing the sky and sun reflected in his eyes.

A smile grew on his face, until it reached all the way into his eyes, and another kind of warmth shot through me. *How I wished he would always look at me that way.*

"We did it!" He laughed, letting go of me.

It was suddenly cold without his warmth, without his magic. A lonely sadness whipped through me, but then the excitement of what we had done took over. I let out a little whoop of excitement, until my exhaustion suddenly slammed into me and I stumbled forward.

I would have fallen down if Dylan hadn't grabbed me. I clung to him for a moment and then, reluctantly, let go as I realized where we were. Sir Dagonet came out of the woods—a quarter of a mile away!

"How did we get all the way over here?" I asked, pushing

away from Dylan and taking a few steps toward the wood.

Dylan looked beyond me to where Sir Dagonet stood calling for us. "I don't know. The storm must have pushed us."

"So far? So fast?"

Dylan just shrugged his shoulders. "That's what happens when you create such strong winds," he said, as he began to walk back to Sir Dagonet. I could do nothing but follow in silence.

Dylan still believed I was responsible for the storm, but that was ridiculous. Why would I create a storm like that? I wasn't even certain that I could.

But if I wasn't responsible, and neither was Dylan, then who was?

<><><>

Nimuë crumpled into the most comfortable chair in her chamber.

She could not move. She barely had the strength to even blink. She was completely drained.

It was too much. A full–blown hurricane at such a distance—it took too much magic. And still they were not close enough.

She had hoped the hurricane would blow them closer so she could send her man out to fetch them. But it was not enough. They were only three miles from Gloucester—so close and yet too far.

"Sister! Are you determined to kill yourself before the three have a chance to do so?" Morgan's voice echoed through her chamber.

With great effort, Nimuë pulled herself up to the table that held her silver bowl. Her sister's image shimmered in the water in front of her eyes.

"I will get them," Nimuë whispered. She was too tired to even speak normally.

"But not this way," Morgan stated.

"No," Nimuë conceded, "not this way." She took a breath as her heartbeat slowed to normal. "But I must get them before they join together."

"Two of them are already together."

"Yes, I can see that. But it is in Gloucester that they will meet the third."

"Do you not think it will be easier to wait until they are all together and to get them all at once?" Morgan suggested.

Nimuë thought about this. "No. Individually they have less of a chance."

"Yes, perhaps that is wiser—they are very strong," Morgan agreed.

Nimuë nodded. She had been shocked to see the two young Vallen working together to subdue her storm. But Nimuë was not worried. She could still easily best them if needed. The trick was to keep them alive—she wanted their powers. She would need to drain them before she could kill them.

"Right now they do not trust each other," Nimuë continued, partially thinking aloud.

"After your storm? Yes, I am certain you're right. They will each think the other responsible for starting it."

"It is just as I had planned. I have planted the seeds of distrust into fertile ground."

Morgan laughed. "And you are hoping they will blossom?"

"They will bloom and grow, I assure you."

"Well, they had better be quick–growing, because you do not have much time. They are sure to meet the third one soon."

Nimuë agreed and then thought about this. Was her sister aiding her? Making suggestions on how to accomplish her goal? No, that was not possible. There must be a trick somewhere.

"Why are you helping me?" she asked Morgan.

"I am not." Morgan's lips quirked into a lopsided smile as she faded away.

Nimuë sat back in her chair, wondering what her sister was up to. She did not trust her. Not for one moment. The golden girl of Avalon, the one who could never do wrong. Oh, how Nimuë hated her sister. Hated her with an anger that seethed and undulated inside of her like a snake writhing in a cage. It would get out someday. In fact, Nimuë looked forward to it. But she had other work to do first.

She had to capture these three—the Children of Avalon—or else how was she to become the most powerful Vallen? *Then one wielding the power of three, the greatest earthly force will be.* It was her destiny, and if it was not, she would make it so.

She would get them and drain them of their magic—and she would start with the blond.

Chapter Fourteen

I looked down into the pale, drawn face of Sir Dagonet. Had his cheeks been so sunken before? I couldn't remember, but I didn't think so. Maybe they just looked that way because of the two days' growth of beard on them. I hoped that was the reason. I didn't want to think of the alternative. I closed my eyes for a moment and said a quick prayer.

Removing the warm, damp cloth from his forehead, I dipped it into the bowl of cold water on the bedside table. The cold bit into my hands as I wrung out the cloth, dipping it once more to make sure it was as cold as it could be, and then wrung it again with all of my strength.

"You're going to tear that piece of cloth right in half if you wring it so hard," the old man croaked. His voice was dry and thick with the congestion in his head and chest.

I gave him my best smile and tried to hide my frustration. "It's all right."

He reached out and patted my cold, chapped hand with his burning one as I gently placed the cloth over his forehead. "You poor girl. You shouldn't be here tending to a sick old man like this."

"It's all right, sir, truly..."

"No. You should be out searching for your parents." He paused as a coughing fit overcame him. His frail body bucked with the violence of it, and the cloth slipped down his face to cover one of his eyes. Such fits terrified me. I'd seen men die from coughing like that.

I plucked the cloth off of him and used it to wipe his face and the back of his neck while pushing my fears to the back of my mind. "Dylan is out doing just that, although I wish he wouldn't. He's supposed to be searching for a healer for you, and yet all he does is come back with news of this person or that who could be my parent." Even I could hear the frustration in my voice. I clamped my mouth shut and wrung out the cloth in the cold water once again.

Sir Dagonet sighed.

I put the cold cloth on Sir Dagonet's forehead once again. "He had no right, no right to keep that rain falling the way he did. Not only was it wrong to try to disrupt our journey, but it was also wrong to fool with the weather that way."

The old man closed his eyes, and I looked toward the window and wondered if all the noise from the city was bothering him. I had the shutters closed, keeping both the light and noise out as much as possible, but it still managed to creep in through the gaps. The clopping of horses' hooves resounded off the buildings. The creaking and clunking of carriage wheels and the cries of wandering tradesmen and milkmaids were still easily heard. Especially after the quiet of the forest, the city was a very noisy place.

"You should be out there," Sir Dagonet said again quietly.

I looked down at him. He stared up at me with such concern in his eyes. I had no desire to be out there, not while my dear old protector was lying here like this.

I shook my head. "I was just worrying about you—how you can rest with all that noise. You need to sleep."

He gave me a weak smile but nodded. "I'll be all right."

"But..." I clenched my hands together in my lap. "If only Dylan would come back with a healer!"

"Scai, my dear girl, do not worry. I will recover from this. Have no fear, I will not be carried out of here in a pine box, wot?"

He knew. He knew my fears. His words were meant to reassure me, but still, if only Dylan...

I blinked to stop my eyes from stinging and then gave him my best smile. "Of course not. How silly you are, sir. You will be perfectly healthy again in no time. It would just be so much faster..."

The low murmur of voices from the taproom downstairs momentarily got louder. I turned to see Dylan coming into the room. He closed the door gently behind him.

His face, flushed with good health, was like a slap to Sir Dagonet, but the good knight didn't seem to mind. I felt the sting for him, but restrained my growing anger by taking a deep breath and reminding myself Dylan was doing all he could to make up for his misdeeds.

I stood up, wincing, as every one of my muscles protested the sudden movement. Sitting still for the past three hours had made me stiff.

"Well?" I asked, taking a step toward him. I hoped the excitement in his eyes foretold good news.

"I found a woman..." he began.

"Can she come right away? Did you explain his symptoms to her?" Finally! Finally, I cried silently. I was so worried about the old knight, I was desperate for someone to come and help him.

Dylan shook his head, losing his smile a little. "No, not a healer. A woman who might be your mother."

"Oh." I dropped back down into my chair, like a sail that had suddenly lost all of its wind. The hard wood of the chair hurt my bones and muscles all the more for having had a moment's respite.

"No, Scai, she sounds very likely to be the one. She said..."

"Dylan, I told you, I don't want you searching for my parents. I need you to find a healer!" How many times was I going to have to explain this to him? I clenched my teeth together and took in a deep breath through my nose.

Sir Dagonet's hand reached out from under the covers once more and patted my knee. "It's all right, my dear."

"I am looking, truly sir, I am. But I can't help it if someone begins to tell me about their lost child, now can I?"

I didn't say anything, just continued to glare up at Dylan, wishing for him to understand the extent of my anger. The fact that he took a small step back reassured me he was finally getting some inkling of my feelings. The heat of Sir Dagonet's hand caught my attention and I turned back to remove the cloth from his forehead once again.

"You will go and see her, won't you?" Dylan asked hesitantly, as I rinsed out the cloth once again. It took less and less time for it to soak in Sir Dagonet's fever. I worried it was getting worse.

"Scai." Dylan took two steps forward, moving from the door to the bed and put his hand on my shoulder to get my attention. "I told her you would be down soon."

I finished arranging the cloth on Sir Dagonet's burning forehead once again and then sighed. I supposed I could go. It was unlikely that Sir Dagonet's condition would change within the twenty minutes it would take me to go and come back. I would be as quick as I could.

The old man gave me a little nod of encouragement—it was all I needed.

"Very well. I'll go. You will stay here and watch Sir Dagonet?" It came out more as a command than a question.

"Of course," Dylan said without hesitation. He took my arm and helped me up. "It'll do you good to get out, honestly, Scai. You're looking pale and tired."

I couldn't help but sigh once more. He was right. It would do me good to get out of this room. It was exhausting work I was doing.

"You'll be all right, sir?" I double–checked with Sir Dagonet.

"Just fine. Don't you worry about me."

As I opened the door, Dylan stopped me. "She's at the grocer's. It's just down the street to the right."

I spun around. "What?"

"At the grocer's."

"You want me...?" I couldn't believe it. He wanted me to leave the inn?

"It will do you good. Just go. I promise, I'll look after Sir Dagonet." Dylan started to push me out the door.

I stood outside of the closed door for a moment, debating whether I dared to go out. Sir Dagonet's condition was not good, not at all. But then I heard his rumbling voice through the thin door: "Be good for her to get out. Get some fresh air."

"Indeed, sir," Dylan answered.

I was not happy as I made my way down to the taproom and out the front door of the inn, but I was doing what Sir Dagonet wanted me to do. As I stepped out of the door, it occurred to me that I hadn't actually passed through this door for nearly three days.

I couldn't believe it had been that long since we'd come to Gloucester. But considering that all I'd done since we'd found this inn was to care for Sir Dagonet, I wasn't entirely surprised.

I stopped and took a deep breath. It did feel good, filling my lungs, giving me energy and life. I just stood there basking in the fresh air that moved all around me, gently caressing my skin, moving my hair—until a man pushed past me as he, too, left the inn.

Recalled to where I was standing, I set out to the right to find the grocer's.

It wasn't a particularly nice day. The sky was clouded over and it was cool, but there was a fresh breeze, filled though it was with the smells of the city. Autumn was definitely in the air—I could smell it even through the city scents.

And, oh, but it felt good to stretch my legs.

Taking deep breaths and walking at a good pace to work out the cramps in my legs, I reveled in every moment of my freedom.

I found the grocer's and the woman waiting for me.

"My friend, Dylan, said that you had given away a baby twenty years ago?" I asked the woman, after we had exchanged the usual pleasantries.

"Yes. It was a very sad day for me," the woman said, sighing.

"What made you and your husband decide to travel to Wales to give away the child?" I asked. Hopefully this would be the one—then Dylan could stop looking for my parents and concentrate on finding a healer.

The woman's eyes widened. "Wales? Husband? Oh no. I've never been married. The babe was, er, an accident."

"Oh." I found myself surprisingly unsurprised by this

revelation. "Then you gave the baby to another couple to take with them? Because I know for certain that I was left on the church steps in Wales by a couple, a man and a woman." My heart sank just a little as I realized that there was no hope that this woman was the one.

The woman's eyes grew sad. "Oh, dear, no. I gave my child to the Lady Adelaide. I just wished I knew what she did with her." The woman's eyes began to shine with tears, but she blinked them away.

"Oh. Yes. Well, perhaps you can ask her." Perhaps someone, at least, could have a joyous reunion with her mother.

The woman's mouth fell open at the thought and she nodded her head. "Do you think she would tell me?"

"I'm sure she would. And you never know, your daughter might still be with her."

The woman's lips trembled into a smile. "Yes, oh, yes." She reached out and grasped my hand. "What a good girl you are. What a very kind girl."

I smiled at the woman, even as my hopes slid a little further away. Each time Dylan brought someone else for me to meet, my hopes became a little more distant. Very soon I would be certain that I would never find my true parents. Twenty years was a very long time, after all. It saddened me more than I would admit, though. I would be alone, without a family, for the rest of my days.

I took my time walking back to the inn. It almost killed me to return to Sir Dagonet and to my nursing duties. It had been so pleasant to be outside once more. Even if it had begun to rain a little on my way back from the grocer's, it still felt wonderful.

But the closer I got, the more my worries began to compound. What if Dylan wasn't watching him? What if he had opened the window and was letting the cool air into the room making an already sick man even sicker? What if he wasn't changing the cloth or soothing the poor old knight?

Once inside the inn, I practically ran back up the stairs. My anger and frustration, too, returned, even stronger than before. Why couldn't Dylan just stick to his job of finding a healer, instead of wasting my time when Sir Dagonet truly needed me?

"Well?" Dylan asked as soon as I came in.

I jerked my head from left to right, taking back my post next to the old knight. I had nothing kind to say.

Chapter Fifteen

I tried not to slam the door behind me like a petulant child. Yes, I had been forced to leave Sir Dagonet's room yet again. Forced to take yet another break to meet a man who could be a link to my long–lost parents. The woman I had met the day before at the grocer's was all wrong, could this man be any closer? Probably not.

But as I stood there fuming, Dylan's voice filtered through the closed door. "It's getting harder to find people to claim to have lost a child, sir. I had to pay this one."

"I'll give you the money. That girl works too hard, I—" His words were interrupted by a coughing fit. I had to force myself to stand my ground until it subsided. "She needs the break. You just keep doing as you have been," Sir Dagonet finished.

"Yes, sir," I heard Dylan respond as I began to move down the hall as silently as I could. I just couldn't believe how quietly caring those two men were. All of my muscles were tired and aching as I went down the stairs. But there was no one at the corner table of the other inn down the street, where Dylan said I would find the man he had spoken with.

I asked a bar maid, but she just shrugged and went back to her work. She had seen the man, I 'heard' in my mind, and she had seen Dylan hand him some money. She hadn't thought anything of it when the man had left soon after Dylan. Shaking my head sadly at the dishonesty of these city people, I turned to go back to the inn and Sir Dagonet.

It may have worried me to leave the knight alone with Dylan, who certainly didn't care for him nearly as well as I, but I had to admit it did feel good to get some fresh air and a little exercise. Despite the fine day, though, my heart ached with concern. Sir Dagonet had had a bad night. After so many days of fever, I just didn't know how much longer...

No!

Nothing was going to happen to him. Sir Dagonet was going to be all right. If only Dylan would concentrate on finding a healer. I picked up my pace and returned to the inn.

I had paused to allow my eyes to adjust to the gloom of the inn just inside the door when I saw him. Dylan was sitting at the bar with a glass of ale in his hand, laughing at something the fellow next to him had said. He must have come down just after I had left, for his glass was half empty and I hadn't been gone long.

A fury like I had never experienced before exploded inside of me. The door to the inn smashed open behind me and a gust of cold wind swept through the taproom.

"What are you doing here?" I asked, my voice low with pent up rage. I stood right next to Dylan, practically whispering into his ear.

He jumped, spilling his drink all over his hand and the bar. I had no memory of walking toward him, but I shoved the momentary confusion out of my mind. I just wanted my question answered.

Dylan looked nervous for a moment, but then took on a defensive stance. "When I left, Sir Dagonet was sound asleep. He doesn't need me hovering over him like a..."

But I didn't wait to listen to the rest of Dylan's excuse. I turned and ran up the stairs.

My heart pounded in my chest. How could he have just left Sir Dagonet all alone? The old knight was very sick. His fever was high; he was restless and had been hallucinating during the night—calling out to someone, promising to find "them." I didn't know who "they" were, but it had taken all of my strength to keep him in his bed.

Honestly, I didn't know how much longer I could last with him like this.

I stopped outside of his room to wipe away the tears that had started to slip down my cheeks. I couldn't allow him to see how worried I was.

I took a deep breath to calm myself. The last thing I wanted to do was disturb the old knight if he was finally getting some much—needed rest.

Another breath was abruptly stopped when I heard voices coming from his room. And laughter? That was definitely laughter.

I turned around and took a step closer to the door on the other side of the corridor, thinking it must be coming from the room opposite. I stood listening outside of the other room, but there was nothing. I walked back to Sir Dagonet's room—laughter! It *was* coming from here. But how could that be?

I opened the door a crack and peered in.

Chapter Sixteen

$\mathcal{S}$ ir Dagonet was sitting up in bed, a glass of ale in his hand, a laugh on his lips. "Ah, Scai, come in, come in, wot?" the old knight said. His voice was still raspy with congestion but otherwise sounded remarkably energetic.

I did as I was bade. But it just didn't make sense. How could this be? When I'd left he had practically been on his deathbed, and now...

"Scai, I'd like you to meet Bridget. She's a healer, don't you know? Heard we were looking for one, and she found me just like that. Remarkable ability, wot?"

For the first time, I noticed the young woman sitting in my chair. Closing the door behind me, I advanced into the room as the woman stood up.

She was younger than me, and yet she had such a strong presence that I could hardly believe that I hadn't seen her right away. Her hair was bright red, her eyes a brilliant blue, and the freckles that were splattered over her nose and cheeks gave her a childlike glow even though she had to be in her late teens.

"I'm so happy to meet you, Scai. Sir Dagonet was just telling me about you. Oh, but..." She paused and cocked her head a little to the side, staring wide–eyed at me like a little sparrow. "Have we met? No, that could not possibly be. I certainly would have remembered you. I've got an excellent memory for faces. Names I sometimes have a problem with, but faces I always remember." She stopped and took a breath. "Yours looks extraordinarily familiar."

If I'd wanted to say something, I couldn't, for her rapid–fire delivery. There *was* something niggling in the back of my mind, but it slipped away as I struggled not to laugh at this girl. I finally got a hold of myself and said, "No. I'm certain we haven't met. And please excuse me for being so straightforward, but you're just so...familiar and well, vibrant. There's no other word for it."

And it was true: I'd never met anyone like Bridget before. Everything about her was bright and filled with energy. But what was it about her that seemed so familiar? It wasn't possible that we'd ever met before.

"Vibrant." Bridget giggled. "That's a good word for it. I like that. No one's ever called me vibrant before."

"Bridget is strongly tied to the element of fire, don't you know?" Sir Dagonet croaked out.

"Fire? Yes, that makes perfect sense!" That explained a lot.

Bridget giggled again. "It's how I heal the sick. Although my brothers say that I'm too full of fire, too impetuous. I like to think of myself as enthusiastic. Now you, on the other hand..." She leaned back and contemplated me for a moment. "You must be tied to the element of air."

"Yes, but how did you know?" I asked. A jolt of fear hit me as if Bridget had just struck me with lightning.

Bridget waved away my worry with a laugh. "Sir Dagonet told me. He was telling me all about your journey here, how it rained and rained for days. You poor things! You must have been so cold and absolutely drenched. I just hate the rain. I won't go out when it's raining if I can help it. My brothers laugh. Of course, it's because I can't stand water or being wet—you know, fire and water just don't mix. Well, but you are..." She closed her eyes for a moment, and took in a deep breath through her nose as if she was smelling something wonderful. "You are like a cool breeze on a hot summer's day. So refreshing."

That made me laugh. "Refreshing? And no one's ever called me *that* before."

"An excellent description!" Sir Dagonet agreed wholeheartedly.

"But I wish I knew where I've seen you. It's just not like me at all not to be able to place a face," Bridget began, but the door opened and Dylan came into the room, soundly dousing all of the good feelings flowing back and forth between me and Bridget.

"Scai... Oh! I beg your pardon," he said, coming to a stop in front of Bridget.

I turned, forcing the smile to stay put on my face. It was so tempting to scowl at Dylan when I wanted so much to give him a piece of my mind. But we had a guest, so I held my tongue. It was also a little difficult to dredge up my earlier anger with him when Bridget was right next to me and Sir Dagonet had a broad smile of his face.

"Dylan, this is Bridget," I said. "She's a healer."

"Oh, excellent! How did you find her?" he asked.

"*I* didn't. *She* found Sir Dagonet." And suddenly what had been teasing the back of my mind popped into the forefront—how *had* Bridget found Sir Dagonet? He said that she'd just found him on her own. Was that part of her magic?

"I heard you were looking for a healer. You did ask around, did you not?" Bridget asked. "I speak to people all the time, and someone mentioned to me that some strangers were looking for a healer, so I came looking. You know," she said, turning back to me, "I may talk a lot—and don't feel bad for laughing at me, I assure you, everyone does—but I do always listen as well." She turned back to Dylan and raised her arms out to the side saying, "And so, here I am!"

"Ah, I see," he said, frowning at her. "Well, excellent. Then I did find you a healer after all." He turned to Sir Dagonet and straightened his shoulders, as if he was going to take all of the credit for bringing Bridget there.

Bridget and my eyes met, and we both just burst out laughing. How ridiculous men were! Dylan hadn't truly found her. She'd come all on her own, and yet, without a moment's hesitation, here he was puffing himself up like anything.

Dylan didn't seem to understand the joke, but Sir Dagonet was chuckling as he drank some more of his ale.

"Sir, I am glad to see you so well recovered," Dylan said, taking a step toward the foot of the bed.

"Owe it all to Bridget, don't you know?"

Dylan gave Bridget a cold, if polite, smile. Turning to

me, he asked, "And how did your meeting with Jonah go? Is he related?"

I shook my head. I didn't reveal what I had overheard through the door before I'd left. I was certain it would anger Dylan if he knew I had been eavesdropping. Instead, I said, "I didn't meet him. He was gone by the time I got to the other inn. But I'm certain that he would have been another dead end."

"He was gone?" Anger flashed onto Dylan's face. "Well, perhaps I could..."

"No. Really, that's all right," I said, perhaps a touch too quickly.

"What's this?" Bridget asked.

"Dylan has been helping me search for my lost family." I explained my search very briefly. "But so far none have been successful," I concluded.

"Well, of course not. He's not looking in the right places. You're Vallen. You should be looking within our community," Bridget said, as if it were obvious.

"There's a community of Vallen?" I asked, taking a step forward. Could such a thing actually exist?

"Oh, well, I, er, wasn't certain..." Dylan stumbled over his words.

Bridget cocked her head, looking at him. "Didn't I see you last spring at the Beltane festival? At the jousting?"

"Oh, er, did you see me? Um, I was there with my foster brother."

"I thought so," Bridget said, nodding. She turned back to me. "I told you, I'm good with faces." She turned back to Dylan. "You're a squire? Or were then, right?"

"Yes," he mumbled, suddenly very interested in his shoes.

"You were here before?" I asked Dylan. I could feel my anger beginning to stir inside me like a leaf caught in the wind.

"Er, yes, but you know, it was busy. A festival," Dylan explained, "I was working. Squiring for my foster brother, who was participating in the jousts."

"We have a wonderful festival every spring. It's so much fun! We have jousting and jugglers and the most wonderful food you can imagine. The locals call it May Day, but in the Vallen community, we all know and celebrate it as Beltane. It's almost the same thing—a celebration of the coming planting season. We pray for a good and fruitful summer and harvest, full of rain and sunshine. And then the real fun begins," Bridget said, enthusiasm leaping from her eyes.

I couldn't help but respond to Bridget's excitement. "We do something similar where I come from, only we do it at Easter, and, of course, we don't have jousting."

Sir Dagonet laughed. "No jousting? Where's the fun then, wot, wot?"

I couldn't help but laugh, even though I was really annoyed with Dylan. All this time he had known there was a Vallen community here in Gloucester, and yet he kept bringing me ordinary people and saying that they could be my parents. He should have known to look among the Vallen! And why hadn't he looked there to find a healer for Sir Dagonet, instead of asking at the inn and the grocer's? We were lucky that word had gotten to Bridget anyway.

"The funny thing is," Bridget was saying, "if you had gone to the Vallen community, you would have found me. Well, me and my family."

I turned to her. "What do you mean?" I felt as if I had missed something important.

"Well, I know that my parents had another daughter before they had me," she explained. "But they gave her away. Something about a prophecy? I don't know. I just know that my oldest brother mentioned it to me once when I was complaining about being the only girl in our family. I have five brothers!" she said, rolling her eyes.

"Ha!" Dylan chuckled. "And I thought having two foster–brothers was bad."

Somehow I didn't find this at all funny. In fact, my mind was whirling with possibilities. "When did your parents have this other child?" I asked.

Bridget shrugged. "A year or two before I was born."

I was beginning to get anxious and little impatient. For once Bridget wasn't going on, adding more information. "And when was that? How old are you?" I asked, feeling like

I was prying the information out of her.

"I'm eighteen. My sister would be about twenty. My next older brother, Matthias, is twenty–two and..."

"But I'm twenty!" I said as the excitement mounted inside of me. "You don't know what they did with the child?" I asked.

Bridget thought about that for a minute, but then shook her head. "I think they went away with her. I know my oldest brother said that they left him in charge of our brothers and went away. That might have been when they went to Wales."

"To Wales?" Sir Dagonet and I said in unison. Even Dylan's eyes had gone wide.

"Er, yes," Bridget said, her eyes shifting among us. "But I'm really not certain. All I know is that they returned more than a month later. Can you imagine, leaving a nine–year–old boy in charge of four younger brothers for over a month? Anyway, I'm sure Thomas could tell you more."

"Thomas?"

Bridget nodded. "My oldest brother."

"Yes, I'd like to speak with him. When do you think I can do so?"

"It will have to be tomorrow. He and the others are extremely busy today. They're finally fixing the roof of the house we rent to the blacksmith and his family. It caught fire last week and the poor things have been living with only half a roof ever since."

"If your parents took this baby to Wales..." I mused, halfway to myself, but my voice petered out when faced with the overwhelming possibility.

"Excellent chance that they're your family, wot?" Sir Dagonet finished for me, saying just what was on all our minds.

Bridget took my hands in her own and looked straight into my eyes. A small smile played around her lips. "You *are* my sister. I can feel it. And that's where I've seen your face before—on my brothers."

Chapter Seventeen

The three young men—hardly more than boys—hesitantly entered the private drawing room. Their heads were bowed and their hands visibly shaking, despite being clasped together in front of them.

Nimuë just shook her head sadly. "Do I frighten you so much?" she asked.

"N–n–no, ma'am," one brave boy spoke up when the others didn't say anything.

"Good. I certainly do not intend to frighten you."

"No, ma'am."

"Are you all enjoying your new positions in the royal household?" she asked, to calm them a little—before she terrified them once again by telling them why she had called them to her.

The tallest of the three let out a breath, while the third said with great enthusiasm, "Yes, ma'am. Thank you, ma'am."

Nimuë smiled. "I am so glad to hear that, truly, I am."

"It was very good of you to get us our positions, ma'am," the first one added.

"Well, you did what I asked of you and for that you received what I had promised." She paused, before continuing. "Now, I am afraid, I have another little job for you. It is something along the lines of the first."

"But we already have our positions," the third young man said.

"Yes, and you would like to keep them, would you not?"

His gaze dropped to the floor. "Yes, ma'am."

"Good."

"But ma'am..."

"Yes?" Nimuë asked. They were determined to test her patience.

"The first time you... well, we had... well, it was..."

"What is it? Just spit it out, boy." She was *really* beginning to lose her patience.

"It's just..."

"We felt urges," the tall one whispered.

That stopped her. "Urges?" How delicious! And unexpected. "What sort of urges?"

"To...to kill," the first one said, clearly disturbed.

The tall boy dropped his head into his hands in shame. Worry lines creased the forehead of the third.

Nimuë caught and stopped herself from laughing. "Oh, yes. That is not entirely surprising." She paced in front of them. "I am sorry to tell you that, once again, you will not be able to act on those urges. I need the girl. The girl you watched for me last time. She is in Gloucester, and I need her brought to me."

"How?" the third one interrupted.

Nimuë frowned at him, but continued, "You will go in the same form as last time. Attack her. Hurt her. But do not kill her. Do you understand? If you do, there will be dire consequences for you." She paused to let that thought sink in. "I will be waiting for her outside of the Northern Gate to the city. Drive her there."

The first and third nodded, their faces solemn. The second still had not taken his face from his hands and his shoulders were now shaking as if he were weeping. Just so long as he did what she told him.

She positioned herself in front of them and began to concentrate on turning these young men into ravens.

Chapter Eightteen

Five enormous, monstrous giants came thumping toward me. Evil smiles revealed sharp, white fangs they gnashed with obvious intent. Their hands opened and closed into fists the size of boulders.

I turned to run, but there was nowhere to run to. I was surrounded by a thick forest with trees so dense I could barely wind my way through them, let alone run. The ground shook with the oncoming approach of the giants as I bounced from tree to tree, trying to escape.

"But, Scai, we're your brothers," one of them said from behind me. In a sweet, alluring singsong voice, he called out again, "We're your family, we just want to taste you."

"Be with you," another one corrected.

"Er, yes, be with you," the first one said. "Dear sister, don't run away. Come back! Come back to us."

I moved as quickly as I could through the overcrowded trees. Somehow, although I had difficulty squeezing in between the trunks, my brothers had no problem moving forward. They were gaining on me and still the trees crowded me in, making escape impossible. I whimpered in fright when I turned and saw how close they were. I had to get away!

Breaking out from the forest, I sprinted away, running as fast as I could. Looking back over my shoulder, I didn't see the line of men approaching me from the other direction until I had nearly run straight into one of them. A man reached out and grabbed me by my shoulders just before I barreled into him.

"Who are you?" he asked, holding me at arm's length.

"Don't you remember, brother?" said the man next to him. "Bridget said she might be our long lost sister."

I looked from one to the other of the five men. Each one was strong and handsome, with blond hair like mine and harsh blue eyes.

The first looked down at me as if he had put something awful into *his mouth, and then he pushed me away. "Go back to where you came from, girl. We don't want you."*

"But..." I began to protest.

"We thought that we'd gotten rid of you for good. We don't want you. Go away." He turned his back on me and walked away. The other men did the same, the last one spitting at me as he did so.

"But wait! I've come all the way from Wales just to meet you," I cried.

"We don't want to meet you. Go back to Wales." The voice that drifted back to me sounded awfully familiar.

I started to run, following the men. Somehow they had gotten very far away very fast. I hoisted my long skirts and ran as hard as I could to catch up to them, calling out to them, "But you're my brothers, my family." But I didn't seem to be getting any closer. I ran harder and faster as the men sauntered carelessly away.

I wouldn't give up. I couldn't! Not after all that I'd been through. I had traveled so far to meet them, they couldn't just turn their backs on me.

"Go back to Wales," the voice called back again, and this time I knew whose it was for sure.

"Dylan!"

I sat up with a gasp, staring directly into Dylan's green eyes.

"How dare you," I breathed. "You entered my dream. You toyed with my mind while I slept!"

"You can't go to meet your family," he said, not looking away.

"How did you do that?" Fear, true blood–chilling fear, crawled me down to my very bones like the North wind in the dead of winter.

"It doesn't matter. You cannot meet your family."

"Why not? Why are you trying to scare me away from them?"

"They don't want you, Scai. Why can't you get that into your head?"

"Because it's not true," I insisted. It's not true, I said again silently, convincing myself as much as I was trying to convince him. No, I *was* convinced! I was. I knew that what I was doing was right.

"How do you know that? They left you, a helpless babe, on the steps of a church in a town they didn't know. Isn't that enough for you? Why do you insist on returning to them?"

"I have to. I have to find out why my parents gave me away."

"But *why*?"

That stopped me. "Why? Because they just left me there. Who does that to their daughter? And why would they travel all the way to Tallent, so far from Gloucester, to give me away?" I unclenched my hands only to wring them together. They were hot and sweaty despite the cold that had invaded me.

"You're right. No one does that unless they are strongly compelled to do so. Think about it, Scai." Dylan leaned forward to make his point even stronger. "They didn't want you and they went to a lot of trouble to get rid of you. Don't you think you should honor their decision? Don't you think there was a very good reason why they went to all of that trouble?" He paused and then added quietly, "Don't do this. Show some respect for your parents and their decision. You know it had to be made for a good reason. Honor that."

"What do you know about this? Do you know my family? Do you know why they gave me away?"

Dylan shook his head. "I know families. I've had two: my real family and my foster family. Believe me when I tell you that you are doing the wrong thing," he said. His voice had softened, filled with concern. "I just don't want to see you hurt when you're not greeted the way you expect to be. I guarantee you, they're not going to kill the fatted calf and welcome you home. You didn't leave—they got rid of you."

Pain slashed through me as I sat at the edge of my bed. He was right. I hated it, but he was right. They had given me away—left me miles away to ensure I didn't come back. Maybe I *should* respect their decision, I thought, blinking away the tears that had begun to sting my eyes.

Clearly my parents had not done this lightly, or easily. But they *had* done it. I took a deep breath, trying to dispel the heaviness that had descended on my chest. I felt for a moment as if I was suffocating. I needed air.

I got up and pushed open the window shutters. I could hear Sir Dagonet snoring in the next room, sleeping soundly. Finally, thanks to Bridget, he was recovering from that awful illness.

Watching the sun as it peeked up over the horizon of the neighboring houses, I thought about my parents. Yes, they had given me away. Yes, they had done so for a reason. But I had to know what that was. I *had* to know why they had gone to so much trouble to get rid of me.

I opened my hands to the cool of the morning. "No. I have to know. I have to find out. I *will* go and meet my family today," I said, as I turned around to face Dylan.

He dropped his head in defeat for just a moment. Sorrow pooled in his eyes as he looked directly into mine once more. "You will not go to see your family. You will return to Wales, today."

His voice was deep and resonant. I could feel the magic in his words. It swirled around me, trying to enter into my mind. Even before the words were out of his mouth, I was concentrating on blocking them out. His words would not flood my mind. They would not!

I took a few steps back, away from Dylan and his mental assault. Although I glared at him, I couldn't stop the smile of triumph that rose to my lips.

I had done it! I had blocked his magic.

Dylan realized this in an instant and came toward me.

I bolted. I didn't know what he was thinking of doing, but I didn't wait a moment to find out. Every instinct told me to run—and so I did.

I ran out of the door of my room and turned down the hallway.

No! I had turned the wrong way! Ahead was the dead end. The stairs were in the other direction and Dylan was practically on my heels.

I noticed light coming from an open door at the end of the hallway. The last room was open, unoccupied.

I scooted into the room and was about to turn and close the door, but Dylan was too fast. He was right there, behind me.

"How did you do that?" he demanded. "How did you block my suggestion?"

"I don't know, but it worked. I told you once before, Dylan, you *may not* put your commands into my mind. I will not stand for it."

Dylan stopped as well. A small smile grew on his face. He knew as well as I did that I was trapped. I didn't like the look in his eyes. He looked...half–crazed and angry. "Go back to Wales." He began advancing.

"No." I backed away from him.

Making a lunge for me, Dylan sprang forward. I dodged around him and started to run back out the door, but before I could even get through it, he grabbed hold of my hair.

A scream of pain escaped from me as he pulled me to a sudden halt. "No!"

I rounded on him, my fist smashing into his ear. Immediately, he let go of me, recoiling in pain.

I was out of the door and running back down the hall as fast as I could go. My only hope was that Sir Dagonet would stop Dylan. I ran at full speed into his room. "Sir Dagonet!" I screamed as I threw open the door.

"Eh, wot, wot?" the old man sat up in his bed.

But a glance behind me showed Dylan right on my heels.

There was nothing else for it. I didn't even pause. I kept running straight past Sir Dagonet's bed and threw myself out of the second story window, praying as I did so.

Chapter Nineteen

With two strong flaps of my wings, I shot up into the early morning sky. Circling around to take a look behind me, I saw Dylan glaring at me out of the window, his hands gripping the window ledge.

"You shall never get it, Scai. Merlin's chalice is mine! It was meant for me, and I shall be the one who finds it. I, alone, shall be the one who wields it." The words poured into my mind like acid—hot, burning, and angry.

I didn't know what he meant, but I didn't have time to figure it out. From above me there came terrifying screeches, and they were coming closer, fast.

The ravens looked identical to the ones I had seen just before leaving Tallent, but I didn't have time to look closely before they started attacking me.

Two of the birds came at me fast. I tried to fly away, but a third was coming at me from the other direction.

I faltered, not knowing which way to turn, and was hit hard by the beaks of two of the ravens. I closed my eyes as searing pain shot through me. When I opened them again the ground was coming toward me fast.

"Flap! Flap your wings, dammit!" Dylan's voice penetrated the fog of terror and pain.

"Dylan!" I wanted to scream, but all that came out of my beak was a screech. I didn't know if I would get any help from him, in any case. No, I was all alone in this.

I lifted my head and pumped down as hard as I could, trying to ignore the pain in order to save my life. The ground began to retreat again, but the birds didn't.

Before I had even gained a proper altitude, I was

buffeted by the ravens once more. I felt like a ball being thrown back and forth between a group of children. Again and again, the birds flew at me, stabbing at me with their sharp beaks. I barely had time to flap my wings to stay up in the air before another bird would attack, its beak jabbing painfully into me.

I made another attempt to fly away from the attack, but my wings were getting heavier by the minute. I was too tired, too battered, and too weak to put much effort into it. It was all I could do to stay aloft, and even that was becoming almost too much for me.

Something else flew by, nearly hitting me. Only after it had passed did I realize that it was a rock. I looked down and saw Dylan standing in the street, another rock in his hand, ready to be thrown. I didn't know if he was aiming for me or for my assailants, but right now I was too tired to even care. I had to get away.

Another bird slammed into me, knocking me sideways.

That was it. I was going to fall. The pain was too much. I was dizzy and sick. Once more I tried to find a space to fly through the circling birds so that I could at least land safely, but once again the ravens were coming straight at me.

I was just closing my eyes, preparing for the pain of their attack, when I saw a flash of white and heard one of the ravens squawk in surprise.

The hawk! The white hawk that had frightened away the ravens in Tallent—it was here! I recognized it at once. It flew up and then banked, descending fast. Its sharp claws grabbed hold of an attacking raven from above and behind. The bird was powerless to stop the attack. With speed and agility, the hawk smashed the raven against the ground.

An idea struck me. I took advantage of the brief moment when the other two ravens were stunned into immobility as their companion was taken away. It couldn't hurt to try. With a last burst of energy, I flapped my tired wings hard to get above the other two birds. They were still staring at their, now immobile, companion.

I didn't know what kind of bird I was, but at least I had the advantage of surprise when I mimicked the hawk's movements. Swooping down on one of the ravens, I reached out with my talons and grabbed the bird. It thrashed and struggled in my claws. I held on as tightly as I could, but my strength just wasn't there. As it pulled away, I heard it caw again. I looked down to see that Dylan had caught the bird as it had escaped from me. I watched in a mixture of horror and relief as he wrung its neck.

The hawk flew past me, also watching Dylan, with the third raven tightly clasped in its talons. As Dylan dropped the dead bird, the hawk deposited the last one into his hands.

I circled once more, my wings aching with fatigue and pain from the attack. I wanted to say my thanks to the hawk, if I could. But as soon as the hawk had left the third raven with Dylan, it didn't stay around for thanks but darted off. It flew away with a speed I couldn't match in my pain and exhaustion.

It took the last vestiges of energy I had, but I managed to fly the half mile east to the bright red roof Bridget had told me to look for. In through the open window, I landed on my own two feet, just as my legs collapsed under me.

Chapter Twenty

Strong arms and warm bodies surrounded me.

"Here, I've got her, James," a voice said very close to my ear. I was being lifted and carried away.

When I next opened my eyes, Bridget was sitting beside me, pressing a cool cloth to a huge gash in my side. Pain shot in every direction.

Concern faded from her eyes as I tried to give her a smile. "Welcome, sister. That was some entrance you made," she said, laughing.

I tried to sit up, but Bridget put a restraining hand on my shoulder. "Wait just a little while longer. Your cuts are almost healed. Just a touch more here and there and you'll be sore but whole again."

With a sigh of relief, I lay back down. I was in a simple whitewashed room, barely larger than a cupboard. The only furniture was a beautiful wood and brass chest and the bed in which I lay.

Bridget noticed me looking around and gave me a little smile. "This is my room. Being the only girl, I get to have my own." She laid her hands on my side where she had just applied the cloth. There was a slight burning sensation, as if someone had touched me with the flame of a candle, but then it was gone. I looked down and saw a trickle of blood, but the cut had disappeared. It was incredible. What a gift.

"There, I think that is the last of them. How do you feel?"

My smile, this time, was true. "Much better, thanks to you."

"Good. Do you want to see if you can sit up now?"

I nodded and, with Bridget's help, managed to sit up with my feet on the floor. My head was light and my stomach rebellious.

"Just give yourself a moment," Bridget cautioned.

As I sat there waiting for my head and stomach to steady themselves, Bridget got up and rummaged in her trunk. She pulled out a pale blue dress of fine wool, much finer than anything I had ever owned. And yet, I noticed for the first time, it was no finer than what Bridget was wearing.

"It'll be short for you, but it'll do for now. Yours, I'm afraid, was in tatters."

She helped me to dress and then gave me an arm to lean on. We went out to a large and airy kitchen where Bridget's brothers were all seated around a scoured wooden table.

They all rose upon our entrance.

"Scai, I'd like you to meet *our* brothers," Bridget said, beaming at the men. "Thomas is the eldest," she said, indicating the first man. He was tall with light brown hair and soft, smiling blue eyes. "Next to him is Piers. He and Peter," she indicated another man, who looked identical to Piers but sat on the opposite side of the table, "are twins. Next to Piers is James, and this"—she indicated the youngest man, who seemed to also be closest in age to me—"is Matthias." Bridget moved to the large fireplace and put her arm around the woman standing in front of it, whom I hadn't even noticed until now. "And this beautiful creature is Joan, Thomas's wife."

Joan came forward and held out her hands to me. "Welcome. Please come and sit down." She pulled out the chair next to Mathias, which I sank into gratefully. Looking at the faces all around the table, I just couldn't believe that these people were *my* family. My brothers and sister! I shook my head in wonder. And they were smiling at me, welcoming me. I wasn't quite sure how this could be. I had been dreaming of this day my whole life, and now that it was here...it was baffling.

"Thank you." I paused to swallow my emotions, which were tightening within my throat. "Thank you so much for..."

"Please, Scai, you're our sister. You don't need to thank

us for anything," Thomas said, his voice filled with gentle kindness.

I just shook my head, now completely overcome. They were accepting me. Without a question or concern. Even after I had barged into their home, uninvited.

"But I didn't even knock," I whispered, horrified at my own lack of manners.

A couple of them laughed.

"I presume you don't normally fly into people's homes," Thomas said, trying to hold back his own laughter.

"No!"

"Pretty incredible that you can turn into a bird," Matthias said with unabashed awe.

I wiped away the tears threatening to spill from my eyes and laughed, amazed that he—that they all—could accept me and my odd abilities so easily. I didn't know what to think. No one had ever been so quick to accept me and my quirks. Even Aron had taken a moment to digest the thought that I might be a witch, and Father Llewellyn had probably taken years before he accepted it—and they had known and loved me my whole life.

"It's all right, truly," Piers said. He reached over and patted my hands as they rested on the table.

I couldn't help it. I didn't know whether to laugh or cry, to be happy or...well, I should be happy, I knew I should, but I was still too confused.

"Are you feeling better now that Bridget has had at you?" the other twin asked.

I gave a little laugh and took stock of my aches and pains. "I'm still feeling very sore and tired, but yes, thank you."

"Are you hungry?" Joan asked, moving to a huge pot that hung over the fire.

And as soon as she said it, I recognized the churning feeling in my stomach as just that, hunger. "Oh, yes. Very."

Matthias turned to the others and said, "Yep, she's our sister all right."

The men all laughed.

But I started to choke up again at being anyone's sister. I squashed down my emotions, not wanting to embarrass myself. But then something odd occurred to me. "I do feel comfortable with you all, as if you really were my family," I said, voicing my thoughts... and then my fears. "But do we know for certain?"

"Well, tell us your story, and we'll see if it matches with ours," Thomas said, giving me an encouraging smile.

So I recounted my story once more. With each piece of it, the men nodded their heads.

"I remember when our parents left with the baby," Peter said.

"I remember how Mama cried for days after she was born," Piers added.

I felt hollow, and it wasn't hunger, for Joan had given me a large piece of bread and a bowl of broth that I had begun to eat greedily. I swallowed, the food in mouth turning dry as sawdust. "Why did she cry? Why did she give me away? Is she here?"

"She and our father passed away some time ago," James answered, his deep, quiet voice reflecting the sadness I could see in the eyes of the others.

"Our mother didn't just give you away, Scai," Thomas said after a moment. "She and our father traveled for nearly a month through Wales searching for a good home for you."

"But why?"

"You were a girl," Matthias said with a shrug.

"No, that's not it. That's not why," Thomas corrected, giving his brother a scowl.

I turned back to... to my eldest brother—chills touching my skin at just the idea—who sat thinking for a moment. "I was only nine at the time, but Papa explained it to me, or at least some of it. Although I'm certain he simplified it." He paused to collect his thoughts before continuing. "They knew that the sixth child in our family would be a girl. She would do great things, but then..." he paused. Looking away from me, he shook his head, not saying any more.

"But then, what?" I asked.

"Yes, come on, Thomas, you must tell us the rest," Bridget said, leaning forward toward her brother.

He looked around the table uncomfortably, and then

lowered his eyes and his voice so that he spoke only to the table. "Papa said she would do great things, but that she would kill herself to save others." He lifted his eyes to mine. They were full of sorrow and perhaps a little fear. "I'm sorry, Scai. But Papa said he and my mother would rather give you away and have you live a quiet life where you didn't have an opportunity to do great things than have you die in such a way."

There was silence in the room as we all digested this.

Bridget was the first to speak. "It must have been a very difficult decision for them."

"Yes! Absolutely." All of the men around the table immediately spoke up, agreeing with her.

I was warmed by their kindness.

"It's true, Scai," Thomas said. "As I told you, our mother cried for days just at the idea of having to give you up. I heard her and Papa discussing it, arguing about it. They didn't want to do it, but they also couldn't allow their child to die young—or by her own hand."

"But were they told I would die young, or just that I would die—what was it? For others?" I asked.

"I don't know for certain, but I know they believed you would die young and they didn't want that, naturally," Thomas answered.

"So they gave me away."

"I'm certain they did so only after ensuring that you would be well cared for," Piers put in.

"You were, weren't you?" Peter asked.

"Yes. I was. I was loved and cared for by a very good man. A priest named Father Llewellyn." I paused to blink the tears out of my eyes as I remembered my dear, sweet guardian. I sent up a silent prayer that he was all right.

"That's very good to hear. But now I want to know who attacked you on your way here," Thomas said, leaning toward me. He tipped his chin down and looked directly at me as if he would not accept anything less than the entire truth. It was more than a little intimidating. I imagined he had to have learned to be so with so many brothers to care for.

I could only shake my head, however. "I don't know

who was responsible. All I know is that three ravens attacked me in the air. A hawk—I've it seen before—saved me."

"Do you change into a bird often?" Matthias asked.

"No. I'm not even certain how I did that. I've only done it once before."

They all sat looking at me, clearly expecting me to go on.

I weighed my words carefully, considering how much I should reveal to my new family.

What a wonderful thought. This was my family. The thought of it threw me off guard again, but I collected myself, knowing they were waiting.

According to Bridget, they were all Vallen. So maybe they knew something about this chalice Dylan had spoken of. Maybe...it was worth a try.

"I, er, well, this morning, I threw myself out of the second story window of the inn where I'm staying," I said. "I was hoping I would turn into a bird, and I did, thank goodness." I gave a little laugh.

None of them joined in, nor even cracked a smile, not even Bridget. They were still waiting for more information.

"I suppose you want to know what led me to jump out of the window?" I asked, trying hard not to giggle at their stony faces. With some trepidation at what they might do about this, I told them what Dylan had done that morning—how he had invaded my dreams and done all that he could to get me *not* to go to meet them.

"Just after I jumped out of the window, he spoke to me in my mind," I told them, at the end of my story.

"What did he say?" Thomas asked, not even giving any sort of recognition that putting words into someone's mind might be odd.

"He said something about a chalice." I tried to remember his exact words. "Merlin's chalice! That was it. Yes, and he said that it was his and that he alone would wield it. I have no idea what he was talking about. How can someone wield a chalice?"

"A chalice?" The other brothers all began to talk amongst themselves, trying to figure out this new mystery.

"The chalice of Merlin is no ordinary chalice." The voice

was quiet, quieter than any other in the room, but it could be heard clearly. Everyone stopped talking and looked over at James, who up to now had hardly said a word.

Chapter Twenty One

James alone had hair and eyes the same color as mine. He was almost frighteningly pale and his white–blond hair did nothing to help that.

Thomas asked what was probably on the tip of every tongue in the room. "What do you know of Merlin's chalice, James?"

"It's no ordinary chalice. I don't know a great deal about it, only what I've heard from Old Maud." He paused and explained to me, "Old Maud is a very old and venerated Vallen who lives here in Gloucester. I've been helping her with some chores around her house, and in return she's told me some of the old stories."

Everybody was silent, and I got the impression that although James didn't say a lot, everyone listened when he did. He had their undivided attention now.

"Merlin's chalice is... well, I suppose it's sort of like the Holy Grail. It's a chalice of legends. We all know the story of Merlin, the great wizard who was enchanted by Nimuë. She learned all she could from Merlin and became a very powerful Vallen."

Everyone around the table nodded, except me. I had never heard these tales of Merlin. My childhood was filled with parables from the bible.

"Merlin was a great prophet and could foresee the future," James continued, clearly for my benefit. "He knew he only had a short time left before Nimuë would trick him and entomb him in an oak tree. So before that happened, he created a chalice. What we now know as Merlin's chalice."

"Wait," I interrupted. "This great wizard, he knew that

he was going to be tricked and imprisoned?"

Everyone turned to look at me. I feared that I was sounding ignorant, but they had accepted me so far, hopefully they would forgive me my stupidity.

"Yes," James answered.

"Then why didn't he stop her, or not allow himself to be tricked?"

"Well, he didn't know precisely what the trick would be, how she would do it. He only knew it would happen."

"But then why didn't he do something about it—I don't know, leave her or kill her or lock her up in a dungeon somewhere? You know, anything to stop this from happening."

James smiled.

"You know, I think I asked the same question when I was told this story," Matthias said. "I was very little, but I imagine everyone asks the same question,"

"Everyone does," Thomas reassured him—and me.

James answered. "Merlin didn't do anything to Nimuë for two reasons, Scai. First of all, he loved her. He loved her with all of his heart and all of his being. He was a slave to this love. He knew this and there was nothing he could do about it. He would have done anything she asked of him."

I scoffed. How ridiculous for a man—a great wizard— to be slave to his love.

"You may laugh, but just you wait until you're in love," Thomas said, smiling at Joan. She returned his smile, and the love that passed between them shamed me for mocking the emotion.

"The second reason," James went on, "is because although Merlin knew what the future held for him, he knew better than to try and change it. The future is what it is and there is very little we can do to change our destiny."

"As we see before us all now," Thomas said. "Even though our parents tried to change Scai's destiny by taking her away and leaving her in Wales, she still came back to us. Destiny will happen whether we want it to or not,"

That left everyone thinking furiously. My brothers' eyes sought out everything else but me. Only Bridget had the nerve to look directly at me. It was I who couldn't hold her gaze.

So I would kill myself. And I would probably be young when I did so. And there was nothing I could do about it. My only consolation was what Thomas had said—that I would die to save others.

That wasn't so bad, was it? At least I would be brave and die a hero's death.

"Before he was entrapped," James said, going on with his story, "Merlin created a chalice. I don't know of what it might be made. No one has ever seen it. But into this chalice he poured his remaining powers—all that he had *not* given to Nimuë."

"Given to her?" Bridget interrupted. "How could he *give* his powers to Nimuë? We are born with our powers. They can't be given away."

James shrugged. "I don't know, Bridget. I imagine that Merlin could do this because he was such a powerful Vallen."

"I don't imagine anyone else could transfer powers the way Merlin did. Don't even think about it, Bridget," Peter put in.

"Oh no, well, I wouldn't want to give away my powers, I can assure you," she said, folding her arms over her chest.

"No—and no one will give you theirs either," Matthias said.

"I wouldn't want them," she pouted.

"No, of course you wouldn't," Thomas said, supporting her.

She gave him a kind smile.

"Ha! She's powerful enough. I'd hate to see what she would do with even more," Matthias said.

Bridget stuck out her tongue at him. There was clearly some animosity between the two of them.

"So what about this chalice, James?" Piers asked, bringing them back to the point.

James nodded. "It is a chalice of the earth. It holds the powers of living things and brings strength to the one who holds it."

"So where is it?" Peter asked.

"And why does Dylan think that it's his?" I asked.

"I can't answer either of those questions. No one knows where the chalice is, and I don't know a thing about Dylan," James said.

"And why was he so determined that you not meet us?" Bridget enquired with heat.

"I don't know. Perhaps because then you would tell me about the chalice? Does that make sense?" I asked the room in general.

No one answered, although a few nodded their assent.

"But I suppose it all fits. With the chalice, I mean," I continued, thinking aloud. "If he thinks I'm going to try and fight him for this chalice, then he would certainly want to stop me from learning any more about it, right?"

"But why does he think you would be going after it?" Piers asked.

And Peter added, "It's just a legend. We don't even know if it truly exists."

"Well, clearly, Dylan thinks it does—and thinks it's his," Bridget put in.

"What else has Dylan done, Scai?" Thomas asked me pointedly.

I just looked at him in amazement. "How did you know he'd done anything else?"

"Thomas knows these things," Peter said.

"It's really annoying!" Matthias added.

"And you'd better tell him everything or else he'll just keep at you until you've said it all," Bridget said. It was clear she'd had some experience with this.

I couldn't help but laugh, but then I answered him truthfully, as Bridget had recommended. "Soon after I first met Dylan, he tried to drown Sir Dagonet and me in a raging river. That was the first time I turned into a bird. I managed to fly out of the water and then pull Sir Dagonet to safety. After that, we went through days without water only to be deluged by incessant, torrential rain for another three days. That was when Sir Dagonet became so ill," I explained to my brothers.

"Tied to water, is he?" Peter said, with a derisive note to his voice.

"I wouldn't trust him. He sounds slippery," Piers added, nodding his head.

I laughed.

"Not everyone tied to water is untrustworthy." James frowned at his younger brothers.

"So basically, ever since you met him he's been doing everything he can to either stop you or kill you?" Thomas asked, ignoring his brothers.

I shrugged. "Yes. I suppose he has." I took a long drink of my ale. "Since we've been here in Gloucester, it seems as if he's been trying to distract me from finding you by having me meet a lot of ordinary people he said might be my family. Although he told me he was trying to find my family, he didn't even look in the Vallen community. And I hate to even think this, but I wonder if he deliberately didn't try to find a healer for Sir Dagonet." I gave an involuntary shiver. "It quite scares me to think he would want to kill good Sir Dagonet. He is truly the kindest, gentlest man. He would never hurt a soul."

"But Dylan tried to kill you as well," Matthias pointed out.

I could only nod. All of Dylan's deeds sounded terrible when they were laid out on the table in this way. But somehow, despite this, there was a soft spot in my heart for him. It was on the tip of my tongue to ask these men to not take retribution for what he'd done. For the moment, though, I kept my thoughts to myself.

Peter and Piers held an identical murderous look on their faces.

Thomas simply looked thoughtful. "And he claims to have done all this so that you don't go seeking Merlin's chalice?" he asked.

"Well, he hasn't claimed anything. He just told me that the chalice was his—as if I would—"

"Wait a minute," Matthias said. "Did he say the chalice was his? Were those his exact words?"

I sat back, thinking about it for a moment. "No. He said that it was meant for him. He would be the one who would find it and he would be the one to wield it."

"But how does he know that?" Peter asked.

"Perhaps he heard it somewhere, or someone told him," Piers answered his brother.

"But if he's scared that Scai is going to try and get it first..." Peter didn't finish his sentence, and no one jumped in to do so. They were all too lost in their own thoughts.

"Thomas, how did Mama and Papa know that Scai was going to die young?" James asked.

"I don't know."

"Could you ask Old Maud, James? Maybe she knows something," Peter suggested.

"It's a good idea," Thomas agreed. "I was really too young at the time..."

"Where's Bridget?" Matthias asked, looking around the room.

All of the brothers rose at once.

I looked around at them all. "What? Why are you so upset? Maybe she just went to, er, to relieve herself?"

"If she'd gone for that, she'd have mentioned it."

"She wouldn't have just snuck out," Matthias added.

"But where—?" I started.

"I don't know." Thomas cut me off.

"Where's Dylan?" James asked, turning back to me. "Is he still at the inn where you're staying?"

"I don't know. I suppose so," I answered, standing up with everyone else.

With just a nod of agreement all five men headed out the door. I joined them, hoping I could do something to help, although I certainly had no idea what.

"I'll stay here in case she returns," Joan called after us.

Remembering my manners, I stopped briefly. "Thank you, Joan. And thank you for the meal."

Joan gave me a smile and an encouraging nod. "You'd better catch up."

Chapter Twenty Two

S he wasn't gone long before you noticed..." I started to say as I and my brothers strode down the street toward the inn. We were a formidable group—five men walking with determination down the middle of the street. But there didn't seem to be anyone about to even notice. It was odd—I hadn't been in the city long, but still, I'd never seen the streets so empty.

I was about to comment on this, when a huge billow of smoke and anxious shouts of fear ahead froze the words on my lips.

The men all stopped moving, and then as one they broke into a run, heading toward the burning inn.

A long line of people snaked from the blazing building. They were passing buckets from hand to hand as quickly as they could without all of the water being sloshed from them. My brothers immediately joined in the brigade.

"Scai, you run ahead. See if you can find Bridget," Thomas shouted above the noise.

"This is certainly her handiwork," Matthias said more quietly. I took a quick look around to make sure no one else had heard him, but, luckily, no one was looking our way. With a sigh of relief, I began to press forward through the crowd.

There were masses of bystanders, all talking or attempting to direct those who were actually trying to help.

As I got closer, the acrid smell of the burning building became stronger and denser. Smoke billowed into the air, threatening to choke me and bringing tears to my eyes. But still I pressed forward. I had to find not only Bridget, but Dylan and Sir Dagonet as well.

I slipped through the throng of onlookers. Luckily, the closer I got to the actual building, the fewer people there were. No one wanted to get too close to the fire for fear of being scorched or having the building collapse on top of them.

"Bridget! Sir Dagonet!" I called. The smoke billowing all around threatened to choke me. "Dylan!" I called out again. The more worried I got, the more frantically I searched. Where were they? They had to be here!

I made my way through to one side of the crowd, breaking through close enough to the building to feel the scorching heat and fear the flying embers. But they weren't here. They couldn't still be inside? No! I prayed not.

I moved even closer, dangerously close to the burning building, calling out again, "Bridget! Dylan! Sir Dagonet!"

The heat was becoming unbearable as I got closer still. "Sir Dagonet! Bridget!"

"Here, wot, wot?"

The familiar voice came through the crowd. With relief, I shoved between two older men who must have been early morning customers. Sir Dagonet was standing in front of the door to the inn, a measly fifteen or twenty feet from the fire.

Grateful that he was safe, I threw my arms around the old man.

"Ah. Yes, er...quite all right, don't you know, quite all right." He chuckled and gave my shoulders a little squeeze before releasing me.

"I'm so glad to see that you are," I said with all my heart. "You haven't seen Bridget, have you?"

Sir Dagonet's smile slipped from his lips. He angled his head toward the burning building. "In there. With Dylan."

"What?" I spun around to look at the inn.

"Exactly."

The entire second floor was in flames. I could see fire licking out from the windows, and spots where the roof, too, was ablaze.

The men of the fire brigade were doing what they could, but that was so very little compared to the ferocity of the flames. Every minute or so the man at the head of the line would toss a measly bucket full of water into a window on the second floor, but he was just one man on a flimsy ladder pouring water into one window. The fire had spread throughout the building.

"Why didn't they come out with you?" I asked, watching the men doing their best to control the fire.

"They did. Well, I thought they had, don't you know?"

"Then what happened?"

Sir Dagonet opened his mouth to explain but then started to cough, choking on a gust of smoke that had billowed toward us. When he could speak, his voice was raw from the smoke. "I followed Dylan downstairs, and I thought Bridget was just behind me. But when I turned around, she wasn't there. I started to call for her, but then we heard a crash upstairs and a scream." Sir Dagonet's knuckles were white as he held tightly onto the hilt of his sword in his hand. He seemed ready to spring into battle, but all he could do was look anxiously into the burning building.

"Dylan ran back up," he concluded in a voice so quiet I almost missed his words.

"He went back in? To look for her?"

Sir Dagonet gave me a sad smile and a nod. "Brave boy, wot? Especially after all she had just said to him. Gave him quite a piece of her mind, she did. That's what started the fire, I'm afraid."

"I don't understand."

"Oh, she was fit to be tied, dear girl," Sir Dagonet said, explaining. "She yelled at him, throwing accusations at him like balls of fire. Some of them hit him, scorched him terribly, too. But some missed, don't you know? They caught the place on fire. First the bedclothes, then the curtains. Soon the whole room was an inferno," he concluded shaking his head.

I looked back at the building, not quite understanding, but just now I couldn't focus my mind enough to question the knight. I was too concerned for Bridget.

Tears sprang to my eyes. I looked up, hoping they wouldn't fall and give me away. As I did so, a fine mist of rain began, despite the fact that the sky was a clear, cool blue.

"Ha, ha!" Sir Dagonet exclaimed, a smile breaking out on his face.

I immediately turned on him. "What? Are you...?" I stopped and looked around us. There were people everywhere, but none close enough to hear if we kept our voices low. I was terrified of being caught as a witch.

"Oh no, I can't do this. But Dylan can," Sir Dagonet said, not even bothering to moderate his voice. I resisted the urge to reach up and put a hand over his mouth. I let my eyes stray around once again to ensure that no one had heard him.

"Means he's all right, don't you know?" Sir Dagonet was saying. "Trying to put it out, wot?"

"But the rain's not hard enough," I whispered back as loudly as I dared. "It's not enough water to put out this blaze."

That sobered Sir Dagonet. "No, you're right. He must be too tired to really bring on a downpour. Oh, dear. You're going to have to do something, Scai."

"Me? But what can I do?"

"What? Oh." Sir Dagonet finally lowered his voice and bent down to whisper in my ear, "Bring on the wind, dear girl. Call it forth to put out the fire. But mind, it's going to have to be a big one to really do the job."

I looked about once again to make sure no one heard, but the people nearest were too busy watching and commenting on the fire to notice what we were saying.

"I can't do that! Not here in the middle of this crowd of people. What if someone were to see me, or suspect something? I could..." I couldn't even say what could happen to me, it was too close, too real. Just the thought terrified me.

"No, no. Who will know? Do it quietly, wot? Just reach down, right down inside of you, my dear, and bring it forth."

Sir Dagonet paused and put his hand on my shoulder. "But just remember, it's got to be big and all at once. Otherwise it'll just spread the fire to the other houses nearby."

My eyes widened and my mouth fell open a touch in horror. Sir Dagonet nodded at my reaction. I hadn't even thought of the possibility of spreading the fire, but he was right. I had one chance, or else the whole town could catch fire.

My heart began to pound in my chest as I wiped my sweaty hands on my dress. "Oh no! Sir Dagonet, no, I couldn't risk... No, I can't, honestly I can't." I would be caught. I was certain that someone would see me. Even if they didn't, surely I didn't have that much magic to bring on a strong enough wind to blow out this enormous fire!

"Of course you can." He turned and looked me straight in the eye. "You can do this, Scai. You have the ability. I have faith in you." He turned and looked up.

The rain had stopped.

"And you'd better do it now. That's not a good sign."

My throat began to close up with emotion, and tears burned in my eyes. I couldn't do this. I couldn't! But if I didn't, Bridget and Dylan were going to die. I had to. Oh dear God, I had to do it, and I had to do it right the first time. And without anyone knowing it was me—I did not want to be burned at the stake. Standing this close to this burning building was the closest I ever wanted to come to a fire.

I began to wring my hands but then knotted them together and concentrated. I took a deep breath trying to calm my whirling mind.

What had Sir Dagonet told me? Powerful magic took a lot of energy. This was certainly powerful magic if there was any.

Remembering how Dylan and I had stopped the storm just before we'd reached Gloucester, I closed my eyes and reached down inside of myself. I knew what my magic felt like now. From all over my body, I could feel my energy. Harnessing the magic, I brought it up and into my chest. From there, I imagined it all flowing down into my hands. My fingers tingled, but I kept a tight control over it. I held it back, dredged up some more, and added that to what I had.

My palms burned with the heat of so much energy. Still, I held on to it and pulled even more from every source I could find—from every part of my body and even from the air all around me. Slowly, ever so slowly, I raised my hands. The burning was intense, but still I held on to it—growing, growing...

And in one great breath, in one great push, I thrust out my arms—shoving all of that energy at the burning building in one great go. As I did so, my hair went flying and my dress flattened itself against the back of my legs as a huge rush of wind blew from behind me and into the building.

"What?"

"Where on God's mighty Earth did that come from?"

People exclaimed all around me as they righted themselves after being caught off–guard by the gust of wind. Sir Dagonet caught me from collapsing where I stood.

"I don't know, but that did it. Look! The fire's gone out," someone close to us shouted.

And from the gasps grew cheers. Suddenly everyone was yelling and clapping each other on their backs as if they were responsible for the wind that blew the fire out.

"Well done, oh, I say, well done!" Sir Dagonet said quietly in my ear.

Chapter Twenty Three

I gave Sir Dagonet my best smile, but I was so exhausted that even that was an effort. In an instant, Sir Dagonet and I were surrounded by my brothers.

"Scai! Was that you?" Matthias said with barely restrained enthusiasm.

"What do you mean? Of course it was, idiot," Piers said, pushing his brother out of the way so he could give me a hug.

"That was incredible, Scai," Thomas said.

"Completely and wonderfully incredible!" Peter added.

I was thoroughly overcome, wanting nothing more than to bury my face in Sir Dagonet's chest and cry my heart out.

It must have shown on my face, because Thomas put a gentle arm around my shoulders and said, "What is it?" His voice was so full of concern that I had the hardest time not bursting into tears right then.

I took a deep, shaky breath and looked all around at my brothers and then past them. "So many things," I whispered. "Everything, really."

I looked up into his eyes. "Was it so obvious that it was me who brought the wind? Will you hide me if they come after me? I'm too young to die, yet, Thomas. I'm not ready."

"What are you talking about?" he said, with a smile, as if he were trying to hold back a laugh. "You're not going to die."

"But if it was so obvious that I produced the wind, they'll think I'm a witch and burn me or have me swum," I whispered. My whole body began to tremble. And the prophecy... it had said I would die young to save others. Was this that? Had I just ensured my own death in order to save Bridget and Dylan?

Peter scoffed loudly, "How ridiculous you are!"

"Don't worry, if anyone tries to harm one hair on your head, we'll have at them," Matthias said.

I gave him a grateful smile, but I still couldn't stop shaking.

Thomas gave my shoulders a little squeeze, and added, "If anyone should come after you—which I am certain they won't—you'll be safe with us."

Gratefully, I rested my head against his shoulder, still looking at the door to the inn. "And Dylan and Bridget still aren't here. Maybe you should..."

But then the door flew open and Dylan came staggering out, Bridget unconscious in his arms.

All of the brothers rushed to them, except Thomas. Luckily, he continued to hold on to me, even though I could feel him start then restrain his desire to dash forward with the others.

"Bridget!"

"My God, what happened to her?"

They all started talking at once, questioning Dylan, who looked ready to collapse. Piers managed to take Bridget before any of his brothers. Gently, he held her cradled in his arms.

Dylan, relieved of his burden, stood panting in the fresh air, his hands on his knees.

"Got hit," he rasped, his voice rough with the smoke. He swallowed hard. "Got hit on the head by a falling beam," he just managed to croak out.

"Come on, let's get her home," Peter said, trying to guide his twin in that direction.

"Yes, let's get you all home," James echoed.

"Are you all right to walk, Scai?" Thomas asked me.

"Yes, I think so, I'm just very tired."

"'Course you are, my dear, wot, wot?" Sir Dagonet said, coming around and supporting my other arm.

<><><>

"How could she?" Nimuë growled. "How *could* she have escaped? And the other ones as well!"

Nimuë prowled around her room like an animal in its

cage.

"They are very strong, aren't they?" Morgan asked.

Nimuë took another turn around the room and tried to ignore her sister. "Yes," she finally admitted. "I can accept that they escaped from my hurricane—they worked together and managed to stop it. But my ravens should not have failed, and they would not have if it had not been for that other hawk. Who was that and why was it protecting the girl?"

Morgan was silent. So Nimuë took another turn around the room. "And the redhead was mine! She was unconscious, and mostly by her own hand too. I needed only to get her out of there, which I could have done easily... but, no, that tiresome boy and his sense of chivalry or whatever that was. He had to go back in there and pull her out."

"You could have had them both." Morgan was deliberately goading her.

"It would have been perfect."

"But once again, Scai came to the rescue."

Nimuë nearly growled in her anger.

"You have to admit her magic was impressive," Morgan went on. "Calling for a gust of wind. And it was strong. Strong enough to put out the blaze without spreading it."

She hated it—and never in her life would she admit as much to her sister—but Nimuë had been impressed.

"It should not have happened!" Nimuë slammed her fist down onto the table. Her silver bowl rattled with the force of the blow, spilling some of the precious water of Avalon. Nimuë steadied the bowl in her hands.

"Temper, my dear sister, temper," Morgan said, trying to hold back her laughter and being completely unsuccessful.

"Why am I unable to capture these children? They are *children*."

"You said yourself that they are not," Morgan pointed out.

Nimuë waved a hand. "To me they are no more than children. Twenty years of age." She would have laughed if she hadn't been so angry—and concerned.

But then she realized she had not had to trick anyone in this manner for some time.

Yes, that must be it. She was out of practice. That was all. She was simply out of practice.

Merlin had been so easy—but then, he had known what was coming.

"This is not a problem," Nimuë told Morgan. "Not at all." She stood in front of the silver bowl and looked down at her sister's shimmering image within it. "I will simply have to work a little harder. Be a little more clever, a little more cunning to deal with these three young *adults*." She practically sneered the word. "I assure you, this is not a problem."

<>
<>
<>

I lay down gently next to Bridget while Joan fussed over us both. Bridget had come to during the walk home and had immediately insisted that she could walk the rest of the way by herself. Her brothers would have none of it.

Cold water was applied to Bridget's head while she concentrated her energies on healing herself. Oddly enough, she wasn't burnt at all. It was just the bump on her head that was bad. I simply needed rest.

"Thank goodness she's got the power of healing," Matthias said, standing at the foot of the bed and grinning down at his sister.

Peter laughed, but Joan shooed them out of the room. "You leave these girls to rest," she said, closing the door on their protests.

Thomas stayed, sitting by my side of the bed while his wife continued to place cold compresses on Bridget's head. Bridget just lay there with her eyes closed, so I didn't know if she was awake or not.

It was a little disturbing seeing Bridget so still. I didn't think I had ever seen her not moving or animated. I turned to Thomas and whispered, "She's going to be all right, isn't she?"

My brother gave me a reassuring smile. "I think so. I've never seen Bridget down for long. I'm sure she'll be up and making us crazy sooner than we'd like."

"I heard that," Bridget mumbled.

I laughed as a whoosh of relief flowed through me.

Looking from Bridget back to Thomas again, I still could hardly believe where I was and who I was with—they were my brother and sister! I closed my eyes a moment in prayer to thank God for this wonderful, no, *incredible* gift He had given me.

Blinking hard once or twice to clear the tears from my eyes when I opened them again, I reached out and took Thomas's hand. His eyes immediately turned from Bridget back to me. They softened, and yet looked inquiringly. "I just wanted to truly thank you," I said quietly, so as not to disturb Bridget again.

"Thank me? For what?"

I gave a little shrug. "I don't know. For accepting me. For being my brother. For everything, really."

His eyes became a little shinier as he squeezed my hand. "I told you before, you have no need to thank me, Scai. You *are* my sister; there is no doubt about it. Even if you didn't look like us, I'd be able to feel it." He gave a little shrug. "I'm not a very powerful Vallen like you and Bridget, but I know my own sister when I meet her."

Such a feeling of love washed over me. A feeling—no, a knowledge—that no matter what, I would always be able to count on Thomas, or any one of my brothers. They would always be there for me. I swallowed hard at the lump that had suddenly tightened in my throat.

"I'm just sorry our parents didn't live to see you return to us," he said quietly, turning his eyes back to Bridget.

"What happened to them?" I asked.

"Mother died in childbirth with Bridget, and Papa, well, he just wasted away after that. He worked so hard to feed us all and take care of us, but without Mother's support..." Thomas shrugged.

"I'm so sorry," I said and, indeed, I felt a hollowness in my stomach at the loss of someone I had never known.

"If it hadn't been for Bridget, I'm sure we would have all starved or lived like pigs. She has taken care of us ever since she could walk, practically." He laughed while looking down at his frowning sister who still hadn't opened her eyes.

Thomas gave a little smile, squeezing my hand again before standing up. "You need to get some rest and we need to stop disturbing Bridget."

<><><>

I awoke to the sound of men's voices. For a moment I lay there not remembering where I was, but a movement drew my attention. Bridget was stirring next to me.

I propped myself up on my elbow so I could look out the window and try to gauge how long I'd been asleep. It must be near evening, I realized, not because of the shadows that I could hardly make out, but because of the rumbling in my stomach. I was absolutely famished, as if I hadn't eaten in a week.

The men's voices grew louder, as if they were arguing. Bridget sat up with a grumble and then held her hand to her head for a moment.

"Are you all right? Can I get you..."

"No, I'm fine. I just sat up too fast, that's all," she said, not even turning around. She stood and wobbled to the door, calling, "All right, all right. Stop arguing and just tell me what it is already."

There was immediate silence as she took a step out the door and into the common room to which all of the other rooms in the house were connected.

I scrambled up and followed Bridget out.

Our brothers and Sir Dagonet were all there, some seated, some standing. It looked like a still-life painting—Peter had even stopped somewhere in between sitting and standing. I burst out laughing at the sight.

Bridget turned to me with a smile. "Yes, they are rather ridiculous, aren't they?"

Peter finished standing up and moved away from the chair he had been sitting in. "Sit down, Bridget, before you fall down."

"I'm not going to fall down, idiot. I'm perfectly all right." But she took his seat anyway.

Thomas glared at Matthias, who reluctantly stood up and offered his chair to me. I was happy to take it since I was feeling a little light-headed.

"Now, what are you all arguing about?" Bridget asked, taking command of the situation.

"Nothing," Thomas said.

"Nothing at all," the rest of the men concurred.

Bridget just looked at me as if to say "Can you believe this?"

I laughed again, but this time I tried to hide it.

"Not very convincing are we, wot?" Sir Dagonet said, laughing as well.

"Not at all," Bridget agreed, beginning to giggle, too.

"Well, it's just that..." Peter started, but he was hit by Piers on the side of his head, so he shut up.

"We might as well tell them," Matthias argued. "They're going to find out anyway, and as Sir Dagonet said, it concerns them so they have a right to know."

"You're damn right we have a right to know!" Bridget said vehemently.

"Bridget! Your language," Joan admonished.

"Sorry," she said, not sounding sorry at all.

"What is it?" I asked.

The men all looked at each other, figuring out who was going to be the one to talk. James finally stood up.

"I went to see Old Maud about this chalice of Merlin's to see if I could learn any more about it," he began.

I took a quick look around. Dylan wasn't there. He must not have followed us home after the fire.

Bridget leaned forward. "What did you learn?"

James glanced at Thomas, who gave a small nod of his head. "Well, she couldn't tell me much more about the chalice specifically, but she did tell me more of the prophecy, which was apparently made a very long time ago." He sat down again on the arm of the chair Thomas was sitting in. "Apparently, our mother was extremely worried about this so she went to discuss it with Old Maud to try to decide what to do."

"What was the prophecy, James? Just spit it out," Bridget said, losing patience with his long–winded tale.

He looked at her and frowned. "There were a few parts to it. One was the bit about Scai," he said, looking back at me. "That we already knew about."

"That I would die to save others," I said, aware that no one else would.

"Er, yes, to save mankind, actually," he admitted a little

sheepishly.

"Wouldn't completely trust that one, don't you know?" Sir Dagonet interjected.

James turned to look at the old knight. "What do you mean, sir?"

"Oh, it's just that, well, Merlin, not infallible, don't you know?"

"I'd heard that everything he'd said had come true," Thomas argued.

Sir Dagonet nodded. "Nearly everything."

They all waited in silence for him to continue.

"Er, yes, well," Sir Dagonet said after a moment. "Said that he and Lady Nimuë would be together for eternity, didn't he? And, well, we all know how that turned out, wot, wot?"

"I'd never heard that," James said.

"Oh yes, common knowledge. Anyway, don't think we should start digging Scai's grave just yet, all I meant to say, don't you know?"

We all laughed a little uncomfortably, but inside of me everything seemed to sigh with relief.

James looked over at Bridget and continued with his reporting. "The prophecy said that the seventh child's heirs would heal the world of the Vallen."

Bridget paled a little. "That would be me? I'm the seventh child in our family."

He nodded and then went on. "There was more, but Old Maud really couldn't remember—she hasn't heard the prophecy since just before Scai was born twenty years ago. The only other thing she could remember with certainty was that the prophecy did mention Merlin's chalice."

"It did?" both Bridget and I said in unison.

He gave a little laugh, "Yes, sisters, it did. Unfortunately, Old Maud couldn't remember what it said," he finished on a more somber note.

"Well, but if it mentioned me and Scai along with the chalice, then surely we should be destined to find it," Bridget said, standing up and beginning to pace around the room.

"Can't tell you how many people have tried to find it over the years," Sir Dagonet said. "No one has, naturally."

"And clearly, Dylan is another one of those treasure seekers," Bridget said in exasperation, as if the chalice were already hers and Dylan was preparing to steal it.

"But because it's been impossible to find, most people think it's a myth—that it doesn't really exist," Thomas said. And, more softly, he concluded, "And it may not, for all we know."

"Well, don't know about that..." Sir Dagonet protested feebly.

I noticed the fingers of his right hand playing with something at his wrist. It was a funny habit he had whenever he was nervous.

"Well, but if it does exist..." I began.

"Then *we* are destined to find it," Bridget finished for me.

"What I was going to say," I began again, "is that if it does exist, then maybe Dylan knows where it is."

"Excellent point, Scai," Sir Dagonet said, sitting up.

"But since it was mentioned in a prophecy that spoke about us, then it's ours, not his," Bridget said with growing enthusiasm. "What does it matter what he knows or doesn't know? We don't want him to get it, do we? It's ours. *We're* going to find it and *we're* going use it."

All of the brothers glanced at each other nervously. Clearly, they knew the direction in which Bridget's mind was going, and they weren't at all happy about it.

"Now Bridget..." Thomas said, as the voice of reason.

"No! Don't you even dare try to talk me out of this one. I'm not going to allow that sneaky, underhanded Dylan find something that rightfully belongs to me—and certainly not something as powerful as Merlin's chalice! Can you imagine what would happen if he got his hands on it? I don't even want to—"

"Bridget, calm down," I said, trying to sooth her with my voice the way Dylan did.

"...contemplate such a thing. He is..."

But I didn't have his magic. "Bridget!" I said again, but she still didn't hear me.

"Usually physically grabbing her and forcing her to look

at you will work," Matthias said, laughing at my attempts to get our sister's attention.

I looked at Matthias for a moment and then smiled as the answer came to me. "I don't need to use physical force." I stood up and caught my sister's eye. Adding a touch of magic to my voice, I said, "Bridget, calm down and please listen to us."

Bridget stopped her harangue and frowned at me.

"Fine. What?" She then paused for a moment, blinked, then cocked her head to one side. "What did you just do to me? Did you use magic on me?"

"Yes," I admitted, wondering if perhaps I shouldn't have. "I'm sorry, but you just weren't listening."

"Oh! Good work," Matthias exclaimed. "I didn't even think of doing that."

Piers and Peter burst out laughing. "That's because you can't," Piers said.

The other brothers all laughed while Matthias turned pink.

A warm breeze filtered into the room as I looked around at all of my brothers. I had never been so very happy as I was now in the heart of my family—*my* family! I almost pinched myself to see if I was dreaming.

"I believe it would behoove you to find out what Dylan knows, wot, wot?" Sir Dagonet said, smiling at me and Bridget and bringing the conversation back to where it should have been. "He was headed in this direction before we even met up with him. Seems to have already been on his quest to find the chalice, don't you know?"

"But why would he help us?" Bridget asked.

Sir Dagonet shrugged. "Because you might have some information that could help him."

"But we don't know anything," I argued.

"You may not think you do, but you might know more than you know, wot?"

"What?"

"Precisely!"

I burst out laughing, as did some of the others. "I don't understand what you're saying, Sir Dagonet," I said, "but I'm willing to try talking with Dylan if he is willing to speak to me."

"Even after all he's done to you?" Bridget asked, aghast.

I shrugged. "It's easy for me to accept that he's done bad things to me—people always have." And then I added, trying not to sound as embarrassed as I felt, "It's when people are being kind and accepting, as you all have been, that I find it harder to understand."

"I thought you said you were treated well in Wales?" Thomas asked, a note of anger staining his voice.

"I was," I said quickly. "Father Llewellyn was wonderful and kind and loving. It was the townspeople. Well, everyone except my closest friend, Aron. He was always kind and always defended me—and got into too many fights on my behalf."

Yes, I could easily understand Dylan. He was going for what he wanted and wasn't going to let anyone get in his way. This new family of mine, on the other hand, just confused me, making me feel awkward and wonderful at the same time. They were like Aron and Father, only even more so. They were kind, accepting and generous—and they didn't even know me very well. "I know it sounds strange, but I like Dylan, and I don't think he truly meant to harm anyone," I added aloud.

"Well, I don't," Bridget said vehemently. "I don't trust him." She crossed her arms in front of her chest. "I think that we should go out on our own to find the chalice."

"Do you really?" James asked, quite surprised.

Bridget looked at him for a moment before answering, but then she said firmly, "Yes. Yes, I do."

"You really want to leave us?" Matthias asked.

Bridget's eyes softened. "No! Oh no, of course not. You all know that I love you and would hate to leave you, but..."

"But this is something that you've got to do," Thomas finished for her.

She gave him a little smile, her spark returning. "Yes."

"Well, but we can't do it on our own," I persisted. "Let's try talking to Dylan first, and if it doesn't work, then we'll try it your way, all right?"

Bridget didn't look happy at this, but she had begun to look tired. Clearly, although she claimed that she was fully recovered, she still needed some more rest. "Very well," she said, reluctantly.

I turned to Sir Dagonet. "Perhaps after dinner you can go and see if you can find Dylan?"

"If he hasn't already left to find the chalice," Bridget added in a sulky voice.

"Yes, of course. Happy to, wot, wot?"

Chapter Twenty Four

P ower," Father du Lac said almost to himself, "it is all about power."

He leaned against the battlements and looked out with a scowl at the rolling green pastures that surrounded Lord Lefevre's castle. "That is why I learned all I could from Merlin—everyone knows that he was the most powerful wizard ever. And he taught me everything. He shared his power with me." Du Lac turned to the wide–eyed cleric who stood next to him.

The man had paled considerably. This was a good sign.

At first the fellow had only looked worried, as du Lac had outlined for him the nature of the position for which he had been called. Spying was not something clergymen were typically asked to do, and certainly not from one of the most powerful priests in the land. Du Lac was known for being secure in his position.

"Surely, Father," the man had stated, "the King would never set you aside. I should not think you have anything to fear."

Father du Lac nodded, conceding his excellent point. "No, you are right. The King never would set me aside."

"But then why do you need me? Are you certain..." the man began.

"Am I certain? Am I certain that I am behaving in a reasonable manner? Is that what you are asking?"

"Well..."

Du Lac cocked his head at the man and studied him for a moment, reading him. "What is it, *Father*?" He tried to keep the mocking tone from his voice.

"It's just that...well, sir..."

"You think I am getting too old," du Lac stated. He nodded, pulling his thick grey eyebrows down over his eyes—almost as if he were in agreement. "You worry for my sanity."

"Well, Father, it's...it's just that..." the younger man began to stammer but could not bring himself to lie.

Du Lac laughed. "But you see, I am actually much older than you think. If I mention Merlin, it is because I knew him, personally. I assure you, however, that my mind is fully alert. And it is not Father du Lac for whom you are going to spy," she said as she turned fully toward the man—the façade she had worn for so many years falling away.

Even as the man watched, du Lac lost nearly a foot in height. His broad shoulders narrowed and a bosom swelled beneath his costly, albeit plain, tunic. His face softened into a woman's face—the sagging jowls turning into a firm jaw line, the old wrinkles smoothing out to reveal sharp, high cheek bones, piercing green eyes and full lips now caught up in a sneer. She was dark and yet knew herself to be beautiful, even as wisps of her long, curly black hair fought with the light wind that swirled around them.

"Oh yes, I am quite, quite old." She paused, but then, ignoring the abject terror on the priest's face, continued with her earlier train of thought as if nothing had happened. "They all cried for poor Merlin when I trapped him in that tree, you know," she said softly, enjoying the fact that the cleric had begun to shake visibly. He backed himself against the outside wall of the parapet, trying to get as far away from her as he dared.

"But he knew what was coming. He knew very well what was happening, and yet he did nothing to stop it. He knew I had the one thing he could not control—his heart. It was mine from the moment we met and he was powerless to do anything about it. He accepted that and I respect him for doing so."

She turned back toward the meadows. "Yes, I, Nimuë, bested the most powerful wizard ever," she said, wistfully. "My sister, Morgan, tried to take my power from me. She tried, but she was not clever enough. I enjoyed destroying her reputation—she went from the beautiful, kindhearted and talented Lady of Avalon to the villain of Arthur's reign." Nimuë laughed, remembering. But then her smile slipped off her face. "And now some children think they can just come and kill me? Ha! They do not stand a chance."

"Ch–children?" the priest stammered. He looked at the door that led down into the courtyard then back at Nimuë.

She took a few steps toward the door before he could move in that direction. She wasn't finished yet. "They're not actually children," she said, with a negligent wave of her hand. "They are powerful, all three of them, but they shall not best me. They shall not!" Nimuë calmed herself and turned back to the cleric. "You will watch them. I want to know what they are doing, where they are going, and what they are planning. And then you will lure them outside Gloucester's Northern gate." She paused and then added, "I will have a little...surprise waiting for them."

The man's eyes widened.

"Oh, just a few friends to help convince them that they should come with me. That is all," she said airily, as if she were planning a day in the park.

But the man's eyes narrowed in disbelief. From somewhere deep inside him, the fellow seemed to have found his backbone. "What do you plan on doing to these children?" he asked.

"Not children!"

"What are you planning to do to these people?" the priest corrected himself.

"I shall capture them," she replied, switching to a lighter tone of voice.

The man's shoulders lowered with relief.

"Then steal their powers and kill them, naturally," she finished.

The cleric's jaw dropped. "But you can't just..."

"I can't? I can't just what?"

"Kill innocent children—people!" he corrected.

Nimuë smiled. She laughed. The man's eyes widened.

"But...but why?" the cleric stammered out.

"Why? Why do I want them destroyed?" she snapped.

She took a deep breath to regain her composure. "Because with their powers I will become the most powerful Vallen in history, idiot. I am the most powerful one here, but I will be the most powerful ever, anywhere."

"But then why do you fear..."

"I fear nothing and no one!"

"And yet you plan on killing these innocents," the man argued.

"It is the prophecy," Nimuë growled. "*This power will render her accursed, unless the trio all die first. Or she will be...destroyed by one and children three*," she recited. "Clearly I have to kill them before they kill me."

"I...I can't allow you..." His whole body once again began to tremble with fright, but he stood his ground.

Nimuë took the two steps that separated them, anger flaring in her gut. "You cannot allow me? You cannot allow me to what?" she whispered, closing the distance between them.

"To...to kill these children," he whispered.

"Oh, really?" she said, putting her fingertips on his shoulders.

He nodded, leaning away from her. His hands fumbled behind him, trying to find the wall that pressed against his legs.

"No one," she said, leaning forward, "no one tells me what I can and cannot do."

The cleric leaned backwards even more, trying to get away from her, but there was nowhere to go.

"You do understand, do you not?"

The fellow's arms began to windmill behind him as he fought to keep his balance.

"I will simply have to find someone else," she said, stepping back as the man finally lost his fight with gravity and fell over the wall. She paused to watch as he fell, his face twisted in terror.

Just as he was about to be shattered on the hard ground, she gestured with her hand. The man stopped his descent in mid–air. Smiling grimly, she twisted his body so that his feet were nearly touching the ground and then released him so that he dropped the rest of the way, landing lightly on his toes.

With only the briefest look back up at her, the priest fled for the nearby woods, running so fast he almost tripped over his robes.

As her anger calmed within her, Nimuë wondered at her generosity. Would he tell anyone what he had seen and heard? Perhaps she should have just let him die.

No, even if he did tell anyone, who would believe him?

Determined and possibly a little power–hungry she might be, but a petty murderer she was not—she only killed when she had to.

Chapter Twenty Five

Following Sir Dagonet's directions the next morning, Bridget and I drove out of the city in our brothers' wagon. I rubbed the cold perspiration from my palms, yet again. I hated this feeling of sweating in the chilly autumn air, but I just couldn't help feeling apprehensive.

The last time I'd really seen Dylan, aside from the few moments after the fire, he'd been doing everything he could to stop me from meeting my family. Now I was trying to put that behind me. Father Llewellyn had always taught me to turn the other cheek, and somehow, despite the teasing and cruelty of the village children, I had learned to do so. So now, I dredged up all of my learned patience and fixed my eyes firmly forward. I refused to let my anger and hurt color my relationship with Dylan. We were going to have to work together to find this chalice. It would do me no good to hold on to negative feelings.

I took a deep breath and felt the wind ruffle through my hair. Opening my heart and mind to it, I let all my emotions blow away on the breeze. I would do much better with a clear and open mind this morning.

I glanced over at Bridget, wishing that I could teach her the same trick. Her eyes stared fiercely ahead as she navigated our way out of the city. Her mouth was pinched, and I could see the embers of anger in the pink of her cheeks.

I took another deep breath, preparing myself for this meeting, as we drove out of the city's Northern gate. Bridget had insisted we come to meet Dylan alone, without our brothers to act as a buffer—as they, apparently, always did. Sir Dagonet had offered to stay back as well.

Dylan was waiting for us when we arrived. I could hear Bridget's tension in my mind. Thank goodness she was reminding herself to watch her tongue.

"How is your head?" Dylan asked, as we approached him.

"Fine, thank you," Bridget said. She might have had her teeth clenched, her voice was so tight.

Dylan was obviously aware of Bridget's suppressed anger and matched it with a tension of his own. He stood with his head held high and his thick arms crossed in front of his chest, just in case either of us girls forgot for one moment that he was the man.

Bridget clearly wasn't impressed, and to prove it she turned away and began looking around. We were in a clearing not even fifty yards from the town entrance, and there was no one in sight. I supposed this was a less—used entrance, with more traffic coming from London in the east and Cardiff and Bath to the south. A forest encroached from one side, but didn't look menacing—or perhaps after my journey from Wales, I had just gotten used to forests.

"Why did you want to meet here?" Bridget asked.

Dylan frowned in her direction. "It's quiet and we can speak openly. Are you unhappy with it?"

Bridget blinked at him innocently. "No. It's just an odd spot. I would never have thought to come outside of the city."

"Well, someone suggested it to me, all right?" He was already beginning to get angry and defensive. This talk was not going well, and we hadn't even truly begun.

I wished I could do or say something that would make Bridget like Dylan more, but just now my mind was blank as to how I would go about such a task. I was grateful when Bridget gave a careless shrug and asked, "So what do you know of the chalice?"

Unfortunately, Dylan raised both his eyebrows and his chin, clearly not liking her question or the tone with which she asked it. Even I had to admit Bridget sounded much too suspicious, as if she didn't trust Dylan one bit. That may have been true, but surely she shouldn't show it so blatantly.

Before Dylan had a chance to answer her, though, there

was a snort and a grunt, and a wild boar came bearing down on us from the forest. Its horn was drawn down aggressively as it charged straight at us.

I froze, unable to move as the terrifying beast came at us at an alarming speed. Both Dylan and Bridget each grabbed one of my arms at the same time—and pulled in opposite directions. A scream burst from me as power jolted through me. I could feel every hair on my body stand on end, but suddenly I was energized like nothing I had experienced before—to say nothing of the pain of having my arms nearly pulled from my body.

Dylan pulled again, harder, just as Bridget stopped, and we all went flying off to one side. This only disconcerted the animal for a moment as it ran past. It paused to turn and charge at us again.

Dylan was on his feet right away, turning toward the forest, his hand held out expectantly. A branch from the closest tree tore itself away. Dylan caught it and turned back to face the boar once more.

Bridget hadn't waited for a weapon. She curled her hand up over her shoulder as if it contained a ball and threw something at the animal. Whatever it was turned into a ball of fire as it flew. The boar dodged at the last moment, but Dylan stood ready with his stick in his hands.

I wanted to help but was wavering over what I could do, when a screech from above caught my attention. A hawk! My friend had come...no, wait—this hawk wasn't white like the one who had saved me from the ravens. It flew with amazing speed straight at us, reaching out with its razor sharp talons to grab at Dylan just as he was about to strike the boar.

My natural instincts kicked in and I raised my hand, sending a rush of wind to knock the bird off course. It faltered but started on its course of attack again, this time aiming straight for me.

"Scai, change into a bird and attack it!" Dylan shouted.

I considered this for the briefest second and then shouted back, "No! I don't have as much strength as a bird as I do as a person."

He didn't have time to answer because the boar was

about to attack—and now it seemed as if it had brought some friends.

Three wolves appeared from nowhere.

Bridget followed Dylan's lead and pulled a branch from the forest to use as a weapon, only she set hers on fire.

"This was a trap!" she called out, swinging the burning branch in front of the wolves.

"Yes, but from whom and why?" Dylan answered. He was doing his best to stave off the boar.

"It doesn't make sense," I said, while doing all I could to stop each of the hawk's attempts to get close to me. Again and again it lunged, its talons coming closer each time.

One of the wolves began to yelp as Bridget's stick set its fur on fire. But the other two only stopped their attack for a moment to glance at it.

Things almost seemed under control, with each of the three of us managing to stave off the attacks of each animal. But then the odds changed.

Two more hawks joined the fray, as well as another boar. Suddenly, we were badly outnumbered.

Dylan swung his branch at one boar, only to be attacked from overhead by another bird, its sharp talons digging deep into the back of his neck and shoulder.

I tried to help him, but one of the wolves had decided I was easier prey than Bridget and had leapt straight at me, grabbing onto my arm. I screamed in pain as it sank its teeth deep, pulling me down to the ground.

Spheres of fire came flying from Bridget, but they did relatively little harm. In fact, they seemed only to anger the wolf even more.

In excruciating pain, I was certain this was how I was going to die. My vision began to dull. The wolf let go of my arm. Baring its bloody fangs, it focused on my neck—when it was suddenly sent flying away from me.

An old man in priest's robes appeared above me, and I realized all the noise in my ears wasn't my imagination. Men surrounded us. Men of every description, wielding pitchforks, swords, and even a blacksmith's hammer.

We were saved. Father Llewellyn had found me and

saved us. With a sigh of relief, I let go of the battle and closed my eyes.

When I opened them again, the priest was kneeling next to Dylan, pressing a cloth to his wounded shoulder, and another man was tightly wrapping cloth around my own arm. Bridget just sat watching from a short distance away, not daring to do any magic in front of such a crowd.

Aside from the one tending to me, there must have been ten more men standing around, all waiting for direction from the priest. But as he turned back toward me, I realized he wasn't Father Llewellyn at all. It must have just been a trick of my imagination—or wishful thinking.

No, this priest had much more hair than my beloved guardian, and he was older, more wizened. "Are you all right, child?" he asked.

I nodded. "Thank you, Father." Turning to the man who was binding my arm and then to the others all standing around, I said, "Thank you all. I don't know what we would have done..."

"We heard your screams," one of the men said.

But I didn't scream, I almost said aloud. I stopped myself, however, just before the words were out of my mouth. I exchanged a glance with Bridget, who was looking a little confused and very worried.

Did I scream? I directed into Bridget's mind.

She looked surprised for a moment but then shook her head, not saying a word. I wondered if perhaps she couldn't speak telepathically as Dylan and I could. Perhaps not.

"You need more help than we can give you here. My name is Father du Lac. I am staying with Lord Lefevre at his home not far away. If you would fetch my carriage," he said, turning to one of the men standing nearby. "I will take the young people there to be cared for."

The man and two others went to do the priest's bidding.

"That's not necessary, Father," Bridget said.

"Very kind of you, sir, but truly we can..." Dylan began.

"No, no, I insist. Lord Lefevre has a servant who is very skilled in the arts of healing. I will have her tend to you, and then if you do not care to stay for the night, I will see that you are driven back to the city. Of course"—he turned and smiled at me—"you are more than welcome to stay as long as you wish."

I nodded, smiling at the old man. It was so good to be taken care of by someone familiar. Even if I didn't know him, Father du Lac was a priest. I knew I could trust him.

Chapter Twenty Six

I was just too tired. My legs were as heavy as rainclouds before a storm and my arm was hurting. I thought it had finally stopped bleeding, but I wasn't certain. And frankly, I was too frightened to peel back the rough bandage to take a look.

I wished that this spritely old priest, Father du Lac, wouldn't walk so fast. I was having the most difficult time keeping up as we followed him through Lord Lefevre's castle.

After what seemed like an interminably long walk down the corridor, Father du Lac finally stopped at a door and opened it. He stood back so that Bridget, Dylan, and I could precede him into the room.

"Oh!" The word popped out of my mouth as soon as I had gone through the door.

I paused, taking in the room. It was beautiful. Certainly the loveliest room I had ever seen in my life.

I was acutely aware at how dirty and ragged I was as I looked at the pristine white cushions on the armchairs that basked in the light and warmth filtering in through the narrow window. My filthy toes curled in my shoes at the thought that they would never feel the beautiful carpet on the floor, which just begged for me to luxuriate in its softness. And then my eye was caught by the tapestry hanging on the wall at the far end of the room. More than anything else in the room, it truly bespoke of a wealth I had only heard of in stories. The room even smelled rich—clean and with the faintest scent of flowers. Only as an afterthought did I see a small, ordinary table that did not fit in with the rest of the room's lush furnishings. It had a bowl of water and some clean linens on it, which made me think it must have been placed there just for us.

"Oh, honestly, sir, this room is entirely too beautiful for us to inhabit even for just the shortest time," I protested, turning around to face Father du Lac, who was standing by the door.

"Indeed, Father, you are too kind," Dylan said.

"Not at all, not at all. Make yourselves comfortable. I shall return shortly with the maid and her healing salves." He closed the door behind him, but the sound that immediately followed made me turn around, perplexed.

Dylan took two steps toward the door and tried to pull on the handle. "Locked!"

"What?" Bridget tried it herself, then frantically shook the handle, before finally, pounding on the door with her fist. "Let us out!" she yelled through the door. But no one answered.

"I don't understand. Why would he lock the door?" I asked, not liking the obvious answer that was clawing around inside my stomach.

Bridget turned around and started to give me a look, but she stopped, her eyes widening in horror instead.

I spun around, almost ready for another wild animal to attack, but what I saw blew everything else straight out of my mind. I fell back a step. "I don't understand," I managed to whisper. "Where did it go?"

There was nothing left in the room. Nothing but one small bare cot pushed up against the far, very empty, cold stone wall. Even the window had disappeared.

"It was a glamour." Dylan's voice reflected his tightly controlled anger.

"I've never seen an entire room with a glamour before," Bridget said in quiet, terrified awe.

"This 'priest' must be an extremely powerful Vallen to have managed such a thing," Dylan said.

As Bridget walked to where the window had been, I bumped into the table with the water bowl on it—that was still there. "It's just incredible," she said, running her hand along the now very solid wall.

"It's a trap." Dylan turned to me. "You led us into a trap."

"But...but Father du Lac is a priest. He would never..."

"Why not? We don't even know that he is a priest. The only thing we know is that he is a powerful Vallen," Bridget said, turning to face me as well.

"Oh, God!" I dropped my head into my hands. I *had* led them into a trap. All of my muscles tensed and I held my breath, trying desperately not to cry.

"I can't believe we just followed her," Dylan said, his voice cracking in his anger.

"Oh, but *you've* done absolutely nothing wrong at all today, is that right?" Bridget said, her own anger flaring up. "Who was it who decided to meet outside of the Northern Gate?"

Dylan didn't answer her.

I managed to look up, although everything was blurry for a moment until I blinked the tears out of my eyes. "I still don't understand why Father du Lac..." I couldn't even finish my sentence. I felt like a leaf that had been blown around by a strong autumn wind, tumbling head over heels, leaf over stem, down the street. Around and around in my mind came the same refrain: "He's a priest. He can't be a Vallen. He would never harm us, or anyone. He's a priest!"

Desperately, I turned back to Dylan. "He'll be back. He said he would return shortly..." But my voice died off as both Dylan and Bridget turned angry faces towards me.

I could only look helplessly from one to the other.

"Why do you think that just because a man is a priest he's trustworthy?" Dylan asked, fury radiating from his voice.

I opened my mouth, but there was no answer. It was just so obvious. Priests were good. There was no other possibility. How could there be a bad priest? It just didn't make sense. It wasn't right.

"He's not a priest," Bridget stated with an absolute certainty that did give me some small feeling of relief. "She made a mistake," she continued, defending me to Dylan.

"A mistake? A mistake?" he repeated his voice becoming tight once again. "A mistake that is going to cost us our lives!"

Dylan advanced on Bridget.

I took a step toward him. "What makes you so certain of that?"

"Well, if he doesn't come back soon with this maid and her healing salves, I'm probably going to bleed to death," he said viciously.

That stopped Bridget. Now that he'd said it, I noticed his shirt was becoming ever more soaked with blood. I had believed that, like me, he'd stopped bleeding. Bridget must have thought so, too, because she let out an exasperated sigh.

"Let me see."

Dylan took a step back. "No. It's all right. I'll manage. I've been hurt before. Worse than this."

"Yes, of course you have. Now sit down," Bridget commanded.

"No, really..."

"Sit down!" Bridget snapped.

Dylan did so, dropping on to the little cot. Clearly, no one had any energy or patience left.

Bridget ripped open Dylan's tunic a bit more so she could see his wound better. Then, without a word, she turned and stalked to the table holding the water. Dipping one of the pieces of linen into the water, she let it soak for a moment before taking it back to Dylan.

She worked silently for a moment, cleaning his wound. "There's got to be a way out," she said finally, but without looking up from her work.

"The only way is through that door," Dylan said through gritted teeth. "And wishing for it isn't going to make that window reappear, Scai."

I jumped and turned toward him. I hadn't even realized I was staring at the wall where the window had been. "No. But there's got to be some way out—aside from the door. Or some way to get someone to open the door." I paused and then asked quietly, "You really don't think Father du Lac..."

"No," Dylan said.

"Scai, please! Do you honestly think he's going to just come back and let us out?" Bridget said, sarcasm burning through her words. She dropped the dirty linen into Dylan's lap and placed both of her hands over his wound.

Dylan sucked in his breath between his teeth, but when Bridget took her hands away, his skin was whole again. Bright red, but whole.

"Thank you," he said, rather reluctantly.

It was my turn next. Luckily, Bridget healed me more gently, although it still burned when she knitted my arm back together.

"So what are we going to do, just sit here and wait until this 'priest' comes back?" Bridget asked, pressing the cool damp cloth to my burning skin once more.

"We could. He's got to come back for us," I said. I was not going to lose faith. "Even if he is a Vallen dressed as a priest—not that I'm ready to believe that yet—he still brought us to this room for some reason. He wouldn't just put us here and leave us."

"I'm not entirely certain that him coming back is a good thing," Bridget said, now nervously eyeing the door.

"Well, it is just a bar on the other side of the door," I suggested.

"Magic doesn't go through solid wood," Dylan said, his voice turning ice cold once again.

Bridget began to pace the edges of the room, like a confined animal.

"There's got to be some way..." I started. Bridget paused to give me a hard stare, but I wouldn't give up. "Come on. We're powerful Vallen. There's got to be something..."

But my words were cut off at the sound of the bar being lifted.

The door opened and Father du Lac appeared. Immediately, he raised his hand toward Dylan. "I would not try that if I were you," he said, his voice sounding much too threatening for a kindly old priest.

Dylan stopped in mid–stride, frozen in place. A moment later, he landed on his raised foot and nearly lost his balance. "Who are you? Why have you brought us here?"

The priest just smiled, looked from Dylan to Bridget and then finally to me. All of my muscles began to tense, and the air in the room somehow disappeared.

"Who do you think I am?" he asked, looking directly at me.

I was suddenly cold and empty. "I...I don't know. I had thought that you were a priest, which is why I allowed you to bring us here."

"Ah, yes, naturally. But you do not think that anymore?"

"No."

"Good. You are learning."

"But..."

"And now I have more I want to teach you, Scai," he said, his voice sounding so kind and sincere once again. For a moment, I almost forgot that this was a Vallen to be feared, he played his role so very well.

"Why her?" Bridget asked coming forward. "Why not me?"

"Or me?" Dylan put in.

Father du Lac looked at the two of them and smiled. "Oh, have no fear, my children. You will have your turns as well. I would not be so cruel as to single out only one of you. It is just that I can only teach one person at a time. Scai is the lucky one. She gets to go first." He then turned back to me and held out his hand. "Come, my dear. You know, I am so very impressed with how fast you learn that I am sure this will not take long at all."

I took a step forward, but Dylan cut in front of me. "No. You can't take her. I shall go first."

Father du Lac just shook his head. Chuckling a little, he said, "Such bravery, such chivalry. But alas, no. I have chosen Scai, and so it shall be her. Come along now, my dear."

I put my hand on Dylan's arm. "It's all right, Dylan." I had gotten us into this mess, perhaps on the other side of that door there way some way for me to get us out of it.

Dylan looked down at me with serious concern in his eyes, despite the trouble I had gotten us into. As he put his hand on top of mine, there was no need for me to be able to read his thoughts or have his emotion−reading abilities. I could see what he felt in his eyes, and I felt it, too. It warmed the cold that had come over me the moment Father du Lac had come into the room.

And it allowed me to push aside my fears and follow Father du Lac out the door.

Chapter Twenty Seven

I turned around after entering the sitting room into which I had been shown but started to choke on my own breath.

Father du Lac was changing!

He lost height, his body melting into that of a woman. Never in my life had I seen anything so terrifying. I stood there speechless, shaking. I wanted to scream, to make some sort of noise, at the very least to run, or even fly, away.

But the woman who now stood before me held me transfixed with just her eyes.

"Poor dear little Scai. What has you trembling so?" she asked in the same sweet tone of voice that Father du Lac had used. From him it had seemed priestly, but coming from her it was terrifying. "Oh, now, it is all right. Have you never seen a Vallen change shape before?"

I managed to give a little shake of my head.

"No, I do not suppose you have. You are still so new to all of this."

My chin dipped as I tried to nod.

"Yes, I know. But you have learned so very much in such a short amount of time," the woman went on. "I truly was very impressed. You went from almost nothing to being a very powerful Vallen in only a matter of weeks. Well done, my dear girl, well done."

"How do you know that? Who are you?" I managed to whisper through my fear.

The woman's black eyebrows went up, wrinkling her flawless forehead. "You do not recognize me, even in my true form? No, of course not. How silly of me." The woman gave a little laugh. "I forgot you have been raised in such a cloistered way." The woman took a few steps toward me. I wanted to retreat, but it felt as if my feet were stuck fast to the floor.

"I am Lady Nimuë," the woman said in her kind voice. "Have you heard of me?"

My mind began to race. I'd heard this name only the day before. My brothers... "My brothers were saying something about someone named Nimuë. But she lived a very long time ago—in the time of Merlin."

"Yes, that is correct. Very good. Merlin and I were very close once." The woman nodded and smiled.

"But you can't be...I mean...That Nimuë must have died hundreds of years ago."

The woman smiled. "There is no other Nimuë, I assure you."

"No? But surely..."

"There is only one Nimuë and I am she. I am the one who tricked Merlin into the tree. I am the one with whom he shared his powers and his secrets. And now you are going to share yours with me." The woman took another step closer.

Her fingers bit into my arms as she grasped onto me.

I tried to move, but I couldn't even pull my eyes away from hers. They were an intense green, holding on to mine with a force that was beyond anything I had ever felt before. My heart began to thunder in my chest as terror flooded my body.

"Give them to me," Nimuë whispered. "Give me your powers."

I just barely managed to shake my head. "No."

Nimuë's eyes darted around, searching my face and releasing the lock she'd had. "How do I get them?" she whispered to herself.

I had to do something. I had to get away. This woman was crazy. She was delusional, thinking herself the great Nimuë. And now she wanted to steal my powers!

I tried to back away, but the woman's grip only tightened.

"No, let me go," I cried, trying to break free.

"Your powers. They will be mine," the woman growled.

"What did Merlin do? How did he give me his?" The woman gave me a shake as if I could answer her. "It has been too long! Why can I not remember?"

This woman was truly mad. I began to struggle in earnest, but still she held on to me with a grip like steel.

"What did he do? We touched hands," she said, letting go of my arms and grabbing my hands in each of her own.

I could feel the searing heat of Nimuë's powers as our palms touched.

"Yes! I feel it. I feel your power." The woman stared at our hands for a moment and then shifted her eyes up to mine. Her growing excitement drove me to struggle even harder. If this woman was pleased, I had to get away—now.

I tried again to pull away, but Nimuë held on to me too tightly.

"Give me your powers. Push them into me."

"No!"

"There is something more. Something is missing." Her eyes scanned mine once again, and I realized that Nimuë hadn't spoken out loud. Her words echoed in my mind.

I wished I had learned how Dylan had put that lock, that suggestion, into my mind. A gust of hope filled me—maybe I could do the same to Nimuë. Staring into Nimuë's eyes, I projected into her mind "You do not want my powers. You do not want them. Let me and my friends go free."

A smile crept onto her face. "Very clever, my dear girl, but you cannot think to influence me with your magic. I am much too strong for that."

And just as quickly my hope dropped to almost nothing. But, no, I would not give up.

My hands were beginning to hurt, Lady Nimuë's grip was so tight. Her eyes narrowed in thought. "He kissed me," she said, remembering. "Yes, that is what he did, he kissed me."

"No!" I twisted and turned away frantically even as the woman came closer, trying to touch her lips to my own. She was coming disgustingly close. I could feel the warmth of her breath.

But then my eyes caught on a gleaming silver bowl sitting

on the table just behind Lady Nimuë. In the blink of an eye, I sent the bowl crashing over the woman's head, showering us both with the water that had been in it.

"No!" Nimuë screamed, letting go of me. "No! Not my precious water!"

I didn't wait to hear more. I took two steps toward the window and was on my way out with one strong flap of my wings.

A strong gust of wind sent me tumbling into the wall. I was on the floor trying to shake the pain from my head when huge hands came down and grabbed me, pinning my wings to my sides. All I could do was squawk my indignation.

Nimuë held me too tightly as I was carried to the room where Bridget and Dylan were still being held. I could barely breathe by the time I was thrown back in with them.

I landed on my bottom on the cold stone floor. Bridget and Dylan were at my side within a moment.

"What happened?"

"Are you all right?"

"What did he do to you?"

"Who was that who brought you back here?"

They threw questions at me faster than I could even think to answer one. I was trembling inside and out, too shaken up to do anything more than bury my head down onto my knees and try very, very hard not to cry.

Dylan pulled me into his lap, wrapping his arms around me while Bridget brushed back my hair and murmured quiet words of comfort. Slowly Dylan's calm eased through my tension, relaxing my muscles.

"Are you hurt? Scai?" Bridget asked gently.

I took stock of myself. Aside from feeling a little unnerved at just how good it felt to be held by Dylan, I was all right. But I couldn't let him distract me. Not now. Not when that... that woman was nearby and we were imprisoned here.

I took a deep breath. It was filled with Dylan's fresh water scent. With borrowed strength from him, I was able to pull away to answer my sister. "I got banged against the wall when I was trying to fly out the window, but other than that she just... just scared me."

"Who is she?" Dylan asked.

"Lady Nimuë. She said that she was Lady Nimuë."

Bridget burst to her feet. "But she couldn't be. I mean, she'd be..."

"Dead. Yes, I mentioned that to her, but she said that she was the one who entrapped Merlin. He gave her some of his powers and now she wanted mine. She couldn't remember how to take them, though. At least, not at first."

"She wanted your powers?" Dylan said incredulously.

"How does someone take your powers?" Bridget asked, lowering herself down onto the floor next to me again.

"She... She tried to kiss me," I said, shuddering as I remembered how close Nimuë had come to doing just that.

"No! That's..." Bridget began, but then paused when she couldn't seem to find the right word, but her face looked like she had just eaten something sour.

"I know." And I did. I knew just what Bridget meant to say and was shocked when I had the wherewithal to laugh. "I smashed a silver bowl over her head."

"Good for you!" Dylan said, a big smile spreading across his face.

"And then I turned into a bird and tried to fly out the window, but she knocked me into the wall with a gust of wind. She's very strong." But so was I, I told myself firmly.

Dylan's hand caressing my back reminded me as to where I was sitting. I was sure my face must have turned pink with my sudden awareness of him. I tried to give him a little smile and hope that Bridget didn't see it or my blush, as I moved myself out of his lap.

"Well, no surprise there, if she really is Lady Nimuë," Bridget said from the other side of the room where she had retreated in her pacing.

"We've got to get out of here. Whether she is truly Lady Nimuë or not," Dylan said, standing up and putting his back to me. I couldn't tell if he was feeling the same awkwardness I had or was just focused on getting free of this room.

"She might come back to take your powers. Or Bridget's. I managed to escape, but I was lucky."

"How can we get out of here? There's only way out and it's locked," Bridget said, continuing to pace the room.

I looked at the very solid wood door. Then something occurred to me. "Bridget," I said, turning toward her, "you started that fire at the inn, and outside of the gate you threw something that set one of the wolves on fire. How did you do that?"

Bridget looked a little confused, but gave a shrug. "I just threw a sphere of magic at the wolf. I'm afraid it was my words which started the fire at the inn."

I didn't quite understand, but I didn't have to time just now to ask what she meant. "Well, do you think you could set fire to that door?"

"I don't think that would be a good idea, Scai. She nearly burned down the entire inn!" Dylan protested with a laugh.

"Yes, but the inn was made of wood. This castle is made of stone. And also, I'm here. Bridget can burn the door, but before the fire can spread, I'll put it out with a gust of wind, and then you, Dylan, can break down the weakened door," I said, explaining my plan to them.

"Brilliant!" Bridget exclaimed. Then she threw a well-aimed fireball at the door.

<><><>

Bridget, Dylan, and I slipped through a smaller door next to the main gate, the guard on duty happily waving to us as we ran down the road leading from the castle. Dylan's suggestions had done the trick, and amazingly we hadn't had too much trouble escaping. There were too many people running toward the still-burning fire to notice three people running away from it—Dylan had suggested leaving the door burning after we had broken through it, just as a distraction.

I wasn't entirely happy with leaving such destruction or coercing people in this way. But I saw Dylan's point. Sometimes it was just necessary.

I took a deep, welcome breath of freedom—and then almost lost it in a scream. A knight on horseback was racing toward us, his helm lowered over his face and his sword raised, ready to attack. A second horse was following, but it had no rider.

The three of us stopped running, coming to a slow halt in the middle of the road. Still, the two horses thundered toward us, coming at an incredible speed.

"That's my horse!" Dylan exclaimed. I couldn't tell if he was angry or excited.

But if that was Dylan's horse...Yes! I knew that knight. This was exactly the way I had seen Sir Dagonet for the very first time—riding toward me at a great speed with his sword raised high in the air, ready to strike me down.

"Sir Dagonet!" I yelled, praying he wouldn't strike us down by mistake. And just like last time, I found myself unable to move out of the way as his horse's thundering hooves got closer and closer.

Someone pulled me to the side just in time. Sir Dagonet rode past, except this time it wasn't an oak tree into which he embedded his sword, it was a man. In one clean swipe of his blade, he took the head off of one of three knights who were approaching us from behind.

In the shock of Sir Dagonet's advance, we hadn't even noticed the knights who had come after us from the castle.

I hid my face as the knight's head flew off into the field to our right. Bridget's arms came around me. I focused my eyes on her, wanting to look anywhere but at the fight taking place much too close. Bridget's face was pale and serious as she watched the combat.

"Behind you, sir!" Dylan shouted.

I spun around to look and was immediately sorry. A second knight was coming around to attack Sir Dagonet from behind as he fought the one in front of him.

Sir Dagonet turned around, lunging with a speed and agility that I hadn't known the old man possessed.

"Didn't anyone ever teach you any manners, young man?" the older knight asked, as he swung his sword at his new aggressor. "Not the thing to attack someone from behind, wot?"

"Stand down, sir!" the knight in front of him cried out as he joined back into the fray, attacking Sir Dagonet even as he was fighting the second warrior.

"Stand down? Stand down, you say?" Sir Dagonet

exclaimed, swinging his sword back and forth from one knight to the other. "Now how could I possibly do that when astride my horse? I am sitting. I cannot stand down, don't you know?"

I slapped my hand to my mouth. Bridget looked as if she was about to burst out laughing.

And poor Sir Dagonet was somehow attempting to fight two knights at once. I could hardly bear to watch, and yet, somehow, I couldn't turn away. Sir Dagonet thrust his sword at one man and immediately followed it up with a strike at the other.

But then I truly did have problems not bursting into laughter when I noticed Dylan standing by the side, hopping from one foot to the other, watching the fight intently. He clearly wanted to get into it, but there was nothing he could do. He was unarmed.

"Give up," the first knight called out again. "We have you outnumbered."

"Outnumbered?" Sir Dagonet stopped for the briefest of moments and looked between the two knights. "Ha! So you do."

As Sir Dagonet lowered his sword, the first knight tried to take advantage and thrust out at Sir Dagonet with his sword. But before he knew it, Sir Dagonet had dodged his attack and thrust his sword forward, straight through a gap in the side of his armor. The man fell to the ground.

"There, that's better. Now the odds are even, wot, wot?"

"Ha! Well done, sir!" Dylan exclaimed.

The remaining knight took a moment to look at his fallen comrade before turning his horse around and speeding back to the castle.

"Well! That's rather unsporting of him," Sir Dagonet said, sounding a little annoyed.

He sheathed his sword. Reaching his hand down toward Bridget, he said in his usual good–natured voice, "We'd better be off before he returns with reinforcements."

Dylan, his face lit with excitement and triumph, was up on his horse in a flash, helping me up behind him. I barely had time for a thought before we were off, galloping down the road. The most I could do was hold on to Dylan for dear life, because I was certain that within moments I was going to be bounced right off his horse.

Chapter Twenty Eight

Nimuë muttered to herself as she refilled her silver bowl with the last of her precious water from Avalon. How could she let that girl get the better of her? She was no match for the great Nimuë. Did she not know that?

It had taken Nimuë a little bit of time to figure out how to get the children's powers, but now she knew. They had to connect in three places—their hands, their eyes and their lips. Yes, that was it.

She was not entirely certain, but she had a niggling doubt that she might have to have the person's consent as well— just as Merlin had yielded his own powers freely. Well, there would just have to be a way of getting that, too. Perhaps a suggestion like the foolish girl had tried to put into her mind?

"Anything wrong, sister?" Morgan asked, appearing in the water before her.

Nimuë pressed her lips together but kept her silence. The last thing she needed right now was her sister's goading. She was almost tempted to pour the water right back into her water skin just to get rid of her.

"Have you not found a way to capture those three yet? Or have they eluded you once again?"

"I have them!" Nimuë snapped.

"Ah." Morgan's eyes grew bigger in surprise. "Congratulations." But then they narrowed once more as she peered up at her sister. "Then why do you seem...unhappy? I would have thought you would be dancing with joy with your new powers."

"I do not have their powers yet. I am still figuring out how to get them," Nimuë admitted under her breath

"Oh, yes, I can see that would be a small matter of concern," Morgan said, not even trying to hide her smile.

Nimuë scowled down at her. "I nearly have it, it is just..."

"Just what?"

"I need to touch their lips with my own," she growled. It was that small catch that made this so much more difficult than it needed to be.

"Really? Is that how you do it?"

"Yes. Some very sick mind must have thought up that little twist."

Morgan laughed. "Oh, dear, yes. Somehow I do not think these three would be overly eager to kiss you. I know I would not." She laughed again.

Somehow Nimuë could not see the humor in this. In fact, it was not funny at all—only frustratingly maddening.

"I almost had her. I had Scai in my grasp. Our palms were together, our eyes, but..." She stopped. She had been so close. So close and yet unable to complete that last step needed to attain her powers.

"But you just could not lay your lips on her," Morgan said, sympathetically—understanding just what she was feeling, as always.

"No," Nimuë admitted with a sigh. "She managed to squirm away from me at the last moment. But do not worry, I will get her. I have plenty more..."

"Father! Father!" Someone pounded on the door to her room.

In the time that it took Nimuë to walk to the door, she had resumed the form of Father du Lac. "What is the matter?" he asked as he swung open the door.

A footman stood there, panting, in a hall filled with smoke. "The three people you were holding, they're gone!" he said, as the smoke curled into the room.

"What do you mean 'gone'?"

"Somehow the door to their chamber caught fire. When I and a few others came running with water, the room was empty."

"You idiot! Have you looked for them? Have you checked the grounds, the castle, the perimeter?"

The man opened his mouth but didn't say anything.

"Why do you just stand there? I want them found!"

The man saluted and then left to carry out his orders.

When Nimuë closed the door once again, she could hear her sister chuckling.

"I will thank you..." Nimuë started.

"Oh no, I think this is very funny. You finally capture them, and within no time at all, they have tricked you and escaped. They are very clever indeed." Morgan laughed.

Nimuë did not find this so amusing. "I will get them again."

"You think they will fall for the same trick once more?"

Nimuë paused. Of course not. So how would she manage to capture them? Perhaps she would not.

"Next time I will not capture them," she said, thinking out loud. "Next time..."

"What?" Morgan asked, no longer laughing.

"Next time, I will just kill them," Nimuë said, thoughtfully. If she could not capture them, then there really was not much choice. It was either kill or be killed, and frankly, she did not relish the idea of being killed by three young people—barely more than babes—and becoming the laughing stock of the Vallen world for the rest of eternity. It was not how she wanted to be remembered.

"They are barely more than *children*, Nimuë. One of them of your own blood," her sister reminded her needlessly. "You cannot—"

"It will not be a problem," Nimuë snapped. But deep down inside of her, Morgan's words were having their intended effect.

Would she be able to kill the three? She had never really killed anyone before. She was not a murderer.

But if she did not....

Chapter Twenty Nine

There was pounding once more on Nimuë's door.

"Sir, the three have gotten away," a man called from the other side of the door before she even had a chance to open it.

Nimuë cursed silently to herself. Opening the door, Father du Lac addressed the man standing outside. "What do you mean, they got away? They are on foot. You just have not looked properly."

"No, sir. A knight met them on the road, fought three of our men, and then rode off with the prisoners. They could be anywhere by now, sir."

"A knight? One of Lefevre's men?"

"No, sir. He was no one we knew."

Nimuë began to turn away, thinking. Who could this be? Who would have come to their rescue?

Surely not...she nearly laughed out loud but caught herself just in time, remembering that she was not alone. She had seen old Dagonet traveling with Scai and the boy. It could not have been he who had bested three of Lord Lefevre's knights.

"You did not learn his name?"

"No, sir. But he killed two of our knights before the third returned to the castle for reinforcements. When they set out again, it was too late—the captives were gone." The man paused and then added, "I've sent scouts out looking for them, but, as I said, they could be anywhere."

Nimuë thought fast, the cold facts pushing the old knight from her mind. They had truly escaped!

She turned away from the man for a moment to hide her

fury, but it took two or three deep breaths before she could face him with any sort of control. "I want them found. They are witches of the worst sort. It is why I captured them. I want them found and killed, do you understand me?" she said, doing her best to keep her voice even.

The man's lips formed a grim line, but he nodded.

"No, wait!" Nimuë changed her mind. It would be so much more fitting if they were caught and brought to her first. She could then decide just how to rid the world of these pesky children. Yes, she would need to think about this.

"No, do not kill them." She looked down at her hands, remembering her role. "No, we must grant them leniency. They are God's children, after all. For now, just do your best to find them then report back to me."

"Yes, sir."

Looking back at the man, she added, in a voice she filled with sorrow, "I will see to the knights who have fallen in my service. Have them brought into the chapel. I will spend the night praying for their souls."

"That is very good of you, Father," the man said more quietly, clearly touched by Father du Lac's generosity. He bowed low as Nimuë began to close the door.

Before Morgan could even say a word or laugh in her face again for having lost the children, Nimuë looked down into the water and said, "You know I cannot let them get away like this, Morgan."

But her sister was not there.

<>< >

"Well, I will be the first to admit I would never have believed that Sir Dagonet could fight like that," Dylan said, sitting back in his chair and taking a long drink of the ale the barmaid had just placed before him—not without a wink and a smile, I noted with a breath of annoyance.

I reprimanded myself, though. There was no reason why that should annoy me—only it did. It *really* did.

"Well, who would have ever believed an old man could move like that?" Bridget agreed.

Dylan sat forward again. "But, no, you don't understand. The man is a buffoon—or at least, he always *plays* the fool."

"He is not a buffoon!" I argued.

Dylan paused for a moment to look at me oddly. Did he sense my annoyance? "Come now, Scai, you of all people know..." Dylan started.

"I know that he is a very sweet, very witty gentleman," I said, sticking to my defense of the kind old knight and trying to calm my unreasonable anger.

"I'm not saying he isn't, but, really, some of the things he says..." he broke off with a little laugh. "Never in my life would I have believed he was the kind of man capable of fighting the way he did today.

"The courage he showed. The strength and agility. Everything. He is a true knight," Dylan said, with unmistakable awe in his voice.

Bridget caught my eye with a look that nearly made me burst out laughing—and if I hadn't been so nervous and preoccupied, I probably would have.

Sir Dagonet had assured us that we'd ridden far enough that Lord Lefevre's men wouldn't find us, but I just couldn't help but worry. I was sure Lady Nimuë would be furious when she found out we had escaped. And with such a powerful Vallen after us...

"Boys! This is all they ever talk about," Bridget exclaimed, interrupting my worried thoughts. "My brothers rehash every fight they see, talking about it incessantly. Did you see the way he did this, and the way the other fellow parried?" She slumped back into her chair. "Yes, Dylan, I saw the whole fight as well as you. I saw every blow Sir Dagonet made and every blow he received."

"All right, I get the point," Dylan said, cutting her off. "I just think it was pretty amazing."

I jumped as a group of men came into the taproom, talking and laughing loudly.

"Scai, it's all right," Dylan said quietly, leaning forward and putting his hand on top of mine, which were clenched together on the scarred table. "We're perfectly safe here." Warmth rushed through me from my hand where he touched me. The feeling was more relaxing than a gentle summer breeze.

I looked into his reassuring eyes and began to breathe again. Forcing a smile to my lips, I said, "Yes. I know. I'm sorry, I just can't help it."

Bridget turned and looked toward the men as well. "They are loud, that's all. I don't think they'll bother us."

I forced my mind back to Sir Dagonet. "Well, it was quite a fight. I've never heard of anyone fighting two knights at once."

"Most people couldn't," Dylan said, clearly happy to get back to the topic. "I tell you, even my foster-brother, Sir Patric, couldn't have done what Sir Dagonet did today."

"Well, but isn't Sir Dagonet a great deal more experienced than your foster-brother?" I asked.

"Yes, naturally, but usually people get slower with age, not faster."

That idea swirled around in my mind. It was so much more pleasant to think about Sir Dagonet than Nimuë or Lord Lefevre's men. I leaned forward and said quietly so that only Dylan and Bridget could hear me, "Do you think it was his magic?"

That made Dylan stop and think for a moment. "I don't know. I didn't think Sir Dagonet..."

"What, wot? Did I hear my name?" the knight said, slipping into the chair next to Dylan.

I sat back again. "We were just wondering about dinner, that's all, sir," I answered, not wanting him to know that we'd been talking about him.

"Yes! I am famished. I could eat a whole side of beef by myself," Bridget said, brightly.

Dylan raised his hand and caught the attention of the barmaid before Bridget could say anything more.

"Sorry I took so long getting cleaned up, wot?" Sir Dagonet said, giving Bridget a big smile. "I appreciate you waiting for me, don't you know. We'll be sure to get you enough to eat."

Bridget gave him a smile and an enthusiastic nod. "Oh yes, thank you. My poor sister–in–law is probably having to do the same for all of my brothers all by herself now, poor thing. And I can tell you that when they are hungry, there is just no managing them. They're like animals, grabbing for what they want across the table, across each other..."

We all laughed at the image Bridget painted, while I tried to ignore the stab of jealousy and sadness that poked into my side. Bridget had grown up with five loving brothers—a family—while I had been an outcast. No. That was not true, I reminded myself. I'd had Father Llewellyn and Aron. They were both important and very wonderful, even though they weren't really my family.

"You must be missing them a great deal, Bridget," Sir Dagonet said.

"Oh, well..." Bridget thought about that for a moment then gave a shrug. "But this is so much more exciting. I've never been away from home before."

"I still can hardly believe Lord Lefevre had you captured in that way," Sir Dagonet said, shaking his head.

"It wasn't Lord Lefevre, sir," Dylan said. "It was a Vallen."

"Who claimed to be Lady Nimuë," I added.

"Nimuë!" Sir Dagonet exclaimed, looking down at the table for a moment, his bushy white eyebrows drawn low, but when he looked up again his eyes sparkled with mischief and he gave me a wink. "A little old, was she?"

"Actually, sir, she didn't look old at all. But she did claim to be the same Lady Nimuë who entombed Merlin in the tree," I answered.

Sir Dagonet nodded. "Well, if it was Lady Nimuë, or even if it wasn't, she doesn't seem to have been a very pleasant person, wot?"

Dylan laughed. "Not at all."

"Best to head off somewhere where she's not so likely to find you, wot, wot?" Sir Dagonet added with a smile.

My stomach dropped. "Yes, but where?"

Much to my annoyance, it was just as these words left my mouth that our dinner was served. All conversation stopped as we began to eat. Although I had been as hungry as Bridget a few minutes ago, my stomach now rebelled at the thought of food.

"Just how powerful a Vallen is Lady Nimuë, sir?" I

asked.

Sir Dagonet sat chewing his food. "Oh, more powerful than you could imagine," he said, his eyes smiling while his mouth could not.

That wasn't entirely reassuring.

"But don't worry, I happen to know three very powerful Vallen, don't you know?"

I widened my eyes at this, as hope rose within me. "Who? Where can we meet them? When..."

Bridget laughed. "I think he means us."

"Oh." I sat back as the three of them laughed. Grudgingly, I smiled as well, but as I thought about this, it became a true smile. My brothers had said something along the same lines—that being able to change into a bird was something only very powerful Vallen could do. And even Sir Dagonet had been impressed with my ability to break Dylan's suggestion. So, yes, maybe I was a powerful Vallen. And possibly, even as powerful as Bridget and Dylan. We'd escaped from Nimuë once, hopefully we'd be able to take her on again if need be.

I was able to eat with a lighter heart after that.

Our companionable silence was interrupted, however, by a burst of laughter from the noisy group of men at the table nearby. One man slammed his tankard of ale down onto the table, he was laughing so hard. "...and that look of absolute terror that old witch gave Tom just before she went under?" the man was saying.

"She should have been scared. She knew where she was going—straight to the fires of hell," another said chuckling.

I spun back around fast, my eyes meeting Sir Dagonet's and then Dylan's. The merry twinkle was gone from the knight's eyes, and Dylan looked as if he was going to be sick.

"We need to leave," Bridget said very quietly.

"You will stay and finish your dinner." Sir Dagonet said, sounding more fatherly than I had ever heard him. "Then we'll all retire and get an early start tomorrow."

"An early start to where?" Bridget asked.

Sir Dagonet looked around, as if the answer were somewhere on the table. He then shrugged and said with a wry smile on his face, "I would suggest someplace far away from Lady Nimuë."

"Why not back to Gloucester?" Bridget suggested. "With my brothers there—"

"That is just where she would look for us first," Dylan said.

"Sorry, Bridget, but your brothers would be no match for Lady Nimuë—if that's who it really was, wot?" Sir Dagonet said at the same time.

"With all of us there and them..."

"Bridget, you saw how powerful she was with that glamour," Dylan pointed out.

"I would love to return to Gloucester and spend more time with my newfound family," I put in, "but what if Dylan is right? I wouldn't be able to live with myself if Lady Nimuë followed us there. And if anyone should get hurt because of us..."

Worry crept into Bridget's eyes at my words. Silently, she nodded her head. "Well then, where?"

"I've heard the king has sent out a decree calling for all witches to be found and burned at the stake," Sir Dagonet said, with a side glance at the men at the next table.

"We should go to Wales," I offered. "They don't follow the English king's edicts so readily there."

"No." Dylan put down his ale with a thunk.

"Oh, and who do you think you are to make that decision?" Bridget asked, suddenly very testy.

"I have as much right to say where we go, if not more."

"More? What, just because you are a man?"

"That's right, because I am a man and I'm one of the oldest amongst us." His eyes bored into Bridget's, but she didn't back down a touch.

"I knew it!" She turned toward me. "I knew we should never have gone to meet him. He won't work with us, he..."

"Bridget, just calm down," I said, putting my hand on her arm. I turned back to Dylan. "Is there some reason why you don't want to go to Wales, Dylan?" I asked, hoping he would have a good answer and not just be trying to manage things as Bridget thought.

"Yes." He gave me the smallest hint of a smile. "I have just come from there and I know that the ch—" He stopped himself with a quick glance at the men at the next table. He turned back to me saying, "I know that we should stay in England."

"Oh," Bridget said, immediately understanding what he'd been about to say, as we all did. The chalice was in England. We needed to be here.

I leaned forward a little. "Do you know where?"

Dylan lost whatever good humor there was in his face. "No. But I know it is in England."

"Well, then," Sir Dagonet said, interrupting before we could question Dylan any further. "It is in England that we stay, wot, wot?"

"Despite that?" I asked, gesturing to the men with a small movement of my head.

"Despite that," Dylan nodded.

Even Bridget nodded her head at that one. But I wasn't happy. I understood the need to find the chalice, but if there was a witch hunt going on... A cold wind blew down my spine. I didn't like this.

Chapter Thirty

The ground slipped closer to me then retreated once again as I gave a strong pump of my wings. It was so tempting to skim my feathers over the tops of the trees, but I wasn't quite confident enough in my flying to do such tricks.

It was just that they looked so green and inviting. The lush forest was filled with oaks and maples, elm and chestnuts—so many grand trees, and I was above them all. They were so much nicer below me than when I was below them.

The forest gave way to a large blue lake. The color of the sky on summer's day, the water calm and placid. I circled the lake, enjoying the fresh, sweet-smelling air that wafted up from it. Taking in a deep breath, I closed my eyes for just a moment to savor that smell. There was nothing sweeter.

I opened them again to a thunderous sound and found myself quickly approaching rougher water. Directly in front of me was the most magnificent waterfall I had ever seen. It must have been at least fifty feet of straight, falling water. The water's spray reached out, cooling me and making my feathers sparkle in the sunlight as if covered with diamonds.

I angled up and caught a current of air to pull myself to the top. There, an ancient circle of stones reached up to the sky—their mystical foundation calling out to me. As I circled the stones, a pure white hawk joined me in my flight.

It was my friend! I recognized it at once. Warm feelings spread through me as I glided myself closer to the hawk. It, too, took a brief look over at me and moved closer so that the tips of our outstretched wings just touched.

The hawk flew a circle around me and then led me down the other side of the hill where there was a green surrounded by lovely white marble buildings. The lake curved around the land and came close to meeting *with the buildings.*

It was a breathtaking sight. The white buildings standing out from the brilliant green of the grass, so closely touched by the deep blue of the lake. I knew this was a happy place, a safe place. Everything within me told me so.

I followed the hawk as it circled down to the shore. My landing was not so graceful, but I regained my balance before turning to stare at the hawk—no, at the beautiful woman standing close to me.

Her bright, blue eyes crinkled into a smile, while her reddish–blond hair flowed around her face, falling all the way down her back, almost reaching to her knees. Everything about this woman moved about her as light as a breeze, from her smile to her hair, to her fluttering white dress.

"Welcome home, Scai," the woman said, her voice deep and warm.

I didn't say anything. I couldn't. I was so overwhelmed. So many thoughts and feelings were rushing through me. Tears pricked my eyes, but they were tears of happiness—tears of such immense joy that I could barely contain them.

There was only one thing I could do, and without a moment's hesitation I did so—I put my arms around the petite beautiful woman, lay my head on her shoulder, and began to weep, releasing all of the tensions I had held deep inside me ever since I had left my home in Tallent.

"Shhhh. It is all right, my daughter, it is all right. You are safe here." She held me, allowing me my moment of weakness, but soon she lifted my chin so that I was forced to look at her. "Remember, no matter what, you will always be safe here. And I will always be here to welcome you home."

"Scai. Scai!" Bridget's voice penetrated my mind.

I fought against waking, but even as I did so, my beautiful dream began slipping away.

Bridget gave me a shake. "Scai, wake up. We need to go," she said.

There was an urgency to her voice that forced me to open my eyes. "Go? Go where? Have we decided where we're going?"

"No. We're going to meet Dylan and Sir Dagonet downstairs to decide, remember?"

"Oh, yes." I did vaguely remember saying we would do so last night, before we all retired to bed. I had been so tired at that point I could hardly make it up to the room I was sharing with Bridget. Between the two of us, we had managed somehow to get to the room, strip ourselves down to our plain white shifts, and fall into bed.

This morning, however, Bridget had already washed and dressed and was urging me to do the same. But it was so nice and warm in bed, and I'd been having the most wonderful dream. I wanted nothing more than to snuggle down and regain my lovely dream.

I let my eyes drift closed once more.

Who was that woman? Was it my mother? She had called me daughter. But somehow that didn't seem right. And my mother was gone from this life, while this woman was most definitely alive.

She was my hawk! And all this time I had believed the hawk to be male. I almost laughed at myself. The hawk was a female—a woman who lived in the most beautiful, warm, and welcoming land...if only we could go there, we'd be safe there.

"Scai!" Bridget gave me another shake.

I groaned. "All right. All right."

It took all of my will to get myself up. As I did so, I lost the lingering good feelings from my dream, and began to worry about what the day would bring. Since a good portion of the previous day had been spent keeping Bridget and Dylan from fighting, I really hoped this day would be better. Well, anything would be better than yesterday—attacked by animals, kidnapped, and then nearly losing all of my magical powers—no, nothing could be any worse than that.

I splashed cold water onto my face. Goose bumps sprang up all over my body, sending me scrambling into my warm woolen dress. The mornings were definitely getting colder as the year moved more firmly into autumn.

As I accompanied Bridget down the stairs, I looked surreptitiously around the taproom. What a relief: the witch hunters weren't here this morning. I joined Sir Dagonet with an easy stomach. Dylan joined us barely a minute later, water dripping from his curls—he had taken the time to bathe. I wished I'd had that luxury as well.

"I had the most incredible dream last night," Dylan

began, accepting the tankard of ale from the serving maid.

"Really? I did too," I said. What a funny coincidence.

"Me, too!" Bridget exclaimed. "It was beautiful, filled with lots of women in flowing white dresses. And they were all laughing and talking and feeding me the most delicious fruit I've ever tasted. There were some who were practicing their archery skills, and others fighting with staves. And they all lived in the loveliest white marble houses that were warm all the time. I think there must have been fires somewhere because I could feel the warmth of them, but I never saw one."

"There were white marble houses in my dream, too, and the bluest lake I've ever seen," I added, finally able to get in a word as Bridget paused to take a breath.

"Yes! A blue lake with an incredible waterfall," Dylan interjected. "I swam through the lake. It was warm and filled with such life and beauty. There was a woman dressed in white in my dream as well." He paused. His eyes lit up as he added, "And there was the sword. Excalibur! It was held aloft by the Lady of the Lake. She said that I would wield it one day."

I had never seen such joy in Dylan's eyes before. His dream must have been as vivid and wonderful as my own.

"That's incredible. Your dream and Bridget's were so like my own! What did she look like, the woman?" I asked.

Dylan thought about that for a moment and then said, "Beautiful, with long reddish–blond hair and blue eyes. Young, but not very young."

I swallowed hard. "Yes. I saw her, too. She's the hawk. The one who welcomed me on my journey when I set out from Tallent and then saved me from the ravens that tried to kill me in Gloucester. I knew her in my dream, only...I don't know who she was." I paused trying to remember. "She called me daughter." Then, just to confirm my thoughts from earlier, I turned to look at Bridget. "Do you think she could have been our mother?"

Bridget just shook her head, though. "Mother had brown hair, like Thomas's."

"But then..."

"It was the Lady Morgan, don't you know?" Sir Dagonet said, with a wistful tone to his voice that I had never heard before.

"Lady Morgan?" we repeated.

He nodded. "Morgan le Fey, the Lady of Avalon."

"But how do you..." Dylan began.

"I don't understand..." I started.

"You're in love with her!" Bridget blurted out the loudest.

"What? No! I worship at her feet, but in love? Wouldn't dare," Sir Dagonet said, turning bright red.

Dylan laughed out loud at that, Bridget giggled, and I just couldn't hide my amazement.

Sir Dagonet in love?

"Now you really must tell us who she is," Dylan said.

"And why and how she's appearing in all of our dreams," I added.

Bridget rested her chin on her fist, her elbow on the table—ready and waiting for Sir Dagonet's explanation.

He looked around at the three of us and turned an even deeper shade of red. "But, but you know! You know very well who she is, wot, wot?"

"Morgan Le Fey?" Bridget asked.

"The Lady of Avalon," Dylan said, looking like he was trying to remember something. His face paled a little. "You don't mean *the* Lady of Avalon. The one with whom King Arthur, er..."

"Yes! Precisely. That's the one." The knight slapped Dylan on the back.

Dylan sat up straighter. "But, sir, she's...well, she was a contemporary of King Arthur's. They had a child together."

"Mordred. Pity that one. Not his fault, though—a tool of Lady Nimuë's, don't you know?" Sir Dagonet said, shaking his head.

"That was a very long time ago, sir. Why would we be dreaming of her now?"

"First Lady Nimuë, and now Morgan le Fey," I said, thinking.

Sir Dagonet turned his now twinkling eyes on me, a

brilliant smile covered his face. "Go on, Scai, wot?"

I was a little startled at his encouragement. "Oh no, I'm just saying…" but then I didn't say anything because I was trying to make sense of it all. They were both contemporaries of King Arthur's. As was Excalibur, of which Dylan had dreamed. There had to be a connection there.

And I couldn't help but wonder why all three of us had had similar dreams. Were we being manipulated? Someone had to have used magic to do this, but who and why?

"How do you know the Lady of Avalon, sir?" I finally asked. "Or do you?"

Sir Dagonet fiddled a little with his tankard of ale. "Well, yes, I have had the pleasure…"

"But she's got to be dead. I mean, King Arthur!" Bridget exclaimed.

"Just like we thought Lady Nimuë would be dead, too," I pointed out.

"Yes. She should be. That can't have been…" Bridget's words petered out at the serious look that had overcome Sir Dagonet.

"Afraid it truly was, don't you know?" he said, quietly. "And now it looks as though the Lady Morgan is trying to get in touch with the three of you as well."

I widened my eyes. "You think it was Lady Morgan who went into our dreams? Why would she do that? Why would she try to hurt us?" That couldn't be possible. I just wouldn't believe it, not after the warmth and love I'd experienced in my dream last night.

"What? Lady Morgan's not trying to hurt you. Never would. She is the most kindhearted soul, wot? She would never…No, no. But clearly, there is something important going on, or else why would she appear to all three of you? Maybe she's trying to warn you against her sister, wot?"

"Her sister?" I asked.

"Lady Nimuë," Sir Dagonet answered.

"Lady Nimuë is Morgan Le Fey's sister?" Bridget asked.

"Yes. I learned about this," Dylan said, clearly trying very hard to remember something. He began slowly, "Lady Morgan and the Lady Nimuë were sisters. Lady Morgan ruled

Avalon, the island, while Lady Nimuë became the Lady of the Lake. She's the one who created Excalibur, although Lady Morgan made its magical scabbard."

"Its scabbard is magical, too?" I asked. I had heard of the fabled sword—who hadn't? But I'd never heard anything about the scabbard.

"Oh, yes, anyone wearing it cannot be killed in battle."

I raised my eyebrows. "That's a very useful thing to have."

"Indeed. King Arthur wore the scabbard and used Excalibur throughout his reign. It was how he reigned for so long and so successfully," Dylan said, his enthusiasm for the topic showing through his eyes.

"Well, King Arthur was also an excellent swordsman, field commander, and king," Sir Dagonet said. "And a good friend," he added under his breath.

"You still haven't told us how you know Lady Morgan, Sir Dagonet," Bridget said, narrowing her eyes at him.

He looked up, startled. "Oh, yes, well..."

"You couldn't have known King Arthur, sir," Dylan said, although it almost came out more like a question.

I, and clearly Bridget and Dylan, was suddenly very curious about Sir Dagonet's past. Could he have...? Well, but that was almost two hundred years ago that King Arthur reigned. What a ridiculous thought, I scolded myself. I nearly laughed out loud at how silly it was, thinking that Sir Dagonet could actually have known King Arthur, Nimuë, and Lady Morgan.

"Well, it's a funny thing, you know," the knight began.

"Sir, that was a *very* long time ago!" Bridget exclaimed.

Sir Dagonet sighed and lowered his eyes to the table. "Yes, a very, very long time ago." When he looked up again, his eyes widened as he caught sight of something behind Bridget and Scai. He pushed his chair out and stood up. "Tell you about it on our way, wot, wot?"

I turned around to see three men entering the room— the same men who had sat next to us the night before. They also seemed intent on having something to eat before leaving—probably on their way to find more witches to murder. My body and mind shuddered.

Bridget and Dylan must have seen them as well, because we all got up together and followed Sir Dagonet out to the stables to retrieve his and Dylan's horses.

"On the way where, sir?" Bridget said, running to catch up to Dylan and Sir Dagonet, who were striding ahead.

Sir Dagonet stopped, causing Bridget to nearly collide with him. "What? Why, to Avalon, of course, wot, wot?"

Chapter Thirty One

The hall had never been so colorful. The brightly colored tunics, embroidered with expensive gold and silver, were almost blinding to Father du Lac's poor old eyes. Nimuë sighed at the peacocks strutting all around her, just as happy to be in Father du Lac's plain brown robes. She didn't mind a little finery every so often, but these men were as close to ridiculous as one could get.

A page of the court stomped his stick against the floor announcing the king. His Majesty, too, was dressed in his finery, outshining all of the deeply–bowing nobles in the room.

As young King Edward sat down at his place on the dais, the lords all found seats for themselves as well. Father du Lac seated himself at the farthest end of the table at which the king sat with his other advisers.

"My lords," the king addressed the men, "it is disturbing to me that we have had to come together in this way." And indeed, the poor boy sounded very sad and tired. Nimuë knew the truth of the matter, but had not expected the young king to show his weakness to his assembled lords. She was not entirely certain this was a good decision, but it was too late now.

"We had planned to face the Danes in less than a month's time, but so far we have not the army with which to do so." He leaned forward across the table. "Why is this?"

He paused and looked around at the now silent room.

"You, my Lord Stirling, promised me two thousand men and yet you have brought with you less than half that. Lord Barret promised three thousand and has brought two. Lord Lefevre, you also promised three thousand men and how many have you brought with you?"

"Half the number, Your Majesty," Lord Lefevre said, almost too quietly to be heard. "But, Sire," he spoke up quickly, "the men who swore their allegiance to me, they are deserting. There is nothing that I can do to stop them."

Lord Barret spoke up. "It is the same with me, Your Majesty."

"And I, Sire. The men were enthusiastic at first, but then something, and I wish I knew what it was, something is turning them against our cause," Lord Stirling said.

Nimuë saw her chance and did not hesitate for a moment. Standing up, Father du Lac spoke loudly and clearly. "Your Majesty, I know the reason for these desertions."

All eyes turned to him, including those of the king. Edward looked troubled, as if his trusted confessor had just betrayed him, when it was in fact just the opposite. Du Lac was going to help him, and help himself—or rather Nimuë—in the meantime.

"Sire, these men have deserted their lords for one reason and one reason only. It is as I said to you not too long ago—it is the witches, Sire. The witches are turning our young people away."

There was laughter in the room at du Lac's words, as well as a lot of murmuring. Clearly these noblemen did not take him seriously, but that was about to change. This time Nimuë was not going to take any chances.

Reaching inside of herself, she pulled forth a touch of magic and intertwined it with du Lac's words. "My lords, it is the witches who are turning our young men away from what they know to be their duty. They are corrupting them. Teaching them the ways of the devil. It is the witches who are the disease at the heart of our society and they must be destroyed!" Father du Lac's voice grew louder and more impassioned as he spoke. The magic woven into his words grew stronger as well.

She had their attention now. There was not one sound in the hall. She moderated du Lac's voice and the magic. "It is up to you, my lords. It is up to you and your men to see that these witches are destroyed—for if you do not, you will see more and more of your men deserting you. But without the witches to teach them, without the witches to guide them, the young men will come back to you. They will fight for you because that is the good and Christian thing to do. Only, first, they must be torn from the sway of these witches."

She paused for the words to take effect and then turned to Lord Lefevre. "My Lord Lefevre knows of what I speak. He has been working with me, helping me to capture a trio of witches. It is most unfortunate that they were able to escape, but you saw them, my lord."

The man nodded solemnly.

"They looked like ordinary young people, did they not?" Lord Lefevre sighed, but nodded his head.

"And yet, they were able to escape from a locked room, walk through a castle full of knights, and escape in the middle of the day. This is magic. This is evil. This is the devil's work! And it is *this* that is stopping your men from joining you in your fight against the Danes! Tell them it is not so, Lord Lefevre."

"It is so, Father. They looked like ordinary people. Two young women, not more than twenty years old, and a young man. They were witches of the most evil kind. They wove their spells on my men, deceived them, and thereby gained their freedom before we could put them to death." Lord Lefevre looked rather sick. "If it is they who are responsible for my men deserting me, then I will double my efforts to find and kill them!"

"Yes, my lord, it *is* they," Father du Lac said. "It is those innocent–looking people—and many more like them. They are the disease in this realm! But once they are eradicated all will be well, Your Majesty. Once the witches have been destroyed, you will see the ranks of your armies swell just as they should." Father du Lac ended his passionate speech, looking directly at the king. Nimuë had added an extra thrust of magic to the final words—then worried for a moment that it was too strong.

The king's eyes were unfocused, but he pulled himself together. Standing up before his noblemen, he said, "So be it. I charge you, my loyal nobles, to take your men and search out the witches. Search for them in every town and village of your domains. Search for them, find them, and give no quarter. They must be found and killed. Each and every one!"

A cheer erupted in the great hall, rebounding among the rafters, bouncing from the stone walls. It was music to Nimuë's ears. Sweet, beautiful music. In no time at all the three Children of Avalon, many more insignificant Vallen, and perhaps a few of those who called themselves witches, would be caught and killed. She alone would rule over the few Vallen who would be left. Oh yes, and very possibly over the country itself, as would be her right as the most powerful Vallen ever.

Chapter Thirty Two

"Do you know the way, sir?" Dylan asked, guiding his horse a little closer to Sir Dagonet's.

"Know the way? Of course I know the way. Traveled this way quite a few times, don't you know?"

To Avalon! Sir Dagonet had traveled to Avalon before and now we were going to that magical land—the land only ever heard about in fairy tales. I just couldn't believe it. It was real, and we were going there.

I wanted to share my excitement. I looked over at Bridget and Dylan, who were riding together on Dylan's horse. The two of them were talking excitedly together. I could see Dylan leaning back a little to say something that only Bridget could hear. The sight of it had me sighing with relief. The two of them had only been at each other's throats ever since they met. It was almost amazing to see them speaking to each other with civility.

I really wanted Bridget to like Dylan, despite all he'd done. He was a good person, a kind person, even though he was also, sometimes, misguided. But there was something about him... I didn't know what it was, but I felt something deep in my soul when it came to Dylan.

Riding behind Dylan had been the only pleasant part of the day before: having my arms wrapped around his body as he sped his horse away from the castle and the horrible woman–priest. If there was anything about that day I wanted to remember it was just that—sitting behind Dylan on his horse. Just thinking about being so close to him sent warm shivers all through me. Just being close to him made me happy. Even now, I couldn't help but admit that I wished that

I was riding behind him today instead of Bridget.

But here I was, with my hands on Sir Dagonet's shoulders instead of on Dylan's. I kept my sigh as quiet as possible.

"About how many days' travel is it?" Bridget called out to Sir Dagonet.

"Oh! Er, uh, quite a few. Let's see, now. How long did it take me the last time?" He began to think about this.

"How long ago was it that you traveled to Avalon?" I asked.

"What? Oh, er, about, well, let's see... The last time I went must have been..." Sir Dagonet tapped his stomach while he thought. It made a funny sort of hollow sound that confused me for a moment, until I remembered he probably had the top of his armor on underneath his tunic.

Dylan and Bridget and I waited for his answer, only beginning to look nervously at each other after a full minute of deliberation.

"Well, it must have been...er"—he paused and looked over at Dylan and Bridget as if they would know they answer—"about a hundred years or so? I, er, honestly can't remember, don't you know?" He ended with a weak little laugh.

"One hundred years!" Dylan exclaimed but then burst full out laughing. Sir Dagonet twisted around on his horse as much as he could to look at me. He had a confused, although slightly bemused expression on his face, which made me giggle even more than Dylan's laughter.

Dylan must have caught Sir Dagonet's expression out of the corner of his eye, because he stopped laughing. Clearing his throat, he asked, "Er, that was a joke, wasn't it, sir?"

This time Sir Dagonet's cheeks pinkened. "A joke, wot? Well, no, not really."

"It's actually been over one hundred years since you've been to Avalon?" Bridget asked.

Dylan pulled his horse to a stop. "Just how old are you, sir?"

"Eh?" Sir Dagonet seemed to be rather hard of hearing today, so I repeated his question.

"Oh, eh, yes, about, well, let's see..." He thought for another moment and then said very decisively, "Yes, about that!"

"About what, sir?" Dylan asked, warily.

"Wot, wot?"

"Sir Dagonet, how old are you?" Bridget asked slowly and clearly.

"Oh! Two hundred and thirty seven on my last birthday. Haven't actually celebrated a birthday for some time, you know. Got rather depressing after a while, wot?"

I sat back, away from the knight who was much older than I had ever imagined. "You don't actually mean..."

"But how is that possible?" Dylan asked.

Sir Dagonet began walking his horse again. Dylan followed, but didn't seem to be watching where they were going. All of his attention was focused on Sir Dagonet—as was Bridget's and mine.

"Ah, yes, well, you see, er, it's rather a long story." Sir Dagonet chuckled.

No one else laughed.

"I think we've got the time—and so, it seems, do you," Bridget answered with a note of sarcasm in her voice.

"Ha! Yes! Ha! Good one, Bridget," Sir Dagonet laughed out loud.

I reluctantly smiled, but I couldn't help but begin to feel a little bit nervous about Sir Dagonet, a man I had trusted completely up until this point. Could I have been wrong about him, just as I'd been wrong about Father du Lac?

I looked over at Dylan. He wasn't smiling. I must have been looking very worried or nervous, because when our eyes made contact, he gave me a little smile and nodded his head as if to say, "It's all right. Don't worry."

It made me feel better, so I returned his smile and pushed away my fears. It wasn't difficult. Sir Dagonet was a good man. Every feeling inside of me told me so, and clearly Dylan believed it as well.

"Well, let's see," Sir Dagonet began. "Where shall I begin?"

"The beginning is usually a good place," Bridget said.

"Why don't you begin by telling us how you got to be so very old? I mean, why didn't you...well..." I began but then faltered when I got to the touchy subject of Sir Dagonet's death, or rather, the lack of it.

"Die?" Sir Dagonet asked helpfully. "Why didn't I die, wot?"

"Well, er, yes," I said, hoping not to offend the gentleman.

"Yes, well, let's see. It was about a year before the Lady Nimuë trapped Merlin inside of the tree, don't you know. He came to me, Merlin did, and asked if I wouldn't mind helping him out a touch."

Sir Dagonet smiled as he remembered. "Kind old fellow, Merlin. You see, I was rather known as being, well, as being a bit of a jokester in my day."

"I'd heard that!" Dylan exclaimed. "So you are *the* Sir Dagonet from King Arthur's round table!"

"Er, well, yes."

"And yet, you denied it earlier."

"Well, I couldn't just tell you that I was over two hundred years old, could I now?" the old man huffed.

Dylan didn't say anything to this. It was clear he understood Sir Dagonet's point.

Before Sir Dagonet could continue with his story, however, there was a shout from behind us. "Make way! Make way for the knights of Lord Lefevre!"

Sir Dagonet and Dylan both spurred their horses forward, moving quickly to the side of the road. We all sat and watched as the three men from the inn rode past us looking important in their armor, their tunics all bearing the same crest.

There was a silence for a good minute after they had passed. The certainty that some poor innocent was probably about to be murdered in the name of witchcraft was heavy in the air.

I shivered as the air temperature around me fell. Sir Dagonet's hand patted my own encouragingly, but even he couldn't say that it would be all right. We all knew that for some unfortunate soul it wouldn't be.

Slowly, we moved back into the road to continue our journey.

"Now, where was I? Ah, yes, Merlin," Sir Dagonet began again, trying to make everything seem normal. "Dear old chap, he saw what was behind my buffoonery, naturally. Said to me, 'Dagonet, old man, you are the one knight I know I can trust beyond all else.' " Sir Dagonet gave a little chuckle. "Little did I know what he was going to ask, but I agreed to it before he had even done so. Was so thrilled to be asked anything by the great Merlin, don't you know?"

"What did he ask?" I said, determined to put those knights out of my mind.

Sir Dagonet turned around as much as he could so that he could answer. "Asked that I look out for you three, didn't he?"

"What?" Bridget exclaimed. "Two hundred years ago? He knew then that we would exist? How could he possibly know that?"

"Merlin was a great prophet, don't you know? He knew everything—or well, just about everything."

"So he asked that you stay alive and look for us...and you just...did?" Dylan asked, clearly not believing a word of this.

"Well, gave a sort of a spell, didn't he?" Sir Dagonet said. "Made it so that I wouldn't die until...well, until the time was right."

All three of us were silent after that. I supposed we were all wondering the same thing—when would the time be right? When would Sir Dagonet finally die?

I didn't want to think about it.

"Why did he want you to look out for us?" I asked.

"What? Oh well, knew you'd be important, didn't he?" Sir Dagonet chuckled.

"Why are *we* important? I don't understand," Bridget asked.

"Does this have something to do with why Lady Nimuë captured us?" I asked, before Sir Dagonet had a chance to respond.

Sir Dagonet flashed a smile back to me—it was one of the proud smiles he gave me whenever I made a connection.

It always made me feel good.

"Exactly so, Scai. You three are *very* important. Merlin knew, naturally. Never knew that man to get a thing wrong. Well, except for the one about him and Nimuë, but I suppose that was just wishful thinking on his part."

"You haven't answered the question, sir," Dylan prompted.

"What? Oh, why are you important? Right! Well, you three are the Children of Avalon, aren't you?"

"The Children of Avalon?" Bridget and I repeated back in unison.

"We are hardly children, sir," Dylan said, obviously a little affronted.

Sir Dagonet laughed. "No, not actual children, of course, but children as in, er, well, of that place, I suppose. The descendants, if you will."

Dylan drew down his eyebrows. "Well, I know I'm a direct descendant of Merlin. The only one, I believe."

Sir Dagonet nodded his head. "That's right."

"That's how I know I'm destined to find and wield Merlin's chalice. It's mine, by right."

Sir Dagonet gave him a broad smile. "Not *just* yours, Dylan. It belongs to the three of you."

"The three of us?" he asked, skepticism lacing his words.

"Yes. The daughters of Morgan have as much right to that chalice as you do, don't you know?"

"Daughters of Morgan? Do you mean Morgan Le Fey?" I was beginning to feel like a parrot, but Sir Dagonet just wasn't being very forthcoming with his answers.

"Yes, that's exactly right. You and Bridget are the direct descendants of the Lady Morgan, don't you know?"

"No, I didn't know!" Bridget exclaimed. "What do you mean, the direct descendants? After so many generations, how could that be?"

"That's why she called me daughter in my dream last night," I said under my breath, almost to myself. I just shook my head in disbelief. I not only had a family, I had ancestors—powerful ancestors.

"Yes, indeed. You are all the children of Morgan Le Fey

and the great wizard Merlin. The greatest Vallen of Avalon."
He stopped, his cheeks turning a little red. "Well, not
together, I mean, well, Morgan and Merlin never were, er, they
didn't actually have... well, not together at least."

"You mean that Morgan wasn't the mother of Merlin's
children," Bridget said, setting Sir Dagonet more at ease.

"Er, yes, that's right," he said with a sigh, and then an
embarrassed laugh. "Just so."

"But then there must be hundreds of Children of Avalon
after so many years. I know I've got dozens of cousins. Both
my parents had many brothers and sisters." Bridget paused
for a breath and then added, "I'm sure Dylan does as well."

"Ah, yes. Excellent point," Sir Dagonet began.

"Actually, I'm an only child. So is my father, and so was
his father before him," Dylan interrupted.

"Right. The male line was all of single children, don't you
know? Through the female line, however, there were seven
children in each family. It is the seventh through which the
magic runs."

"But I'm the sixth child," I pointed out, feeling a little
easier. Maybe I wasn't part of this after all. It was Bridget...

"Er, yes, the *strongest* magic, I should say, wot, wot?"

"Oh." So it was that her magic wasn't as strong as
Bridget's?

"That doesn't mean you're not as strong, mind you," he
added, as if he could read my thoughts. "Lady Nimuë was the
sixth child in her family."

"Oh," I said again, not exactly reassured.

"Yes, and, er Lady Morgan was the seventh," he
continued. "But I was the eighth! Ha!"

"You aren't related, are you, sir?" Bridget asked.

"No." Sir Dagonet chuckled. "Just the eighth child in my
family."

A giggle bubbled out of me. I couldn't help it; it was just
so silly.

"Nearly named Octavius, too, don't you know. That was
a close one, wot, wot?"

Even Dylan began to laugh a little at that. Bridget just
rolled her eyes.

Still chuckling, Sir Dagonet went on. "The prophecy actually talks about the sixth and seventh child of the female line. Your mother was the seventh child, and her mother before her, and so on back six generations, wot, wot? Bridget is the seventh child of the seventh generation, *very* powerful."

So I was one of the "Children of Avalon." I didn't know what to think about this. Within just a matter of weeks I had gone from an outcast with no family, to a descendant of Morgan Le Fey with five brothers and a sister. It was all a little...uncomfortable in a way. I didn't feel like myself any more, but I wasn't exactly certain I understood this new person I was turning out to be. It just wasn't... me.

"What has the prophecy got to do with it?" Bridget asked, looking a little uncomfortable herself.

But her question didn't get answered. The road we were riding on became the main road of a little village, and within moments we were entering the hamlet.

Chapter Thirty Three

I glanced around, amazed at how ordinary everything looked. We passed a blacksmith's workshop and then an inn that reminded me very much of the inn in Tallent. The grocer's and baker's were next on the other side of the street. There was only one thing missing in all of this normality.

People.

There wasn't a soul to be seen. A chill wind blew down my back.

Sir Dagonet slowed his horse to a standstill and Dylan followed suit. "Where has everyone gotten off to, do you suppose?" the old knight asked, looking around.

"I hear people up ahead," Bridget said, nodding in front of us with her head.

Dylan turned around and held his hand out to Bridget. "I think you and Scai should stay here while Sir Dagonet and I go on and see what this is about. I don't like what I feel coming from there."

Bridget hesitated, but then, for once, did as Dylan suggested. Perhaps she could feel it too. I certainly felt something—an icy tension in the air.

"Why don't you two wait at the inn, wot?" Sir Dagonet suggested.

I gave a nod but didn't really think that Bridget would consent to waiting by so meekly.

Just as I had suspected, Bridget grabbed my hand as soon as the two men had ridden off and started after them.

A loud cry went up from a great number of people farther ahead, and Bridget broke into a run. I couldn't deny that I was just as curious to see what was going on, but as soon as we rounded the bend in the road, I almost wished we had stayed at the inn after all.

In the center of the town green, a huge bonfire had been built with a pole standing straight up in the center of it. Tied to the pole was a young woman struggling for all she was worth.

Dylan had acquired a sword from somewhere, and he and Sir Dagonet were fighting the three knights from the inn in front of the bonfire. There was a large crowd of people standing all about, talking and arguing over the fight. Some men tried to help the knights. Others started to fight against them bare–fisted. Most of the women had pulled to the back, but one or two stood their ground and fought alongside their men.

"Can you take care of them? I'll see to the girl," Dylan called out, while taking an enormous swipe at the guard directly in front of him. The man went down.

"Not a problem, lad. Off with you, then," Sir Dagonet called back.

Dylan maneuvered through the crowd toward the bonfire and jumped down from his horse just as he reached it. He had to fight off a few overzealous townsmen as they tried to protect their prisoner, but he moved them out of his way with the flat side of his sword and his fist.

With one stroke, he cut the bonds holding the girl to the stake and then held out his arms for her. Without a second's hesitation, she jumped straight into them, and I heard a gasp and a startled "Oh!"

I was about to look around for who had made the noise and then realized it had been me. How ridiculous! He was saving the girl; of course she would jump into his arms and hold on for dear life.

Dylan had a moment's problem trying to free himself from the girl's grasp, but he managed to do so and swung them both up onto his horse.

As soon as I saw them settled on Dylan's horse, I turned, took Bridget's hand and ran back toward the inn. We would have to make a quick escape from this town, although I didn't quite know how we were going to manage with an extra person—the horses were already overloaded, each carrying two people instead of just one.

We were out of breath but had reached the inn just as Sir Dagonet and Dylan rode up.

The girl slid off of Dylan's horse. "Oh, sir, how can I ever thank you?" she cried, tears streaming down her cheeks.

"No need at all," Dylan said, his cheeks flushing pink.

"Oh no, it was nothing, wot?" Sir Dagonet said, giving his usual little chuckle.

Dylan looked at the old man and smiled. "All in a day's work, eh?" he said with a little laugh.

"Quite right, my boy, quite right," Sir Dagonet agreed. "Now, little lady, is there somewhere we can leave you before that crowd realizes you're gone and comes looking for you?"

The girl looked around to get her bearings and then said, "Oh no, right here is perfectly fine. The innkeeper is a good friend. She'll take care of me."

"Right, then," Sir Dagonet said, giving her a nod.

Chanting voices calling out "Burn the witch! Burn the witch!" came tumbling toward them, and the head of the mob could just be seen at the bend of the road.

A fresh wave of terror covered the girl's face. I had to hold on to my own hands in front of me to stop them from trembling. A cold wind blew through my veins. I took a step closer to Dylan, who was still sitting on his horse.

"Ah, right. Well, we should be off, then, wot, wot?" Sir Dagonet said, with a little smile.

"Oh yes! Please! And thank you once again!" The girl said, before quickly disappearing into the inn.

I was halfway on to Dylan's horse before the girl had even finished speaking. Bridget must have been doing likewise, because both Dylan and Sir Dagonet were able to take off at a brisk gallop within moments. Shouts followed us out of town, but soon faded as neither Dylan nor Sir Dagonet let up on their horses for a good mile or more.

I held on to Dylan, perhaps a little more tightly than was strictly necessary. I didn't even want to allow myself to think about what would have happened to that girl if Dylan and Sir Dagonet hadn't stepped in.

"These witch hunts," Bridget started, but if she ever finished her sentence, I didn't hear it. I just buried my face in Dylan's back and tried very hard to stop trembling.

That could have been me, or any one of us.

"Scai, are you all right?" Dylan asked over his shoulder.

"Yes, I'll be fine," I managed to say. I didn't know why, but the thought that I would give my life for others didn't bother me nearly as much as the terror of being burned at the stake. Thank goodness I had Dylan to hold on to just now. He would keep me safe. I knew he would. His warm hand covered one of my own, and my fear eased just enough to stop my trembling.

We turned and continued heading north as soon as we could, riding through a forest with almost no path to follow.

"Well, so much for stopping to buy something to eat, wot, wot?" Sir Dagonet said a little sadly.

"I brought a bit of bread from the inn this morning," Bridget offered.

Sir Dagonet turned around in his saddle and gave her a brilliant smile.

She laughed and admitted, "I knew I wouldn't be able to last very long without something, and I didn't know when, or even if, we would find food along the road."

"Good thinking, my girl, good thinking, wot?" Sir Dagonet said.

There wasn't really a good place to stop to eat, so after a while, we just stopped where we were. I had, by then, gotten over my fright, but now I was beginning to feel sore and knew that Bridget was, too—the surreptitious rubbing of her bottom gave her away. It felt good to take a little walk around and stretch my legs.

The 'bit of bread' that Bridget had brought along turned out to be a fine meal of bread, cold meat, and cheese as well. Dylan had brought a skin of wine, so it turned out to be a rather merry party after all.

"Sir Dagonet, you were about to tell us about the prophecy," Bridget reminded him, after we had begun to eat.

"Ah, yes. The prophecy." Sir Dagonet put down his cup and absently began fiddling with his left wrist. "Well, let's see, that's where Nimuë comes in to our little story, don't you know? The prophecy that Merlin made just before she entombed him described the three of you, and Nimuë as well, but it ended like this."

He paused to clear his throat and then recited in a grand voice:

"But Avalon's child will not fail
To discover my stony grail.
Then one, wielding the power of three,
The greatest earthly force will be.

My power will render her accursed,
Unless the trio all die first.
Or she will be, I prophesy,
Destroyed by one and children three."

He ended with his arm outstretched in a fanfare of excitement.

"What does that mean, 'unless the trio all die first'?" Bridget asked, clearly not liking this line at all.

I couldn't say that I did either, but I said, "No, don't you see, the chalice will render Lady Nimuë's power accursed unless we die first. So either she has to kill us, or we...we kill her." I really didn't like it, but I was certain that was what the prophecy had meant. A shiver ran down my spine.

"That...that is what it means, isn't it, sir?" I asked, hoping he would say no.

"That's it precisely!" he said cheerfully, picking up his cup and reaching for some more bread and cheese. He looked sympathetically at Bridget, who had gone very pale.

"So that's why she captured us. Lady Nimuë's got to kill us," Dylan said.

"Take our powers and then kill us. 'One wielding the power of three,' " I added, putting it all together. Now everything made sense. Everything made entirely too much sense.

"What, wot? Why are you all looking upset? It's nothing, really. Oh, it'll be a little bit of a dust up for certain, but nothing to turn yourselves inside out about."

I just stared at Sir Dagonet. I couldn't believe he didn't think this was something serious.

"I don't kill people," Bridget stated unequivocally. "I'm a healer."

"Oh, well, when the time is right, I know you'll do what—"

"No!" Bridget interrupted Sir Dagonet. "I will not kill *anyone*. Anytime. For *any* reason."

"Bridget, none of us ever wants to kill anyone," Dylan began, "but sometimes it's just what you have to do."

"Well, not me. Not ever!" Bridget turned her face away from the others and stared off into the woods.

Dylan looked at me. But I did not, for once, meet his eyes. I didn't ever want to kill anyone either. In this argument, I was firmly on Bridget's side.

<><><>

We traveled with only short breaks to rest for the next two days, until Sir Dagonet stopped at a fork in the road. He sat on his horse staring long and hard down one road and then turning to look down the other.

"Do you not know the way, sir?" Dylan asked.

"Er, used to," the old knight answered hesitantly. "Not sure I remember this, though."

I exchanged nervous looks with Bridget and Dylan from my place behind Sir Dagonet.

"Well, shouldn't we be heading north?" Bridget asked, looking down the right–hand fork.

"Er, well, yes, but it's either at this fork where one of the roads looks like it heads north and then swings around to the west, and so we take the south fork, or at the next fork where we take the west fork, which then swings around to the north, don't you know."

I felt as if I'd just been blown around in a quick circle and had completely lost track of which direction I'd been facing to begin with. "But then how do we know which fork to take?"

"We take the one heading toward the sea, wot, wot?" Sir Dagonet answered decisively. But then didn't move.

"And which one might that be, sir?" Dylan asked.

The knight's shoulders slumped down a little. "Don't know."

"Toward the sea," I repeated, trying to figure out how we could tell if we were headed toward the sea. A slight breeze ruffled my hair giving me an idea. "I've got it!" I closed my eyes for a moment and called upon the wind from down the road to our right. Gently it tickled my cheeks, bringing with it the sweet smell of an apple orchard not too far away.

"No, that's not right," I said to myself. I then turned in the other direction and asked the wind to come from the other road. My hair flittered into my face.

"I smell it!" Dylan exclaimed. "The sea is that way." He turned and gave me a brilliant smile.

"Ah! Well done, Scai, well done, wot, wot," Sir Dagonet exclaimed. He gave his horse a small nudge and off we went.

"Good thinking," Bridget said. "I wouldn't have thought of that."

"But you're not associated with the element of air," Dylan pointed out.

"No, I'm not," she conceded.

"I'm a little surprised that I did think of it," I admitted. "It's pretty amazing the way I've taken to this," I said, finally voicing an idea that had played tag with me ever since I'd met Sir Dagonet.

"The way you've taken to what?" Bridget asked.

"To magic. To having it and using it," I answered.

"That's right, you didn't grow up with this, did you?" Bridget asked.

"I didn't even know I had any until I was confronted by an angry mob of townspeople accusing me of being a witch."

"That must have been terrifying," Dylan said.

"It was. But I had Father Llewellyn there to calm them down. Unfortunately, their calm only lasted until they could build the bonfire where they planned to burn me."

My admission was greeted with horrified looks.

"I escaped before the light of day," I told them.

"Close one, wot?" Sir Dagonet said, shaking his head.

"Too close," I agreed.

"No wonder you were trembling when we left that last

town," Dylan said. "I could feel your fear, but I didn't realize..."

I tried to give a negligent shrug. "It's okay. I'm glad you were able to save that girl."

"Indeed," Sir Dagonet agreed before we all lapsed into our own thoughts.

We rode on in silence for a few more minutes before Bridget said, "I can't imagine growing up without magic. Didn't you feel as if you were missing something?"

"I did feel that way," I admitted, "but I thought it was just my family that I was missing. I didn't realize it was more than that."

"Well, now that you've found your family and your magic, you must be feeling really good," Bridget said with a happy spark.

I thought about that. Did I feel good? Did I feel complete? "I don't know, Bridget. There's still something missing..." I didn't feel entirely comfortable in this new skin I was wearing—the one with a family, and a destiny—I still didn't feel quite right.

"Could it be the chalice?" Dylan asked. "I'm certain I'll feel as if I've accomplished one of my life's goals when we find that."

"Yes, it must be that," I agreed, but I wasn't really certain that was it.

"And, of course, we have to get rid of Lady Nimuë," Dylan added as an afterthought.

Bridget and I exchanged a look and were in complete agreement—we truly didn't want to have to kill anyone.

"Well, I, for one, am grateful you've taken to this so easily, not that I thought you wouldn't. Quite useful, your magic, and you wield it cleverly, wot, wot," Sir Dagonet said, breaking into the awkward silence. He gave my hand a fatherly pat. "We'll soon find the chalice. And Nimuë... well, we'll see about her when the time comes, don't you know."

Chapter Thirty Four

Nimuë paced back and forth in her room. It still amazed her that those children had managed to escape. At least now there was a good chance they would be caught once again. Now, she had not only Lord Lefevre's men out looking for them, but also the men of all of the nobles in the country.

They couldn't escape now. Within no time, they would be out of her way, burned at the stake for being witches.

What was odd was that she had not spoken to her sister since the day the trio had escaped her. It was unlike Morgan not to gloat just a little and point out Nimuë's failures to her. Oh yes, she always said she did so in order for Nimuë to learn a lesson, but honestly, who could believe such nonsense? No, her sister thought herself better and loved to rub it in. Nimuë would have done the same thing had their positions been reversed. The children would soon be caught and killed, however, and then she would not have to hear from her sister again for another two hundred years, at least.

She turned to her silver bowl. Blowing gently onto the water, she willed it to show her the trio again. For the past two days she had left them alone, but now it was time to find where they were and make sure they were stopped—now that they were far enough away so no blame for their deaths could fall on to Father du Lac.

The water showed them in a forest, but it was impossible to judge where. Nimuë's eyes skimmed the background looking for clues, but there were none.

Nothing but trees.

She watched as Sir Dagonet looked up at the sun.

"Continue heading north, sir?" Dylan asked the old man.

"Er, yes. North. Need to turn to the west in a bit—or is that east? First east and then west? Er, one of the two, but not quite yet, don't you know. Soon, but not...quite...yet. Don't worry," the old man said. "We'll find it, no doubt about that, wot?"

He did not sound so sure of his directions, Nimuë thought with a laugh.

Where in the world was he leading them? She began to think seriously about this. Where *would* that old buffoon take those children?

Nimuë gripped the edge of the table. There was only one answer.

He knew where the chalice was. He was taking them there.

"You are deep in thought," Morgan's voice startled Nimuë, but only for a moment.

"It is time," Nimuë answered.

Morgan went still for a moment. "Time for what?"

"Time those children were killed. Dagonet is leading them to the chalice. They must die before they get there."

"Nimuë, you cannot kill them." Her sister's voice had an urgency to it that Nimuë had not heard before.

"Do not worry so, dear sister," Nimuë purred. "I will take care of this. And the prophecy is clear—I am, after all, just following what Merlin foretold would come to pass."

"He spoke of your downfall."

"Unless the children died first. Now which do you think I would choose?"

"Nimuë," her sister said with a sigh. "Do you not understand? The children must live. We have got to see to that."

"I do not see anything of the sort." And frankly, Nimuë was getting tired of this argument.

"If you do not see it, then I do. And I—"

"You will do nothing!" Nimuë said, losing patience altogether. "You leave this to me, Morgan. This is my fight. My life. My—"

"Your death," Morgan said with finality.

Nimuë was stunned. She could not say a word.

Morgan sighed. "Nimuë, the Children of Avalon are the future, do you not see that? They are the future. We are the past. We must let go."

"I will let go of nothing!"

"I know that. Which is why I have to do everything in my power to pry you away. I am sorry, Nimuë, truly I am. But if I have to step in here, I will. In the interest of the future."

Chapter Thirty Five

Dylan looked back at Sir Dagonet. Muttering under his breath, he turned us around to rejoin the old knight and Bridget riding with him. Sir Dagonet was either unwilling or unable to travel any faster while Dylan was eager to move—perhaps too eager.

"I don't understand why he's so very slow," Dylan complained, as we rode back.

"He's old, Dylan..."

"Yes, I know," he interrupted me with a sigh.

Dylan had been doing this a lot over the past two days—riding forward and then coming back. He seemed tense and anxious. The others didn't notice. I did, but I was beginning to think that I had become particularly sensitive to him and his moods.

I was, therefore, not at all surprised when I awoke in the middle of the night to find Dylan sitting up, staring into the fire. Pulling my blanket around my shoulders, I wordlessly settled myself next to him.

He looked over, a little wisp of a smile playing on his lips. "Couldn't sleep?"

"No. I'm worried about you."

"Worried about me? No one worries about me," he said in such a matter of fact way I wished I could see his expression. He had turned back to the fire, though. All I could see was his profile, and it revealed nothing of what he might be thinking.

"Well, maybe it's about time someone did," I offered.

Dylan shook his head. "There's no need." He paused and turned toward me again.

His eyes softened, like liquid pools in the flickering firelight. He reached out and took my hand. "It's very sweet of you think about me."

"Of course I think about you. I care about you."

"Do you?" He sounded surprised, but the rough pad of his thumb moving in circles around my palm was sending tingles through me, making it hard to concentrate on what we were saying.

"Yes, I do." The words came out more softly than I had intended. Even my voice was being affected by his caress.

The little sounds of Bridget and Sir Dagonet sleeping nearby wove into the silence of the crackling fire.

Dylan moved his hand from mine to cup my face. I could only watch as his eyes came closer. The green of them was intense. Beautiful. His eyelids fluttered closed just as his lips met mine.

A gust of warmth blew through me, as hot as the sun on a midsummer's day. His lips, though, were a soft, soothing counterpoint to the fury of heat and light. A tingling sensation spread from my mouth downward, waking up my whole body. At first I just thought it was the fact that I'd never been properly kissed, but then I realized that this wasn't any ordinary kiss. This was magic.

Gently, Dylan nibbled at my lips until I parted them for him. A soft moaning sound vibrated through in my throat as his tongue danced around mine. He tasted so good. Slightly salty, but sweet as well.

A happiness such as I had never felt before washed over me. I was tumbling down a stream of joy, laughing, flowing with the water, flying through the air. I was a fish. I was a bird. I felt everything Dylan was feeling. Everything I felt, he experienced. Our emotions, our very senses, intermingled, even as our arms and bodies intertwined.

His hand ran down my back and another slid up my side. My skin came alive with every touch. One hand came around to cup my breast, and I gasped as heat shot down to a spot between my legs. Another moan vibrated through me, but this one might have come from Dylan.

He broke off his kiss just long enough to say, "You are

so beautiful, Scai. I don't know how I can keep my hands off of you."

I giggled because he *wasn't* keeping his hands off of me. In fact, they were everywhere. I gasped as his thumb caressed my taught nipple. "You aren't," I pointed out to him.

"No, but it's been so hard having you so close and not touching you," he answered, his voice little more than breath.

The hand on my back slipped away only to reappear a moment later sliding up my leg—under my dress!

His fingers reached higher even as his tongue swirled around mine, sending shivers of delight through me. But when his fingers came to the apex of my legs, I couldn't suppress the shiver and moan that erupted from me.

Dylan's lips left mine for a moment. "Shhhh." I could feel his smile against my lips.

"Oh, Dylan, I..." But I didn't know what I wanted. He was doing the most amazing things to me. I wanted to press myself against him. I wanted to touch him as he was touching me. I wanted to hold on to him, and never let go.

"It's okay," he whispered. As a tremor of pleasure shot through his body, I could feel it vibrating both inside and outside of my own.

I pried my fingers from his shoulder where I'd been holding on to him and let them trail down his chest and then back up again. Up and down my fingers skimmed, each time coming closer to his waistband where I knew, from his own feelings and thoughts, that his manhood was standing at attention, reaching for me.

I knew little of men but had some vague ideas, and I was eager to learn more.

His hand disappeared from my chest for a moment and then found my own. He guided it down to his manhood. Curling my fingers around it, he showed me how to caress him. He was hot and the sweet smell of his arousal had me moaning again into his mouth. I loved touching him and feeling how good it felt for him as well.

He guided my hand faster and faster, even while keeping his other fingers gently pressed against my most intimate place, only pausing once to flick and rub at me until I could barely keep still. The sensations were overwhelming, drawing me higher and higher, until I was sure I would explode.

His mouth pressed harder against mine. I peaked with squeak, which would have been a scream if not for him. With his guidance I brought him to his peak. Shuddering against me, he let out only the quietest moan of satisfaction.

For a moment, he leaned his sweaty brow against my cheek as he got his breathing under control once again. "Oh, Scai."

I just kissed his forehead in response and straightened my skirts.

As we lay there, the pull of sleep began to overtake me.

"I need to go," Dylan whispered into my hair.

I roused myself enough to ask, "Go? Go where?"

"I need to find the chalice."

That woke me.

"What? But that's where we're going."

"No. I need to do this on my own. It's my birthright. *I* am the sole heir of Merlin. *I* need to find the chalice, and I need to use it to get rid of Lady Nimuë once and for all."

He lifted himself up on his elbow and looked me in the eye. "I feel this, Scai. I feel it deep in my soul. I never should have dragged you, Bridget, and Sir Dagonet into this. This is my quest, not yours."

I shook my head, heat of another kind entirely beginning to pool inside of me. I tried my best to keep my anger to myself. "It may have *been* your quest, but it's not any more. We're all in this together, Dylan."

He turned, staring at nothing. I wished he would look at me. I needed to see his what was going on in his eyes. He couldn't honestly think to leave us behind—it wasn't right. What had happened to the happiness at being together? It seemed to have cooled as quickly as the heat we'd generated together.

"You don't understand," he said, finally. "This is something I have been told about since I was a boy. I have worked toward this my whole life. I have trained for it. This is *my* quest, *my* legacy. I am Merlin's heir, not you, not Bridget."

The heat inside of me grew into small whirlwind in the pit of my stomach. "Well I *didn't* grow up with this. I didn't even know I was Vallen until Sir Dagonet told me so only a few weeks ago, but that doesn't make me any less Vallen than you."

"No, of course..." Dylan began, but I wasn't done.

"And you may have always known your destiny, but that doesn't mean that I am any less entitled to mine. And mine lies with that chalice just as much as yours does."

"No, Scai, that's where you're wrong. I'm Merlin's heir. It is his chalice that he left for his descendants. I am his only descendant. It's mine."

"He left it for the three of us. He practically names us in the prophecy."

Dylan just shook his head. "You don't understand. Please, don't make me force you..."

"Force me?" I scooted away from him and sat up. "You mean like the way you nearly drowned me and Sir Dagonet? Like the way you tried to force us to turn around by alternately taking away our water and then making it pour for days on end so that Sir Dagonet became deathly ill? Is that what you want to do, Dylan? Is that what you are thinking? Because I'm going to tell you right now, no matter what you do, Bridget and I are not going to give this up. This is our legacy, our destiny—and you cannot stop us."

I stood up and moved away, unable to be near him. I had thought he'd changed his mind. That he'd repented for his earlier behavior. That he understood now that we were all in this together.

I had thought I liked him and he liked me—after what we had just done.

Clearly, I was wrong.

I choked back an angry sob. This wasn't the way it was supposed to be. We were all supposed to work together, and be together. I knew this for certain.

I heard Dylan moving behind me, gathering up his things. After a minute there was a silence. I could feel his presence behind me.

"I'll leave you my horse," he said quietly. "I'll go into

Stafford and buy myself another one there."

I refused to say anything. I couldn't, without giving away the fact that I was on the verge of crying.

"If it turns out that you're right and I need you and Bridget in order to find the chalice, I'll come back and find you."

He would come back and find us? *If* he needed us? I couldn't believe him! My anger rose up again, shoving past the deep hurt inside.

I heard him start to move away.

"Don't bother," I said, turning around and locking onto his eyes with my own.

He paused for a moment to look at me. I could see the hurt in his eyes, even in the dim dark of the night, but he said nothing more.

He just turned around and left.

<><><>

"Where's Dylan? Have you seen him this morning, Scai?" Bridget asked as she was tying our bags onto the horses and getting ready to move on.

I piled another handful of dirt onto our campfire. "He left," I said simply, while trying to ignore the ache that still lingered in my stomach from last night after my anger had blown away.

"Left? What's that you say?" Sir Dagonet joined us from the woods, now fully dressed and ready to go.

I looked from Sir Dagonet to Bridget again. "He left. Last night. He said that he needed to seek out the chalice on his own."

"He's going to search for the chalice alone? Without us?" Bridget said, letting a bag drop to the ground and advancing toward me.

I stood up. "Yes. He said he'd come back if he needed us." I could hear the monotone in my voice, the hurt and the remnants of my anger. I didn't have the energy to even try to hide it.

"Oh, he did, did he?" Bridget exclaimed, putting one hand on her hip. "So he thinks he can just go off on his own to find the chalice, and then if he *needs* us we will just accept him back, just like that. I'll tell you what..."

"Now, Bridget..." Sir Dagonet began.

"No! No, that's just not right. We're supposed to be finding this chalice together—that's what the prophecy said, didn't it? So what does he think he's doing?" She turned to Sir Dagonet. "If he finds it, can he wield it on his own?"

Sir Dagonet's eyes widened. "I, er, don't really know now, do I? But I shouldn't think...well, the prophecy does say that it needs the three of you..."

"The three of us to find it, but one alone will wield it," she corrected him.

"One with the power of three." He turned around and corrected her.

"Yes. One with the power of three. So unless he has..." She paused and turned toward a few sticks lying on the ground next to me.

I jumped when they burst into flames. "Bridget! You almost caught my dress!"

"Sorry. I was just checking." She held her open palm toward the flames and closed her hand as if capturing something inside of it. The flames disappeared, leaving the smoking remnants of the fire that had been there a moment ago.

"Checking what?" Sir Dagonet asked.

"My powers. Dylan didn't steal them while I was sleeping."

"What? Of course not," Sir Dagonet scoffed.

"Bridget! How could you even suggest he would do such a thing? He's stupid, but he's not cruel," I scolded her.

"Well, he needs the power of three to wield the chalice," Bridget explained.

"He is not going to wield the chalice. Clearly, he can't. But he does feel it is his right, as Merlin's only descendent, to find the chalice first." Somehow I just couldn't bring myself to even look at Bridget as I gave Dylan's reasoning. I could feel Bridget's burning gaze on me, however, and looked up.

She crossed her arms in front of her but said nothing.

"Bridget, just let it go," I said, finally letting my exasperation get the better of me. "He'll rejoin us soon enough."

"Yes, because he won't be able to do anything without us," my sister retorted, stooping down to pick up the bag she had dropped.

"Right. So what's wrong with him going out on his own for a bit, wot, wot?" Sir Dagonet said with forced enthusiasm. "A young man's got to stretch himself a little, perfectly natural, don't you know? Can't always be tied down to the ladies."

It wasn't a pretty look that Bridget gave Sir Dagonet, but she didn't say anything more.

<>< ><>

"It's my fault," I said.

We'd been riding all morning in silence, Sir Dagonet alone on his horse, Bridget and me on Dylan's. Bridget had been brooding and angry the whole time. I could practically feel the constant burning of her thoughts, sometimes burning higher, sometimes sputtering. My own mind had been whirling around as well, and now I was certain that what I'd been thinking was right. It was my conscience which forced me to speak out.

"What?" Bridget asked.

"It's my fault Dylan left," I said again, but quietly so that Sir Dagonet would not hear.

"Why do you say that? He left because he's a jerk, thinking that only he is entitled to the chalice." Bridget's words were so full of venom I was surprised I didn't see any flames spring to life anywhere.

"That's what he said, what he told me. But I've been thinking that maybe it was something else." I paused. "Me."

Bridget tilted her head sideways to get a better look at me from behind. "What did you do?" Her words were not accusing. They weren't even harsh as perhaps they should have been. They were simply open and questioning.

I took a deep breath. "Dylan and I were, um, intimate last night." That was a lot harder to admit than I'd anticipated.

I could feel Bridget pull away from me. "Are you kidding me?"

"No."

"You... and Dylan?"

"Yes."

"Why?" Bridget sounded so incredulous I had to laugh.

"Why? Why not? He's handsome, and sweet, and strong."

Bridget was silent for a moment. "I suppose." She sounded very unsure. She gave a little shiver and violent shake of her head. "No. No. Sorry, I just can't see him that way. He's annoying and full of himself."

"No, he's not. He does think he's right more often than not..."

"All the time," Bridget interrupted.

"All right, frequently," I admitted. "But he *is* right a lot of time. He's got more experience than..."

"Not more than me," Bridget protested before I could even finish my sentence.

"Well, more than me. And he knows much more about this chalice than either of us do."

Bridget just harumphed.

"But that's not the point," I said, bringing the conversation back to where I had started. "The point is that... that I'm thinking he might be feeling uncomfortable around me now. I don't know. Maybe he didn't like what we did, or he's worried that I'll feel... I don't know, too attached to him or something." There was silence behind me. "I don't know. I just feel that this is my fault. I shouldn't have done... anything with him."

"Did you like it?" Bridget asked quietly.

"What? Yes."

"*Are* you feeling more attached to him?"

I thought about it for a moment. I really didn't know how I felt about him, aside from the fact that I really liked him. But I'd liked him before we'd become intimate. I didn't think I liked him any more afterward, and I certainly wasn't feeling particularly favorable toward him just now.

"No. It was a moment, Bridget. That was all."

"You're sure?"

"Yes. Absolutely sure. I liked him before it happened. I liked him just as much afterward. And right now I'm so angry at him for abandoning us that I could... could... I don't know do something to hurt him because he hurt me. He hurt us. He had no right to just leave like that."

Bridget laughed, making me try to turn around to face her, but being on a horse made that a little difficult.

"I'm sorry. You're just really funny when you're angry." She became serious again. "But you are right. He had no cause to leave us, and if we run into him again I'm going to do more than just something. I'm going to set fire to his toes."

Chapter Thirty Six

I burst out laughing. "He didn't do that!"

Bridget's shoulders were shaking with her own laughter. "He did. You wouldn't believe the stupid things boys will do."

"No, I wouldn't. My friend Aron would never have done anything that dumb."

"No? Well, then I've got to meet this paragon, because I could tell you so many more stories of my br...of *our* brothers, you just wouldn't believe."

I shook my head in disbelief then started laughing again.

Bridget reached out and grabbed my arm, stilling my hand from piling up more sticks onto the campfire. "Scai, I— I just want you to know I'm really happy you're my sister."

I looked into Bridget's eyes. She had become serious, even though her smile still covered her face.

Sir Dagonet had gone off to see if he could hunt down a rabbit or some other animal for us to eat, leaving us alone for the first time. I loved having the time to get to know my sister. It was magical to hear the stories of her childhood, growing up with five brothers.

I dropped the sticks in my other hand and took hold of Bridget's. "I know *just* how you feel."

Bridget gave me a quick squeeze and let go.

"It's just so funny," I began, picking up the sticks again. "We're so different and we've been raised so differently, and yet...I feel closer to you than I've ever felt to anyone. I almost feel as if I've known you my whole life."

"I know. I've felt that way since the moment you walked into Sir Dagonet's room at the inn in Gloucester."

"Yes!"

Bridget magically pulled a medium sized branch down from a nearby tree. "Do you always do things with magic?" I asked.

With care, Bridget brought the branch to the ground. "Yes. When it's practical. Don't you?"

I just laughed. Bridget realized what she had said and started to laugh as well. "I suppose not," she said, answering her own question.

"No," I said, still giggling. "But perhaps I'll learn." I wondered if Bridget would offer to teach me. I had figured out how to do a lot of things on my own, and I had also learned a bit from Sir Dagonet. Dylan had taught me some magic as well, although now that he was gone...

I was just wondering what everyday things I could do with magic when I heard a sound coming from the trees behind me. "Sir Dagonet must be..."

Bridget screamed, and then something hit me in the head and the world went black.

<><><>

When I came to, I wished that I hadn't.

Even before I opened my eyes, I knew that everything was wrong—there was too much noise, I had a pounding headache, and I couldn't move my arms even though they were hurting terribly. Only after my mind slowly took in all of these sensations, and processed them in a vague and muddled way did my eyes fly open.

I immediately closed them again.

This was a dream. It had to be a dream. A horrible, terrible, awful...but no, my head hurt too much for this to be a dream. I opened my eyes again.

This wasn't a dream—it was a living nightmare.

I looked out at a sizeable crowd of people, all staring up at me. A glance down confirmed my greatest fear—I was standing on a pile of firewood. And yes, the reason I couldn't move, the reason why my arms and wrists hurt so badly, was because I was tied to a stake.

I was going to be burned as a witch!

In my panic, I struggled against the bonds that held me

in place. I wriggled and twisted trying to get free. All I managed to do, however, was hurt my wrists even more against the very tight, knotted ropes that held them.

I couldn't breathe. Air, my precious air, deserted me. My throat closed up as sobs grew heavy in my chest. Tears slipped down my cheeks, but I could do nothing to stop them.

"Aye, that's right witch, cry, for you will burn in hell this evening!" a man yelled out from the crowd.

I looked up. They were all watching me, laughing. I pressed my lips together and held my breath. I *would not* cry in front of these people. Don't give them the satisfaction, I scolded myself.

Bridget. I had been with Bridget when I'd been captured. So where...?

She was there, to my right, tied to an identical stake on another pile of wood just next to me. "Bridget!" I shouted, still squirming even though I knew it wasn't going to do any good. My sister was still unconscious. "Oh, God, Bridget, wake up!"

"Ah, well, at least one of them is awake. That is so much more gratifying," a man said, approaching the bonfire. He looked to be a nobleman, dressed in a fine dark blue tunic with gold embroidery at the neck and hem.

"Please, please, sir, let us go!" I called out, desperation weighing down my words. This was my one chance. Perhaps, just perhaps, I could convince him to release us. "We have done nothing wrong!"

The man threw back his head with laughter. The crowd around us had grown and they too chuckled as if I had made a joke. They were there to be entertained.

"She has done nothing wrong!" the nobleman called out, baiting the crowd. "Tell me, girl, do you proclaim yourself to be a good God–fearing person?"

"I do! I am!" I cried, trying once again to pull my hands free. My wrists burned with the repeated scraping and twisting of the ropes, but I had to get free, I had to. I couldn't let myself be burned at the stake!

"And what do you say to the charge of witchcraft, girl? My men say they saw you and your friend beside you engaging in the worst sort before they captured you."

I didn't say anything. I didn't know what they'd seen. I stopped struggling. "I am not a witch!" I'm Vallen, I added silently to myself. But they wouldn't know what a Vallen was. They wouldn't know the difference. Those who captured us must have seen Bridget use her magic. Naturally, they thought her a witch. "I know no potions or spells."

"You lie!"

"No! It is the God's honest truth."

A knight next to the nobleman turned to the crowd. "I saw her with my own eyes," he said loud enough for everyone to hear him clearly. "I saw her and the other one move sticks without touching them with their hands. They are witches!"

The crowd gasped, thoroughly enjoying the show.

"What say you to this charge?" the nobleman demanded.

I swallowed. I didn't know what to say. He was right: we had moved sticks without touching them.

"There you have it! Her very silence is her admission of guilt," the nobleman called out to the crowd, which responded at once with cheers and jeers. Curses were lobbed at me, as were rotten fruit and vegetables.

I ducked my head and tried to think. There had to be some way to get out of this. My only hope was Sir Dagonet. Dylan was long gone—probably miles away by now. No, it had to be Sir Dagonet. But where was he?

I didn't know how long I'd been unconscious. Could he have come back from his hunting by now? And if he had, would he even realize that we had been taken against our will? Would he think to look here in this town? I stopped and looked around. I didn't even know where I was, how far I'd been taken from our camp. How could Sir Dagonet possibly know where to look?

Oh, God, he wouldn't.

I dropped my head once again as sobs broke from me. It was hopeless. I was as good as dead. If only Bridget would wake up, we could face our death together.

The nobleman picked up a torch and held it toward the knight who struck a flint setting it on fire. Turning back to the crowd, the nobleman raised the flaming torch dramatically.

"For God and King!" he called out triumphantly.

"For God and King!" the people echoed back in one voice.

"Bridget!" I screamed. But it was no use. She was still out cold. "Bridget, wake up, oh God, please wake up!" My tears had started again.

There was nothing I could do. I was going to die.

The man came closer and closer to the bonfire and in a grand gesture sure to please the crowd, lowered the torch first to my pile of wood and then to the one surrounding Bridget.

In horror, shaking with fear, hardly able to breathe for the sobs wracking my body, I watched the fire grow. The heat of it was gentle at first, nothing more than the warmth of a campfire, but too fast it became too warm. And before I knew it, it was lapping at my feet, the acrid smoke burning my eyes and nose.

Reaching out with my foot, I tried to stamp out the flames. I tried and tried, but it was impossible. The only thing I succeeded in doing was to make the crowd laugh and shout with enjoyment at the show I was providing them. Calls of "Dance, witch!" were added to the general jeers and curses that the crowd was still throwing at Bridget and me.

I wanted to scream, but I forced myself to stop—I couldn't give the mob that satisfaction. Somehow I managed to take a deep breath and stop crying.

I held up my head and looked directly at the throng. I might die tied to a stake, but I would die with dignity. Yes, somewhere deep down inside of me there was pride and strength, and I refused to be laughed at as I died.

Deep down inside of me... the fog of panic began to skitter away and my mind started to work. Deep down inside of me wasn't there an incredible well of energy and magic— enough energy and magic to put out the huge fire in Gloucester? Why couldn't I do the same thing here?

I turned my mind inward, reaching for all of my energy, just as I had done standing outside of the inn in Gloucester. I pulled it forth, brought it up, and then focused it into my hands...my hands, which were tied securely behind my back.

How could I put out a fire with my hands tied behind

my back? I couldn't! I needed my hands to direct the magic. Occasional magic I could do with just my mind, but something big like this...

Well, maybe I didn't need something big. Anything would do just now.

I looked up into the sky and called on the wind. Closing my eyes, I concentrated with all of my heart. Come wind, come to me.

My hair waved gently in my face and the smoke began to blow away from me, but that was it. A light breeze was all I could manage without my hands. I needed my hands!

What else could I do? I thought furiously, looking up into the traitorous sky.

"Look at how she prays to her pagan god," the nobleman called out to the people.

They all laughed at my futility.

"Give up, witch," someone called out from the crowd. "Your god cannot help you now."

"My God is the same as yours! I do nothing more than pray for help, pray for just one among you to have the compassion to set me and my sister free," I called out. I looked around at the crowd, but there was no response in their expressions. No, I would find no help there.

I returned my eyes to the sky, searching for a fat rain cloud that could possibly somehow be coaxed to drop its life–giving water upon us. But I didn't have Dylan's powers of coaxing a cloudburst from nothing. All I could see in the blue expanse above were but a few gentle wisps of cloud.

The fire began to singe the hem of my dress.

"Scai?"

I turned toward my sister. Thank God, she was awake. "Bridget! Oh please, please do something! I've tried, but I can't bring on a wind strong enough without my hands. And there aren't the clouds to bring rain!"

Bridget shook her head as if trying to clear it and then looked down at the flames around her. She then looked up at me and smiled. "It's still small enough. It shouldn't be a problem." And as she said it, the flames, which were lapping at her own feet, disappeared altogether. A moment after that, the fire underneath me was gone as well, leaving only smoldering, smoking wood.

The murmur of the crowd became intense. "Witches! They are indeed witches! Did you see that? She put out the flames!"

Women cried out in fear, and some men picked up stray, unburned sticks from the bonfires with which, I supposed, they intended to beat Bridget and me. The nobleman appeared again and in a loud voice called out, "To the river with them! If they will not burn, they will surely drown."

The crowd cheered its relieved approval, and a moment later I found myself untied from the stake and pulled off the bonfire. I struggled briefly, but I couldn't muster up either the strength or the magic to resist with my hands tied behind my back. As I was being dragged away through the town, I glanced back to see that Bridget had also failed to break free and was being forced to follow.

Now what were we going to do? I couldn't swim. I didn't know if Bridget could or not. But no matter what, we would surely drown, just as the nobleman had said.

As we were hauled through the town, I looked around, desperate for anyone or anything that might save us. I thought I saw a man peeking out from behind a closed doorway, watching. Our eyes met and I was certain that he was Vallen—and as terrified of what was happening as I was. He wouldn't help.

As we turned a corner, I nearly tripped over a rock. And then I noticed there were rocks lining the street on either side.

"Bridget," I projected into my sister's mind, *"the rocks! Hit people with the rocks!"*

I twisted around to see if my sister had heard.

Her eyes were wide, staring at me for a moment, and then they shifted to the rocks along the street. One lifted itself and came soaring toward one of her captors. I followed suit with my own barrage of rocks, and soon men were screaming as they were hit by the magically flying rocks.

A man holding onto me saw a rock coming toward him and let go of me to run away screaming. I dropped the rock, but before I could even start to escape, another man grabbed my arm. Without missing a step, he continued dragging me ever faster toward the river and away from the street with the rocks.

There was nothing more I could do. There weren't enough rocks and there were too many men determined to see us drowned.

Our journey ended by the side of a swiftly flowing river. It was wide and terrifyingly treacherous. I knew that even if I had known how to swim, the current would probably be too fast for me to survive, bound as I was.

I took a long look at Bridget, who was still struggling and fighting against our captors. My heart filled with tenderness and regret. I, myself, was about to die, but I hoped my newfound, and now, deeply loved sister would be able to swim away from our terrible fate.

But no matter what, I would die fighting.

Chapter Thirty Seven

I screamed in fury as the men holding on to me began tearing at my clothes. I might be burned at the stake or drowned in the river—but I would not be stripped by strange men. This final indignity I would not tolerate.

I fought, kicking, screaming, and biting anything that came within reach. My hands were still tied behind my back, but I fought like a hurricane. Bridget was holding her own.

"My God, it is a hell–born witch!" one of the men cried out after getting his arm bitten fiercely and his shin kicked as well.

"Leave them clothed!" a woman's voice called out.

"Aye! What is the point in stripping them naked? They are just going to die anyway," another agreed.

I paused in my fight, panting hard. Hardly able to breathe, I prayed that the men would listen. But if they didn't, they would have to physically hold me down while they stripped me.

They looked at each other in indecision until the nobleman spoke up. "Strip them to their shifts. We will leave them that modesty."

This was done, although neither Bridget nor I made it easy. Both of us then found our legs being tied to one of the stakes that had been brought from the town center. Standing next to each other, Bridget turned to me, her face streaked with tears. "We're going to die," she whispered.

"Hush. It's all right. God in His grace will see us through this."

"How?"

I wish I knew.

"Dylan's gone. Sir Dagonet will never find us, and even if he does..."

"If anyone were to find you, it would be your dead body sunk to the bottom of the river," a coarse man said, interrupting Bridget.

"Then we will live forever in God's company in heaven," I said with a great deal more bravado than I felt.

The man scoffed, and the fellow next to him laughed out loud as he continued with his chore of tying our feet securely to the stake.

My mind flitted briefly to Dylan. He had parted from me in anger—was that how he would always remember me? Was it possible that I did feel strongly toward him? I liked him, but did I love him?

Did it really matter now?

I wished that I'd had the nerve to tell him how I felt. Maybe he would have stayed if I had told him how much I liked him. Then, perhaps, we wouldn't be in this situation—about to die.

Bridget bowed her head and truly began to weep. Her shoulders shook with her sobs, but I, with my hands tied as they were, wasn't able to do anything to comfort my sister.

I looked around desperately, searching for a friendly face. There had to be someone somewhere who would save us from this! If only Dylan...but no, there was no one.

No one was going to save us from this except ourselves. *Come on, Scai, think*, I cajoled myself. There had to be something that either I or Bridget could...

"Do you denounce your craft, witch?" the nobleman demanded of us, so everyone surrounding us could hear.

"Denounce my craft?" Bridget asked sniffling back her tears.

"Will you give up being witches and embrace the true and right religion?" he demanded.

"We are Christian," I cried out.

"You are witches!" the man said, appalled at my pronouncement.

I lifted my head and said with a great deal more confidence than I actually felt, "No. We're not witches!"

"How can you lie so boldly when you are about to meet your maker?" the man next to me hissed in anger.

"But..." It was impossible to explain; I didn't even try. Instead I called out, "In the name of God's mercy, set us free and let us go on our way. We swear we will never come near your town again."

"Heretic!" the nobleman cried out in horror. "Go to your rightful place in hell!" He turned his back on us and three burly men came up. One picked me up, another Bridget, and at the same time, the third picked up the stake that was tied to our feet.

Bridget struggled in the arms of the man who had picked her up. I fought and kicked and squirmed with everything I had.

I began to pray—and to cry. I couldn't help it. I wanted to be so brave, but when it came right down to it, I was terrified.

The water was flowing fast, churning and bubbling in a race down its banks. I was given a moment to take a deep breath before Bridget and I were thrown into the water.

The shock of the ice–cold water nearly made me lose the breath I had just taken, but I held it tight. It was ridiculous; there was no way I would be able to hold my breath forever. And right now, it looked like it might just be that long before I came out of this river.

As we sank to the bottom, I struggled against the bonds that held my hands tied behind my back. Desperately, I hoped the cold would make the ropes slack. I did seem to be able to turn my hands more easily, but still the ropes were too tight to allow my hands to come free.

Bridget squirmed next to me. She must have been trying to free her hands as well.

The stake we were tied to hit the bottom of the river with a bump. Still, I twisted this way and that. I wasn't going to give up. Bridget's squirming seemed to have slowed down or stopped. I couldn't feel her moving next to me anymore.

Terrified that she was just going to give up, I opened my eyes and was trying to turn toward her when something slid along my leg. I jerked myself away in fright and looked around.

A fish bigger than I had ever seen in my life had swum up next to me. It was enormous with sharp teeth. Bridget had seen it, too, and was watching it with huge eyes—that was why she had stopped moving.

The two of us watched in horror and shock as the fish took hold of the end of the rope that tied us to the stake—and swam away with it.

As it did so, Bridget and I were dragged downstream. Within moments, the fish stopped and then nudged its mouth right up against the ropes around my leg. Razor–sharp teeth scraped against me, cutting the ropes with a snap. I was free! The fish did the same to Bridget. We both kicked for our lives to the surface.

It wasn't easy reaching the surface without the use of my hands, but somehow, with nudging from the fish, I made it.

I took a huge gasp of air, before sinking back down. But the fish was right there. I could feel its body along my arm and then my hands were free. It must have bitten through those ropes as well.

Using my arms, I pulled myself up to the surface once again—and that's when I heard Sir Dagonet yelling my name. I caught sight of him standing in the water only about twenty feet away, holding out his hand for me. I was so tired I could barely stretch out my arm to him.

I forced myself to paddle toward him. My feet touched ground just before our fingers touched, but I was too tired to even try to stand. I grasped his hand just as Bridget reached for it as well. Somehow, the old man managed to pull us both out of the water. We all tumbled back onto the shore.

A splash at my feet had me turning in time to see the fish that had saved us jump out of the water onto the little beach, changing into Dylan's form as it landed next to me.

"*Dylan!*" I screamed his name in my mind too tired to even speak. "*Thank God you're here. Oh, thank you, thank you.*" He was here. He'd saved us.

"*It's all right, Scai, it's all right.*" Dylan's warm, soothing voice entered my mind, blowing free all of my fears.

"What...? Dylan?" Bridget asked. Lying on her stomach,

her back heaving as she took in deep breaths of precious air, she turned her head so that she was looking in my direction.

I couldn't stop shaking. I was cold. So cold. And soaked through.

"It's okay. You're safe." Dylan's soothing voice warmed my ear.

Relief eased through my body, relaxing my tensed muscles, letting me breathe, finally. But I still couldn't stop the tears from coming. I hated to cry, but I'd been so terrified. I'd been so certain I would drown. That I'd never see Dylan again. Never... It had been too close. If he hadn't.... But he had. He'd come back and saved me.

I rolled over, snuggling closer into his arms, letting his soothing words calm me. He was warm and he held me tightly.

He smelled of the water—ever so slightly fishy, but clean and fresh. I loved his smell, and right now there was nothing so comforting. I rubbed my cheek against his soft skin, against the strong muscles of his chest.

"I didn't think you would come," I said, trying to stop the sobs that were still shuddering through my body.

"I will always be there for you. You know that," he murmured into my wet hair.

"But you were gone!" I'd been so hurt, felt so guilty when he'd left, but perhaps I'd been wrong. Perhaps he hadn't truly left me? Perhaps I hadn't run him off.

"I felt your pain. You cried out to me. How could I ignore that?"

So he did care?

"I did?" I looked up into his warm green eyes, my sobs finally quieting. "I didn't even realize it."

He laughed, caressing his fingers down my cheek. "Whether consciously or not, you called out to me and I came back for you, as I always will."

Relief surged through me. There was hope for us after all.

"I'm so glad you did," I breathed, as his lips descended onto mine. His mouth was sweet and hot, warming me like sunshine. I reached up and ran my fingers through the soft, dark curls that fell to his shoulders.

"I can't lose you, Scai. I... can't."

I didn't know why, but I suddenly found myself shaking. My whole body trembled and I could do nothing to stop it.

"Oh!" Bridget said. "Er, yes, thank you, Dylan."

Dylan pulled away and looked over at Bridget, his cheeks turning bright red. Clearly he'd forgotten, as I had, that we weren't alone.

Bridget rolled away from us and managed to gain her feet. "I'll just, um, go and get dry."

"Fine idea, wot, wot?" Sir Dagonet said. "I'll go find firewood and, er, make a fire to warm you all. We'll camp here tonight. Or, er, perhaps further in the woods. Yes, further in the woods. Wouldn't want to be seen here on the bank of the river by anyone from the village." He stood up and started to go but then turned back to us. "You'll just find us a little ways in, right? Right, right!" He turned and scurried off in Bridget's wake.

I couldn't help but giggle at both Bridget's and Sir Dagonet's discomfort.

"I'm so glad you're all right," Dylan said, caressing my cheek.

I just closed my eyes in bliss and pulled him closer. It felt so good to be pressed against him. He was warm and comforting. He even smelled good—sweet and spicy, fresh and so very...Dylan. I rubbed my face right up against his chest.

And then jerked away from him in surprise. He was naked! That had been bare skin I'd just nuzzled! I dared take a peek down and was relieved to see that he had his leggings on, although they were soaking wet and clung to his form, making it clear just how happy he was to see me.

I swallowed, looking back up into his eyes. He opened himself up to me, allowing me to "hear" what he was thinking, showing me that what his body was displaying was at the forefront of his mind as well.

"Your clothing is hiding about as much as mine is," he said, his cheeks flushing once again, although not quite as red this time.

I looked down to see that he was right. My shift was clinging to me and had become so transparent I might as well have been completely naked. I looked up again to see his Adam's apple bobbing in his throat.

"I think it might be best if we got out of these wet clothes so that they can dry," he said.

I could do nothing more than nod. I was sure that it wasn't merely my face that was flushing, but perhaps my entire body. I felt the heat all the way down to my toes.

Dylan shifted then managed to stand up and peel the leggings from his lower body. I could do nothing but stare. I'd never seen a naked man before. He was beautiful—and fascinating.

Dylan's pack was nearby. After laying out his clothes to dry on the ground, he pulled his blanket from his pack and spread it on the ground away from the water.

It was my turn, but my modesty was so fierce I could barely bring myself to move, let alone pull off my shift. I reprimanded myself, though. Even though I had something on, it didn't do anything to cover me. I might as well be as naked as Dylan and have a chance to get warm and dry.

My legs were still shaky as I stood, but they managed to keep me upright long enough for me to pull my soaking wet shift from my body and lay it out next to Dylan's leggings.

I joined him on his blanket snuggling up close in the hopes that he wouldn't look down at my nudity. Naturally, he did.

Pulling away from me, he ran his hand down my body. "You are so beautiful," he said, a note of awe in his voice.

Again, I was certain I was flushing furiously, but the feel of his hands on me felt so good I didn't want him to stop.

He knew just what I wanted, and I realized he was probably reading my emotions just as I had been able to read his the last time we'd been intimate. His hand found my most intimate place, and his lips my breast. His sucking at my nipple had me arching my back wantonly. I swallowed my shyness and reached out for him, feeling his need for me to touch him.

A soft moan escaped from his lips as I touched his manhood. The sound grew into a steady purr as I caressed him as he'd shown me before. I wanted to do more, but too soon he gently took my hand and moved it away from his penis. I didn't understand. I knew he liked what I was doing. I couldn't have been doing it wrong.

I looked askance at him, but he only smiled and moved on top of me. Holding most of his weight on his arms, he used his legs to separate mine. My mouth fell open as I became aware his intent and his feelings. He wanted to be inside of me with a desperation beyond anything I'd ever felt before.

The tip of him pressed against my heat. Did I want to lose my virginity? But then I looked up into his eyes and knew that this was right. *He* was right. Dylan was definitely the man I wanted to spend the rest of my life with. I didn't know how short or long my life was going to be, but whatever it was, I wanted it to be with him.

I reached up and pulled his head down to mine, kissing him as he slowly entered my body. There was one sharp tinge of pain; then the rest was pure pleasure. I could hear the sound of the sea rushing in my ears. Fell the warm breeze against my skin. I felt as if I were floating free. I *was* the air. I *was* the water. Never had I been so happy. So full. So complete.

I felt too good. I climaxed quickly and expected him to follow, but instead he pulled himself from my body and came in his fist.

And at once I was alone in my body and in my head. I was bereft for a moment but recognized that it had had to end. I let out a soft sigh.

As he rolled over onto his back, I couldn't help but ask, "Why did you do that?"

He looked at me and caressed my cheek with is free hand, the other still wrapped around his penis. "I don't want you to become pregnant. It would make things awkward and difficult for all of us, I would think."

"Oh!" I hadn't even thought of the possibility of conceiving a child, but of course, he was right.

He got up and went back to the river to clean himself. It was cold without his warmth next to me. Cold and lonely.

When he came back he pulled the blanket around me. "I'll get dressed and then get your things so that you can do the same. We should sleep the night closer to Sir Dagonet and Bridget."

I nodded. He was right. It really wasn't safe for us to be separated like this. Both Dylan and Sir Dagonet were fully capable of defending Bridget and me individually, but still, having us all together would be safest.

<><><>

We rode as fast as we could through the whole of the next day, with hardly a word shared. We were all eager to get as far away from the village—any village—as possible.

Even after a day of hard riding, I just couldn't sleep that night. I tossed and turned and couldn't stop fidgeting.

As I stared restlessly at the dying embers of our campfire, I saw a shadow rise behind it. I inhaled, ready to scream—then I saw Dylan's wan face in the dying firelight.

I released my breath. I could still barely believe he'd come back.

And I wondered what had made him come back. *Was* it me? Or was it because he'd realized that he couldn't find the chalice without Bridget and me? After the previous evening's activities, I *hoped* it was me, but I was worried about getting my hopes up too high.

He knelt down and put another log onto the fire and poked at it until it caught.

I stood, shoving aside my fear of finding out the truth.

Dylan looked up, startled by the whisper of my blanket on the ground. But his lips turned up into a smile as I came around and settled myself next to him.

He cupped my face in his hands, kissing me, nipping at my lips with his teeth and being so playful I felt bad about pulling away. But I had to ask. I had to find out why he'd come back. And I had to know if I could trust him not to do so again.

I pulled away, trying to think of a way to start. What could I say? How could I ask this without hurting him?

"I'm sorry," Dylan said with a sincerity that dispelled any and all doubts. He looked deeply into my eyes. "I shouldn't have left."

Had he read my mind? My thoughts? He was looking at me with a seriousness I'd never seen before.

"It was stupid and selfish," he continued before I could say it for him.

"Yes, it was." My tense muscles begin to relax. Could it be that he'd come to his senses? Dare I hope...?

His fingers caressed my cheek. My heart began to pound in my chest again, but this time I ignored it.

"But you came back," I said, searching for an answer, for some sign that my dreams might just be founded in some sort of reality.

"Once I realized what an idiot I was." He dropped his hands from my face. Shaking his head, he looked down at the ground. "It's too dangerous for you and Bridget to travel alone with only Sir Dagonet to protect you."

All of my muscles stiffened once again. "Is that why you came back?" I asked.

He nodded his head and lifted his eyes to mine. "And because I missed you."

That felt good, but it still wasn't enough. I didn't say anything. I just waited, holding my breath and praying for more.

Dylan sighed, finally admitting defeat, although it was clear he didn't like doing so. "And because the chalice is your destiny, too. Yours and Bridget's."

My breath came out as a gentle breeze, making the fire dance for joy before us. Now I allowed myself to smile and fully relax. "I'm so glad you realize that, Dylan. It's important."

He nodded.

"And I missed you, too," I admitted, tightening my fingers around his.

He looked up. "Scai, I..." He paused, and leaned toward me, gently pressing his lips to mine.

I lost my breath as he deepened his kiss. In my mind's eye, the sun came out shining, bright and joyful, and the wind danced around us, sending warmth all through me from my head to my toes. He did care. He did like me. Perhaps even as much as I liked him.

This was happiness through and through.

<><><>

After traveling north for two more days, the road we had been on turned eastward. I didn't realize this until the sun came out from behind some clouds to warm my back late one afternoon. I turned around and squinted up into the sky.

"Sir Dagonet, shouldn't we be heading north? Or west?" I called out from where Bridget and I were riding together.

We were a little distance ahead of Sir Dagonet, so he spurred his horse forward and called out, "What's that?"

"North! Shouldn't we be heading north?" Bridget repeated.

"North. Er, yes. Or west. We'll need to turn west very soon, don't you know?" he called back.

Dylan had ridden ahead as usual. I wondered if he was trying to scout out the route, because it was obvious we were going in the wrong direction.

Bridget brought our horse right up to Sir Dagonet's and said with pained patience. "But we're heading east."

Sir Dagonet looked up at the sun. "Eh? Oh, er, yes, so we are. Well, I'm sure the road turns back north somewhere up ahead, wot?"

"Are you certain this is the right road?" I asked.

"Yes, yes. This is the road that will take us north, and then later we'll head west." I lost the end of his words, as he had turned back and continued heading east along the road.

Bridget turned to look at me for a moment. "I wish I could say that I have complete confidence in him."

I just gave a shrug of my shoulders. I was beginning to worry as well. It had been a very long time since Sir Dagonet had traveled to Avalon. Some things might have changed— the direction of the road, for instance.

Chapter Thirty Eight

Father, I am very sorry to bother you," Lord Lefevre said, coming into du Lac's sitting room.

"Not at all, my lord, please have a seat." Father du Lac stood up and went to a side table. "May I offer you some wine?"

"No, thank you. I'm afraid I am here with some unpleasant news." Lord Lefevre sat down in the chair next to the one Father du Lac had just vacated.

Nimuë was not at all happy to have further bad news brought to her, especially from Lord Lefevre. This did not bode well. She poured herself some wine and drank most of it, bracing herself for the news. She would have to maintain a strong hold on her temper. She was Father du Lac and he never lost his temper.

She took a deep breath and then said with a priest's calm, "What is it, my son?"

Like a child who has been forced to apologize for a wrong, Lord Lefevre stared at his hands for a moment before answering. He spoke to his hands, not even looking up into the priest's eyes. "Those young people you asked us to look out for, the witches. They escaped again."

Nimuë closed her eyes and prayed for patience. Another calming breath. "How did that happen?" she asked with deadly quiet.

"My man had them. Well, he had the girls and was certain the young man would come to rescue them, but he did not. We're still not certain how the girls managed to escape. They were thrown into the river to drown, tied to a stake, but somehow...well, he tells me he is certain that they are not at the bottom of the river as they should be."

Nimuë felt another stab of exasperation pierce her side. "How does he know this?"

Lord Lefevre shrugged and held out his hands. "I believe he has a young man who is a strong swimmer. He searched for the bodies but found none. He thought perhaps the water carried them downstream, and he searched there as well, but they were nowhere to be found."

At this, Nimuë had to forcibly keep herself from uttering the scathing remarks that were desperate to leap out of her mouth.

"Could they...could they have disappeared? Magically, I mean?" the man asked hesitantly.

Nimuë wondered about that for a moment. It was possible Scai could move with the wind if she were powerful enough, but not the other one. She was tied to the element of fire. Deep in the water, she would have been powerless to do anything. No, there must have been...

"The young man! He must have saved them," Father du Lac said.

"But how?"

"I do not know. But that is the only explanation. These witches are wily creatures." She finished her wine and then began to pace back and forth, trying to think of what could be done.

Clearly the trio was too powerful and too clever for ordinary men to handle. The animals she had set on them had been able to hurt them, but it was entirely possible that they would have found some way to defeat them if she had given them more time. No, there was only one choice left.

She had hoped to keep herself, or rather, Father du Lac, out of this fight, but now there was no other choice.

Father du Lac stopped his pacing and turned toward Lord Lefevre, who was still sitting, watching him in silent expectation. "Well, it looks like I am just going to have to see to this myself."

Yes, the more she thought about it, the more logical it sounded. It was inevitable that she would have to become involved. She should have known she could not trust others to take care of something as important as this.

"How, Father? If my men can't capture them or kill them once they have been captured, what do you think you can do?"

Nimuë forced a smile onto du Lac's face. "Show them the way to God. What else can an old priest such as myself do?"

Lord Lefevre opened his mouth. Nimuë didn't know if it was in shock or to tell her what a ridiculous idea that was, but whichever it was, he clearly thought the better of it. He snapped his mouth shut again and stood up. "What can I say, Father? I'm not entirely certain that good luck would cover it."

Father du Lac laughed. "I do not need luck, my son. I have God." And more power than you could possibly imagine, Nimuë added silently to herself.

"So that is it. As soon as you figure out where they are, you are just going to go and kill our children," Morgan's voice said soon after Lord Lefevre left the room.

Nimuë walked over to her silver bowl. Her sister's reflection was shimmering in the water, not looking happy at all.

"I do not see that I have much of a choice, do you?" Nimuë admitted with more honesty than she probably should have.

"Of course you have a choice."

"Morgan, they are destined to kill me if I do not kill them first," Nimuë pointed out to her sister—surely, this was not the first time she had done so?

"But you are forgetting something," Morgan said.

Nimuë frowned at her sister and began to think. "What? The prophecy clearly states..."

"It clearly states the Children of Avalon will find Merlin's chalice and 'then one, with the power of three, the greatest earthly force will be'," her sister quoted. "That is what you are after, is it not? To be the greatest earthly force?"

Her sister knew her entirely too well. "Yes, of course, that is what I want," Nimuë sighed.

"Then what you want is not the children, but the

chalice," Morgan pointed out.

That stopped Nimuë for a moment.

"The prophecy states that it is the one who holds the chalice who will be powerful. It is that magic, Merlin's magic, that will make our children truly powerful, unless you kill them first. But if *you* get the chalice first..."

"Then I will become the most powerful. Why did I not think of that?" Nimuë shook her head. How could she have missed this most important piece? She did not need the children at all—except to find the chalice. "But where is the chalice?"

"That I do not know," Morgan said with a shrug of her shoulders.

"Wait, Dagonet knows. He is taking them there." A smile began to spread onto Nimuë's face. "I suppose I will just have to ask him."

Chapter Thirty Nine

I just don't understand," Sir Dagonet said, scratching his head. "Should have turned north by now, don't you think?"

"I think we're on the wrong road," Bridget said.

"It's looking ever more likely, sir," Dylan agreed.

Sir Dagonet turned and looked at them. "Did we take the wrong fork?"

I turned and looked toward Dylan so that Sir Dagonet couldn't see the utter, bewildering sadness in my eyes. Dylan gave me the smallest of reassuring smiles, but clearly he was just as upset as I was, if not more.

Sir Dagonet had no idea where we were going. We were completely lost and had been for two days now, four if I counted since the day Dylan had saved Bridget and me.

"We went the wrong way at the last fork? You said that you were certain it was this road. I thought you knew where we were going and how to get there! I thought..." Bridget's voice escalated, as did her fury.

I put my hand on my sister's shoulder to stop her. "I suggest we turn back and—"

"Turn back! But we've been going in this direction for two days! It's too late to turn back," Bridget cried.

"All right. Then let's just begin to head north. Leave the road and just head straight north," I offered.

Sir Dagonet looked utterly dejected, but he nodded his head and turned his horse off of the road. "Can't tell you how sorry I am about this, wot? Things seem to have changed," he said, looking around.

"It's been a long time, sir. It's all right," I said.

"It would have been all right if he had just admitted from

the beginning that he didn't know where he was going," Bridget said under her breath. Her chest was still heaving with anger, but she was clearly working on controlling it.

I turned around a little to frown at my sister. "It's all right, Bridget."

"We've come this far. We will certainly make it," Dylan put in.

Bridget, wisely, didn't say anything.

We continued north, edging a little toward the west for most of that day. By late afternoon we discovered another road.

"Ha! Look at this! This road is heading in the right direction, wot?" Sir Dagonet exclaimed with a lot more joy than he had shown for a while.

"This must be the right road. The road to Avalon," I said. I paused to take a deep, thankful breath of air and nearly laughed out loud as a light wind whipped my hair into my face. It was as if the wind itself was telling me that we were now going in the right direction.

Dylan, too, perked up as the road began to follow a stream a little farther on.

<><><>

"Bridget," I cooed softly. My sister had never slept late before. How funny. It was usually Bridget who woke me up. "Bridget, time to wake up," I sang softly in her ear.

My sister just turned over, presenting me with her back. "No. Go away," she mumbled.

"Come along now, Bridget. Got to get going, don't you know?" Sir Dagonet said in cheerful, hearty voice.

Bridget sat up. "What? Get going? Where...oh, right." She rubbed her eyes and stretched.

I just sat back and laughed before getting up to tie our bags back onto the horses.

"Oh, I was having the most lovely dream," she said.

"Really? You'll have to tell us about it on our way," Dylan said from behind her.

She jumped a little then scowled at him. "And so I will," she said, before sauntering off behind some trees to refresh herself.

We were on the road quickly after that.

"So, Bridget, going to tell us about this wonderful dream of yours, wot?" Sir Dagonet asked.

"Oh, yes," she said, around a mouthful of bread. "Well, let's see, I only remember snatches of it. There were some trees. I remember that. Oddly shaped trees. They bent and twisted around themselves like a knot and..." She stopped speaking and gasped.

Gripping my shoulder, she said, "It was the chalice! That's what the tree was wrapped around."

I turned halfway to face her. "What?"

"The chalice? You saw it?" Dylan asked, almost stopping his horse in his excitement.

"Yes! That's what was at the center of the knot of branches. It was a stone cup." She closed her eyes and tried to remember. "What little I could see of it was white—sort of a creamy white stone. But I couldn't see very much because of all of the branches wrapped around it."

"But where were they, these branches? How do we get there?" Dylan asked.

"I don't know. I don't remember seeing anything else but these trees and following the branches inward to find the chalice."

"Don't believe I've ever seen trees like that on Avalon," Sir Dagonet put in.

The three of them turned to him, but he just looked back at them, wide–eyed, with a bit of a smile on his face. "Sorry?"

"What do you mean you've never seen trees like that? Does that mean you've never seen them, or that they aren't there?" Dylan asked.

Sir Dagonet gave a shrug. "Be pretty surprised if something like that grew there. Now, I'm not saying that they don't. Haven't been all over the island, mind you. But it just doesn't sound like something that would grow on Avalon, don't you know?"

"So, is it possible these trees are not on Avalon? That..." I just couldn't say it out loud. I shared a desperate look with Dylan.

"That we've been heading in the wrong direction all this

time?" Bridget finished for me. She had no qualms about stating that most uncomfortable thought.

"Er, well, I don't know. I mean, well, the Lady Morgan did call you to the isle, so we couldn't be traveling in completely the wrong direction, wot?"

"But we don't know that we are heading in the right one," Dylan clarified.

"Well, no, not precisely."

Dylan turned to Bridget. "You've got to remember more of your dream. What else was there besides these trees? Where were they? Were they in a forest? On a plain? In the mountains? Where?"

"I don't know! I don't remember any more than what I've told you," she said, beginning to get angry and defensive.

"It's all right, Bridget," I said, trying to calm her down. I gave Dylan a look telling him to stop his questioning. "Maybe tonight you'll dream of it again, and then you can try to remember more."

"Or I can go into your dreams and see for myself," Dylan offered. "That would be a lot faster."

"Go into my dream? No! Absolutely not."

"But why not?" he asked. "I can do that."

"Yes, I know you can do that. Scai told me all about how you went into her dreams to try and convince her not to come meet our family." Bridget glared at him for a moment. "Thank you very much, but I will not allow you to get into my head. Ever!"

Dylan looked nonplussed for a moment, and perhaps a little guilty as well. "I promise you, I wouldn't do anything but look around and try to figure out where those trees are."

"No."

"But Bridget, if that's the only way we're going to find out where the chalice is..." I wouldn't particularly relish the idea of Dylan entering my dreams either, even after all that had happened between us—unless it was really important. But this was, most definitely, truly important.

"No! And I'm not going to talk about it anymore. It's out of the question."

"But, Bridget," Sir Dagonet tried.

Bridget just kept her gaze steadily in front of her and refused to even acknowledge anyone.

Dylan sighed heavily. I felt the same way, although I didn't vocalize it. There was nothing we could do but continue on in the direction we were heading—until Bridget allowed Dylan into her dream, or she could figure it out for herself.

That night, as we were settling down to sleep, Dylan called over to Bridget from next to me where he'd been sleeping since he'd rescued us from the river. "Bridget, are you certain..."

"Completely. You stay out of my dreams, Dylan!" Bridget called back. "And I will know if you even try."

I didn't know how she would, but I figured that since she grew up in a Vallen family, she knew how to protect herself from unwanted magical invasions into her mind.

Dylan sighed but settled down to sleep. It hadn't always been easy just sleeping next to him, we both wanted to do so much more, but we didn't have the privacy to do so. Instead, we'd had to settle for stolen kisses and "accidental" brushing up against each other.

The following morning, we all looked to Bridget with the hope that she'd be able to tell us more. She, however, kept her eyes on the ground. "All I saw were the trees," she mumbled before going off to refresh herself.

We continued heading west, sometimes bearing northwest, but still generally staying in the one direction. Each day brought us closer to the seashore. The cool sky above became clearer and bluer, if that was even possible. The forest thinned out as we continued to follow the river that would eventually lead us straight to the sea. Each day the wind grew stronger, and we could all feel the heart of autumn descending upon us.

If only we knew where we were going. If we even had an inkling where these trees were. But Bridget was absolutely dead set against Dylan entering her dream and nothing I, Sir Dagonet, or Dylan could do would change her mind.

"I just don't trust him, Scai," Bridget said, without me even asking. She spoke so quietly so that neither Dylan nor

Sir Dagonet, who were both riding a little ahead, could hear her. "I know you two are involved, but I just don't trust him."

"I understand that, Bridget, really I do."

"No, you don't," Bridget said. "I know you like him—a lot, but I just...well, I just can't."

"You don't even like him at all?" I asked, a little astounded at this admission.

"No. I mean, I do like him a little. But I can't trust him. He hasn't earned it."

I was silent. I knew Dylan had done quite a few things that warranted suspicion, but somehow, I knew deep inside of me that he was a trustworthy person—a good man. I tried to convey this to Bridget, but to no avail. Nothing I said could convince her otherwise.

"But Bridget," I said, finally after much debate back and forth, "if you don't trust him, we may never find the chalice."

"No. We'll find it. I'm absolutely certain of that."

As we traveled, I had the oddest feeling we were going in circles. Oh, I knew we were heading west, but every so often something would look familiar, like I'd seen it once before. I just couldn't place where.

There still had to be something I could do to convince my sister to open up to Dylan and allow him into her dream.

I called him over to help me clean up after the evening meal one night. "Dylan, I wanted..."

"I know," he said, interrupting me. He reached out and took my hand. "I've been wanting to be with you, too. It's just awkward with Sir Dagonet and Bridget with us every moment." He gave me a knowing smile and then turned to see if the others were watching us.

I turned, too, but Bridget and Sir Dagonet were involved in their own pursuits and not even looking toward where Dylan and I sat. As I began to turn my head back, Dylan's lips caught my own, startling me. I pulled back, but only for a moment. It was so wonderful to kiss him. To be close to him, but I had more important things to discuss with him.

"Dylan," I started again, continuing before I could be put off or distracted. "You've got to do something about Bridget. You've got to make her trust you."

He stopped trying to kiss me, and instead, just looked at me. "And how do you propose I do that?"

I, too, sat back. "I don't know. But it's because she doesn't trust you that she won't allow you to enter her dream."

He scowled at the knives we were supposed to be cleaning. "Well, I'm sorry about that, but there isn't anything that I can do."

"Please." I put my hand onto his arm. "Can you try talking with her, at least?"

He took my hand and lifted it to his lips. Ever so gently, he pressed a kiss onto my knuckles. "I'll see what I can do, but honestly, I don't have great hopes that it will change anything."

I made sure to leave Dylan and Bridget some space the following day so that they could have a private talk. Bridget wasn't very helpful, though. Each time Dylan tried to get her apart, she moved away from him. Finally, with a strong look from me, she stopped avoiding him.

I didn't know what they said to each other, but neither one looked particularly happy after their conversation. Once again that night, as he did each night, Dylan offered to go into her dreams, and Bridget flatly refused.

Chapter Thirty Nine

"What...?" Dagonet jumped, turning around. A startled "Oh!" popped out of his mouth when he caught sight of her.

Nimuë just stood there for a moment, watching all the color drain from his face. Within moments his rosy cheeks had turned a sour shade of white, not too different from the color of the old man's beard.

"Good evening, Dagonet," she said pleasantly.

"My, my lady," the knight stammered, bowing to her. His eyes shifted to look around him but never moved very far, as if he were afraid to take them completely off her. Smart man.

"Where am I? Where have you taken me?"

Nimuë walked in a slow circle around the man. She had to admit that this was one of her better ideas. She had not taken Sir Dagonet anywhere—she could not, actually, and it was lovely he did not know that even after all this time. She, herself, could move like the wind, taking mere minutes to go someplace that would have taken days on horseback, but she could not move anyone else that way. No, she had simply surrounded them with a glamour that had blackened out everything around them, giving the impression they were someplace else—or nowhere at all.

Nimuë could not help but laugh at her own cleverness.

It had taken her over a full day of watching him and the children to figure out where they were—the river had helped a great deal. And then nearly another day to find Dagonet alone. But now, finally, she was going to find out what she needed to know.

"Tell me where you are taking these children, and I will return you." Direct and to the point. There was no reason not to be.

Dagonet's eyes widened for a moment, but his mouth stayed stubbornly closed.

"Oh, please," Nimuë said, "just say it and we can both get on with our lives in no time." She paused and then added, "Or you can make this difficult and make me force the information out of you. But truly, I would prefer if you would just tell me."

The knight reached across his body, grasping at the empty space where his sword normally hung. But he had already taken it off for the day. Nimuë had, in fact, caught him just as he was getting himself washed and ready to go to sleep. He was clad only in his leggings and the plain rough cotton tunic he wore under his armor.

He let out a frustrated grunt as he realized he was unarmed.

"You *are* going to make this difficult," Nimuë sighed. "It is really not very nice of you. Neither one of us is going to enjoy this. Will you not please reconsider? Note that I even said please."

Honestly, torture was so unpleasant. She did not enjoy it at all, even though, she had to admit, she was remarkably good at it.

"I'll *not* tell you!" Dagonet said, taking a wider stance and stretching to his full height, nearly a foot taller than herself.

Nimuë almost laughed at his bravado. But no, it was not funny, she told herself. It was sad.

She pointed at his head. "Let us see... your most terrifying experience," she said, her voice laden with magic.

The old knight's eyes widened and began to bulge from his head. He dropped to his knees and his hands gripped themselves behind his back. He threw his head back as blood began to seep from a shallow cut that had just appeared across his throat.

Shaking her head in wonderment, she just looked down at the knight at her feet. "Dagonet, let me stop it. Tell me where you are taking the children."

Dagonet pursed his lips together. His eyes were wide with fear, but still he said nothing.

"Very well." She closed her eyes for a moment and gathered together a small portion of her power. "We will add to this the saddest experience you have ever lived through." She moved her fingers, directing her magical energy into his mind, forcing him to recall that heartrending moment in his life.

Tears began to slide down the old man's cheeks. Nimuë watched his mouth working to keep himself from sobbing like a child.

"Tell me, for if you still refuse, we shall add to this your greatest fear. What is it, Dagonet? What do you fear more than anything else in this world? Your own death? Me?"

The old man interrupted her musings. "Avalon," he whispered. "I am taking them to Avalon."

Nimuë's attention snapped back to the man at her feet and a slow burning began in the pit of her stomach. "Why? Is that where Merlin hid his chalice?"

Dagonet tried to shake his head, but it was as if someone was holding it steady. He could just barely move it from side to side. "No. The Lady...Lady Morgan called for them."

The name exploded in her mind. Morgan! She should have known.

As fury engulfed her, she let go of Dagonet's mind and watched him fall onto his face. The world faded back into existence a moment before she flew off on the wind.

<><><>

"How dare you!" Nimuë said a moment later, appearing just behind her sister.

Morgan spun around. She had been speaking with three of the priestesses of the isle on the green just outside of her own home. The evening, as always on Avalon, was perfect—crisp and clear with just a nip in the air to remind you of the oncoming winter.

"Nimuë!" she exclaimed.

She turned to the priestesses who had begun to back away from Nimuë the moment her name had been spoken. "We will continue this later," Morgan said. The women nodded and bowed low to them both before walking away as quickly as they could.

Morgan indicated her home. "Please, let us go inside where it is warm."

Her sister's calm was almost more than Nimuë could bear, but she managed to hold on to her temper until they were alone in her sister's sitting room.

"How could you?" Nimuë growled out once again.

"How could I what?" Morgan asked, feigning ignorance.

"You know very well what. You called to them. Had Dagonet bring them here. How dare you interfere."

Morgan had the grace to stay quiet. She lowered her eyes to the ground. But then she turned and poured out a glass of wine from the decanter on the table next to her.

Holding it out to her sister, Morgan said, "Honestly, Nimuë, you need to calm down."

Without a thought, Nimuë knocked the wine from her sister's hand, sending the blood red liquid flying all over the low white cushioned chairs. "I do not want to calm down. You have explaining to do." Nimuë did not take her eyes off her sister.

Morgan lifted her chin a touch. "Very well. I could not let you kill them. I told you when we spoke that I could not, but I knew you would try to do so anyway. So I called them here—where I can protect them."

"Protect them? You think to protect these..."

"Yes, Nimuë. I am planning to do so. Not only that, but it is imperative that I do." Morgan's temper was beginning to flare as well. It was not a common occurrence, and Nimuë felt a brief shiver of pride at having provoked it.

"It is only imperative for you to take from me from everything I most want," Nimuë said, feeling her old anger growing inside her. "You have always done so—two hundred years have not changed anything."

Morgan let out an exasperated sigh. "You know that is not true. I have not interfered in your life for all this time, have I? I have let you play your little games with the king, and whoever else you have wanted to manipulate."

"Then why are you bothering me now?" Nimuë cringed

inwardly as she heard the plaintive childlike tone of her voice.

"Because this is important, Nimuë. The Children of Avalon are our future. I cannot simply allow you to kill them."

"Our future? You mean *your* future. It is I who they are destined to kill, did you think about that? Do you even care if I die?"

"Of course I do. I care a great deal," Morgan said, taking a step toward her.

"Then why do you want to protect them? If you truly cared about me—if you loved me—you wouldn't be protecting them, but *helping* me to kill them. For if I do not kill them, they are going to kill *me*!"

"I know that, and it saddens me more than I can say..."

Nimuë scoffed at her sister's false words. "Lies! What lies!"

Morgan's face grew troubled. Why? Because she was telling the truth, or because Nimuë had seen through her false words?

"I am sorry you think so," Morgan said quietly.

"Stay out of this, Morgan," Nimuë warned her. "And stay away from those children."

And with that she turned and left her sister's home. Fury and hurt warred within Nimuë as she stalked down to her precious lake.

Her sister was doing what she always did—had always done. She was consolidating her own power and making sure Nimuë did not get any. It was so clear. And so painful.

Morgan wanted to have the powerful Children of Avalon under her sway. She would have control over them, their powers, and the chalice—and through them, Morgan Le Fey would once again be the most powerful being in the world.

In a fit of anger, Nimuë dove into the crystal clear water of the lake and turned it black. Wherever she swam, she left the ice–cold water surrounding her black and dead.

Dead. That was how she wanted those children. Before Morgan could get a hold of them and Merlin's chalice.

Chapter Forty

Sir Dagonet stepped out of the woods and just stood at the edge of the camp. It was such an odd thing for him to do that I paused in my work.

And then I noticed he was shaking. I took a step closer and saw blood on his collar.

"My God! Sir Dagonet, what happened?" I cried, rushing over to him.

He just stood there, his cheeks completely drained of their color. Gently I guided him forward. His hands were like ice.

"Bridget!" I called out as I led Sir Dagonet closer to the fire. I needn't have, because Bridget was right there. I just hadn't seen her come up from behind.

"What is it, sir?" my sister asked, taking Sir Dagonet's other hand.

Still he said nothing.

We seated him by the fire, and Dylan handed him a cup of wine to soothe his nerves. Dylan pulled me away and said quietly, "I'm going to take a look around. Don't move away from here until I return, do you understand?"

I nodded, feeling my muscles tightening in fear. He pulled his sword from his pack and stepped into the wood from where Sir Dagonet had come.

Sir Dagonet had dropped his face into his hands while I had been speaking to Dylan. Bridget was holding his empty cup and kept a comforting hand on his back.

"I can find nothing wrong with him—physically, that is," she said, clearly worried. "If there's something that's bothering his mind, I can't tell, I'm...I'm not good at that."

"Dylan is, but he's just gone to see..."

"There's nothing there. She's gone," came an anguished whisper from Sir Dagonet.

I turned back to the old man. "What do you mean 'She's gone'? Who was there?"

"Lady Nimuë," he whispered so softly I could barely hear him.

But just at the name, Bridget jumped up and looked around as if she was about to appear right next to us.

"Where was she, sir? What happened?" I asked, as I fought hard to keep from trembling.

Sir Dagonet lifted his head and took a shaky breath. "She was there, in the woods. She, she...oh, God, what have I done!" His face dropped down once again into his hands.

Dylan came back just then. "I couldn't find anything or anyone. Whoever it was, they must be long gone."

"It was Lady Nimuë," I told him.

"What?" Dylan had just been about to put down his sword, but he took it right up again.

"Sir Dagonet says she met him in the woods, but we don't know what she did to him."

"Dylan, is there something you can do?" Bridget asked. She had returned to soothingly caressing Sir Dagonet's back. I was surprised, first at Bridget speaking so nicely to Dylan, and second that she was trusting him to take care of Sir Dagonet.

Dylan paused to look at Bridget and then looked down at the old man. He nodded. Putting aside his weapon once more, Dylan took my place on Sir Dagonet's other side. He placed a hand on the man's shoulder. Then he closed his eyes and concentrated.

After a moment, Sir Dagonet let out a relieved sigh. He wiped his cheeks with a shaky hand as he looked up at the three of us. It was clear he was still very upset, but at least now he was able to look up.

"Thank you," he said, patting Dylan on his arm. "It's horrible what she does to a man, don't you know?"

"No, I don't know. Why don't you tell us what happened?" Dylan suggested.

Sir Dagonet shook his head. His fingers were fiddling with one another, those of his right hand disappearing up the other sleeve in his usual nervous habit. Finally, he gave a great sigh and said, "All I can tell you is that I've done a terrible thing."

"What?"

"Told her where we were going," he said, shame weighing down his words.

The three of us sat there in silence, digesting this. I wasn't entirely certain what it meant. So, Nimuë now knew we were going to Avalon. Did that make a difference? Surely, Lady Morgan would protect us?

"Don't you see, it's now even more important that we find that chalice—before she does," Sir Dagonet explained.

"She's going to try to find the chalice?" Bridget asked, with a bit of a squeak in her voice. "How could she do that? It's not destined for her."

"Doesn't matter. It's got power, wot? That's all she cares about, don't you know?"

We all turned toward Bridget. She was the only one who could help us to find the chalice. She had the answer in her dream, if she would only let Dylan in to find it.

"It's the three of you who will be most in danger if she finds it before you do," Sir Dagonet said, his face more serious than I had ever seen it. "She'll have Merlin's power, and she won't hesitate to use it to kill you."

I looked at Dylan, but there was no comfort coming from him. It was stark truth Sir Dagonet shared. One that couldn't be denied.

"You need to work together," Sir Dagonet continued. "You need to be a team. No more of this not trusting one another." He looked at Bridget. "And no favoritism as best as you can help it." He looked from me to Dylan. "I know there are feelings here. Deep feelings, but you have to work together, the *three* of you. No matter what. You must have each other's back and support each other in every way possible. If you don't..."

"There is no question, sir," Dylan said without hesitation. "Together we will fight or together we will fall."

It sounded like something Dylan had learned when he'd trained to be a knight, but it was the truth. It was the way we had to live. I knew it. Recognized it.

And so did Bridget. She sighed and nodded her head. "All right, Dylan."

Dylan reached out and gave her arm a gentle, reassuring squeeze. "I will look to see where these trees are and that is all, I promise."

I cleared my throat. I should probably have done this in private, but it seemed that now nothing was private. "Dylan, I think we should put... whatever it is we have aside."

Dylan looked at me, his eyes straying momentarily to Sir Dagonet and Bridget. No, he was not happy to have this discussion in front of them, I knew it. But I'd started it, and so I would finish it.

"After the chalice is found and Nimuë is taken care of, we'll have the rest of our lives to... do whatever we want. But if we don't deal with Nimuë first..." I paused and tried to put this into words he'd understand. "We started on a quest. We can't let anything... *anything* distract us from it until it's completed." I looked at him, sadness filling my heart. It wasn't easy, and it wouldn't be easy being so close to him and yet unable to do anything more, or to be anything more than just friends, but it was essential. I knew this. I just hoped Dylan would recognize it, too.

When Dylan nodded his head in acceptance, I released the breath I'd been holding. "You're right." He shifted once again to look at Bridget. "There will be no favoritism. No... anything until we find the chalice and defeat Nimuë."

Sir Dagonet let out a satisfied sigh. "Good decision."

<><><>

I had hoped to be awake when Dylan went into Bridget's dream, so I could watch him and find out where we would have to go.

But when I opened my eyes it was to the bright morning sunshine. I sat up immediately. I had moved back to sleeping closer to my sister. Sleeping so close to Dylan would have just been cruel—to both of us.

Bridget was just lying back under her blanket, staring up

into the trees.

"Well? Did Dylan go into your dream? Do we know where the chalice is?" I asked.

Bridget turned her head toward me. "I don't know really. I mean, I saw him there in my dream, but then he walked off while I stayed with the trees, following the branches through to the chalice as I have every night. I suppose you'll have to ask him."

I turned to look for him, but he was nowhere in sight. For a panicked moment, I wondered if perhaps he had left again. But then I saw his horse nibbling at the grass, and relaxed.

A few minutes later when he came out of the woods, I got up. "So? Do you know where we need to go?"

"Yes. We need to head due west from here to reach the shore. From there it shouldn't be too far," he said, giving me a smile. "It's very close to a jut of land that sticks out a bit into the water."

"Remembered the jut of land," Sir Dagonet said, joining us. "Just didn't remember where it was."

"Have you been there, sir?" I asked.

"Oh, yes. It's from a little village there that I have taken the boat to Avalon."

"So this tree is, in fact, very close to the island?" Dylan asked.

"Should be, wot?" Sir Dagonet smiled. "Merlin must have chosen it because of that. Very fond of the island, he was, don't you know?"

I was so relieved to see Sir Dagonet back to his old self again that I laughed at his silliness. "Yes, I suppose he would be, since that was where Lady Nimuë lived and they were very close at one time, weren't they?"

Sir Dagonet winked at me. "Just so. Just so."

As we mounted our horses, even Sir Dagonet's optimism had returned. "We'll get there long before Lady Nimuë even figures out where we're headed, wot, wot?"

"That's right, sir," Dylan agreed, but the look I saw in his eyes didn't seem to be quite as optimistic.

"Of course we will," I concurred and gave Dylan a very

determinedly cheerful look.

He just laughed and shook his head before clicking his horse into a walk behind Sir Dagonet.

We rode as fast as we could that day, pushing the horses and ourselves. It was clear we were all eager to get there.

By afternoon, we broke free of the forest. I stopped my horse and took a great deep breath of the salty, fresh sea air. The water shifted in front of me in its unending dance. Forward and back, a lick up here, a pull there—I was mesmerized by the beauty of it, at the delicate lapping of the waves and at the immense strength of the water as it pulled back on itself before bounding once again onto the beach.

But as I stood there watching the sea dance before me, something else was lapping at my memory.

I had seen this before, but where?

I looked around me at the forest, the trees, the rocks that were scattered about on the shore. No, this wasn't quite right. But it was close. We were very close; I was certain of that.

The wind picked up, welcoming me to its shores. I jumped down from my horse, landing on the soft sand at my feet. Bridget joined me, as did Dylan and Sir Dagonet.

"It's magnificent!" Bridget said in awe as she looked out into the endless sea.

"Incredible!" I agreed.

"Neither of you ever see the sea before, wot, wot?" Sir Dagonet asked. Even he seemed to be a little in awe of the majesty before us.

"No," Bridget answered.

I didn't say anything. I'd never been to the coast, but somehow this was all very familiar, though I just didn't know how it could be.

"It's hard to tell, but I think that jut of land is just a little to our north," Dylan said squinting up and down the beach.

"Yes. That's exactly right," I agreed.

Everyone turned to look at me in some surprise. I laughed nervously. "It...it seems like the most reasonable thing," I said, with a shrug. I didn't want to admit to having been here before, because I couldn't remember when I had— if I had. It was all rather confusing.

As we traveled on, everything became ever more familiar to me. And just as a huge wave crashed over a boulder that had been negligently tossed on to the shore, it came to me in an instant.

I had seen this all in a dream. I had traveled this path, walked down this shore. I would know the place where the chalice was the moment we reached it.

Bridget was getting ever more antsy behind me, fidgeting this way and that, even making the horse nervous. The closer we got, the more she fidgeted. She finally gave up and just jumped off.

I pulled up on the reins. "Bridget!" I hadn't even stopped the horse. We had been at nearly a trot when my sister had jumped down. She could have easily been hurt.

"Wot? wot? Is this it?" Sir Dagonet exclaimed.

Bridget flipped around to face the old knight. "No, I just, I just can't stand it. We're so close!"

"We are, I can feel it," I added.

"I recognize where we are, but it's farther down the beach," Dylan said, about ready to jump off of his horse as well. The animal did a little sidestep, but he controlled it firmly and kept moving forward.

Bridget picked up her skirts and started to run. Her bright red hair, which had been tied into a neat braid, now had tendrils dancing wildly all around her, like the flames of a campfire. We slowed our horses to match her pace, but Sir Dagonet was overly eager and moved ahead.

And then Bridget stopped. She just stopped in the center of the beach, her hands on her hips, panting from her run. At first I thought she'd just gotten tired, but then I felt it.

We were there. We had reached the place.

There was nothing but a feeling, a tingle in the air that told me I was right.

Sir Dagonet, however, had ridden right by.

"Sir Dagonet!" I called out, but he didn't hear me above the sound of the water.

"Sir Dagonet!" Dylan and Bridget called out in unison.

"Eh?" he turned.

"We're here!" Dylan called out.

Bridget had already turned toward the forest. Slowly, reverently, she approached the trees, as if they were royalty.

And, indeed, they wore such vibrant colors they could have been royal. Brilliant red, gold, and orange leaves flared toward the sea like flames. The wind picked up and the branches swayed, bowing their greeting. And all the while, behind them, the water crashed upon the shore and yet retreated with grace so as not to get any of us wet.

It was a most perfect place.

I closed my eyes, just feeling the wind on my face, smelling the fresh air, the richness of the earth, and the salt of the sea. My ears were filled with the constant thunder of the waves. But beyond all of this, I felt the thrumming of magic. It was like a vibration that made my blood rush through my body and my heart sing with joy. I felt free and happy. I felt...home.

Yes, this was the feeling of coming home.

A feeling I'd reveled in after meeting my brothers. It was happy and sad, exhilarating and overwhelming. A rush of emotion thrilled through me such as I had never felt before.

I opened my eyes to share my joy. Dylan was looking rather pale. I climbed down off my horse and went over to where he stood peering into the woods.

"Are you all right?"

He shook his head clear and then turned to look at me. He seemed to force the smile to his lips, but he said, "Yes. It's...it's a little overwhelming, isn't it? So much magic, concentrated into one place."

"Yes," I said, reaching out and touching his arm. I wanted to calm him, to reassure him, somehow.

His smile became true, reaching into his eyes as he placed his hand on top of mine.

"But these aren't the trees." Bridget's voice broke into the moment.

Dylan turned to look and then moved forward to stand next to Bridget at the edge of the forest. He reached out to touch the beautiful leaves. But she was right. These weren't the leaves of the intertwining trees that I remembered from my dream. These were the leaves of ordinary oaks and beeches.

"They must be here," Dylan said, with a slight panic to his voice. He plunged headfirst into the thick growth that bordered the beach. But the branches were too thick for him to go very far very fast.

Bridget was smaller and more lithe. She passed him, ducking under and climbing over the branches that formed the dense barrier. "Here!" she called out.

"Is it there? Do you see it?" I asked from just beyond the tree line.

"Wot, wot? Is it there?" Sir Dagonet said, coming up from behind me.

"I don't see the chalice yet, but the trees are here. They're..." she paused.

I had lost sight of her, but Dylan was continuing to climb in after her. I could hear him moving among the branches. I gave up waiting for them. Holding up my long skirts, I journeyed forward to try to see where Bridget had gone and to try to catch up to Dylan.

It wasn't easygoing. I could barely take a step forward for all of the branches that poked out at me, twisting this way and that and stopping me from reaching the treasure that lay inside.

"What is it, Bridget?" I asked as I came closer. My sister was just standing, half crouched under a particularly large branch. She turned as Dylan and I drew near. "They're dead," she said softly. "The trees from my dream. They intertwined in this same way, holding the chalice. Do you remember, Dylan?"

"No. I didn't get close enough to see them. I went off to try to find where they were," he said.

"Oh, well, there were three of them, just like this. In fact, I know that these are they. Only, in my dream, they were alive with green shoots among the brown of the branches. But these trees—well, they're dead."

"And so will you be, soon," a low voice said just behind us.

We all turned at once.

Shivers shot through me. I fought hard to keep myself

from shuddering too obviously. Lady Nimuë stood on the beach, looking into the tangle of dry branches where Bridget, Dylan, and I stood.

"I thank you for finding Merlin's chalice for me. Honestly, I could not have found it on my own. But I knew it would call out to you. That it would tell you where to find it. And here you are!"

Chapter Forty Two

Nimuë smiled and opened her hands out in an almost welcoming gesture. "The chalice is there?" she asked.

Not one of us answered her. In fact, we hadn't even seen the chalice yet, but we all knew it was there. We could feel it—or at least, I could, and I was pretty sure the others could as well. But none of us were going to admit as much to Lady Nimuë.

"Have you children no manners? I asked you a question," Nimuë said, her voice hard and demanding.

"But we shall not answer it. Now, be gone!" Dylan said with none of the fear that was making my stomach ache.

"I would do as he says, my lady. I don't want to hurt you," Sir Dagonet said, holding his sword at the ready just behind her.

"*You* do not want to hurt *me*?" Lady Nimuë laughed. "You have been very helpful, Dagonet, but I am through with you for now." With a negligent wave of her hand, Sir Dagonet was suddenly frozen into place.

"Sir Dagonet!" I cried out. I spun around for help from Dylan, but as I did so, my eyes passed not just Lady Nimuë, but four of her!

One was standing outside of the tree line on the beach, but another was standing near Dylan, and there was a third on the other side of Bridget. And, just a few feet from me, staring at me with those implacable eyes, was the fourth.

Four Lady Nimuës. I couldn't imagine anything more terrifying.

Until the world exploded.

Rain poured down, the wind whipped at us, and

lightning shot out from the sky, targeting us and the tree. Huge waves crashed against the shore, sending ice–cold water pouring into the forest. I stood frozen in fear and confusion, as the wind whipped my hair into my face.

But with that slap of wind, a gust of clarity burst open my mind. I could do something about this. It only took a moment's concentration.

Reaching deep inside of me, I pulled my energy together. With a quick wave of my arm, I made the wind stop. Looking up into the sky, I willed for the clouds to disperse and the rain to cease. And beside me, I realized that Dylan was making the sea water recede while Bridget froze the lightning.

But it wasn't going to be that easy. It couldn't be.

The Nimuë standing closest to me pulled back her hand and sent a sphere of concentrated energy straight at me. It glowed a swirling blue, red, and yellow as it flew.

I didn't know quite what to do for a moment, but my instincts kicked in—with a wave my hand, I sent a blast of wind gusting toward the sphere. It disappeared.

But immediately, it was replaced by another, and then another. I wasn't fast enough. Lady Nimuë was sending the spheres more quickly than I could extinguish them.

As the energy spheres hit me, they hurt, burning my skin and causing excruciating pain. I ducked one coming straight at my head and caught sight of Bridget battling the same things coming from the Nimuë closest to her. I didn't have time to even look to see if Dylan was in the same situation, I just assumed that he was.

From off to my right, I heard Sir Dagonet's war cry. Somehow he must have gotten free of the spell. But then there was a grunt before I heard, "What the…?" She's not real! I can't hurt her."

"No," Dylan called out, "It's a glamour, an illusion."

"Three, no four of her, wot?" Sir Dagonet said, his voice heavily laden with awe. "That's four too many, I say."

"Which is the real Nimuë?" Bridget called out.

The air filled with laughter as all four Nimuës threw back their heads and laughed out loud.

Sir Dagonet, brandishing his sword, forged into the

trees. He took a swipe at the Nimuë battling Dylan, but his sword just glided right through her.

"Old man, you are beginning to annoy me," all four Nimuës said, in unison. A glowing sphere of fire and energy flew toward Sir Dagonet. It hit the brave knight squarely in the chest and sent him flying out onto the beach. My heart lurched into my throat.

"Sir Dagonet!" Dylan shouted and reached out toward him, but got his hand caught by the branches.

My fear for the old knight made me involuntarily take a step backward. I started to trip over a limb that was just behind my knees, but grabbed hold of the branch directly in front to stop my fall.

A frisson of magic shot through my hand and a low creaking sound began under the earth where we were standing. The ground began to shift. I held on to the branch, but the movement stopped.

Nimuë looked up, catching my eye. For a moment I couldn't move. I was locked in Nimuë's gaze, helpless even as the witch pulled her hand back to form another energy sphere. Fear trampled through me, but my arms would not respond.

"Dylan, hold on to your branch again," Bridget called out, with excitement lacing her voice. "And keep holding it!"

Nimuë turned to look at Bridget, freeing me to see Dylan swing back around and grab the branch that he had just been holding. I sagged with relief as I turned back to my sister, who was holding on to a knot of branches just next to her, also trying to keep her balance. My fingers gripped onto my own branch ever more tightly, ignoring the rough bark that dug into my hands.

The creaking sound started again, and once more the ground gave a slight tremor under my feet. For a moment, I wondered if the earth was going to split apart and swallow us all with the way it shifted and buckled under me. This was almost as terrifying as Nimuë's magical spheres.

"No!" the Nimuë closest to Bridget suddenly screamed—and that was when I noticed that shooting up out of the ground were what looked like the tree's roots. They were wrapping themselves around Nimuë's legs, climbing her body. The other glamours faded away as the real Nimuë tried to push the roots off. She even aimed some of her energy spheres at the tree, but that only seemed to make it grow even more quickly.

"No! Stop them! Stop them!" she screamed, trying to escape, but they were too strong.

I didn't know what the roots were doing to Nimuë, but for the first time I had a feeling that the woman was just as scared as we had been. It was stunning to see her truly frightened.

If I weren't so terrified myself, I might have done something to help Nimuë—I just couldn't stand to see anyone so upset, no matter how much they deserved it.

Nimuë looked up at the three of us with pure fury on her face. "I will not allow you to win. *I* am the most powerful Vallen in this world and you are nothing but *children.*"

And then she disappeared. Just like that.

I looked around. Was this another illusion?

"She's gone!" Bridget shouted and let out a whoop of excitement.

"Is she really?" I asked. I could hardly believe it.

"No, wait. It's got to be another trap," Dylan said, climbing toward me.

Bridget stopped and looked around, but all was quiet. The tree root that had held onto Nimuë silently slipped back into the ground, like a harmless earthworm.

For almost a full minute, we all stood there, ready for any sudden attack, sure that it was going to come.

Waves crashed onto the beach with a gentle thunder. Yet there was silence in the trees all around us. A leaf began to unfurl itself from the branch still in my hand.

"The tree!"

Dylan was next to me in a moment. Bridget looked all around her and gasped, "It's coming to life!"

"Did we do that?" I asked, unable to keep the awe from my voice.

"We must have," Dylan began.

"With our magic," Bridget finished.

"And Nimuë?"

Dylan's smile spread across his face, lighting up his eyes like the sun reflected in a calm pool of water. "She's gone!"

Chapter Forty Three

The tree attacked Lady Nimuë and she retreated," Dylan said, as amazed as any of us.

"She wasn't meant to be here, I suppose," I said, trying to make some sense of what had happened.

"No, but we are," Bridget said, moving forward once more.

"But what about Sir Dagonet?" I called after her.

Bridget turned around for a moment. "It's all right. He's coming to."

I turned around, and indeed, the old man was beginning to stir.

"Let's get the chalice, shall we? Then we'll take care of Sir Dagonet," Dylan said, beginning to climb toward me.

There was nothing I could do but go along, telling myself he would be all right. I turned back toward Bridget and started to climb farther into the wood.

All around us, the trees had begun to come alive. The branches showed new life. They bent, instead of breaking, when I pushed past them—and I could even see some new shoots beginning to grow out of them. It was just incredible. It was as if, with our combined touch, the trees had taken a deep breath and begun to live once again.

And they were beautiful, folding in on themselves, bending this way and that, forming complicated knots, the branches leading us further in toward the center.

With one more twist of myself between two closely growing branches, I stopped next to my sister. She stood, finally upright, staring into the center. There the trunks of the three trees stood, at their center— the chalice.

It was just as I had dreamed. Branches intertwining, wrapping around its base, up and around the cup of white stone. As I got closer, I could see that some of the lines moving up the cup weren't branches at all, but the veins in the stone. It all blended together so perfectly, that it was almost difficult to distinguish the stone of the cup from the branches supporting it. It was, truly, a cup of the Earth.

Dylan reached out his hand and tried to take the cup from the branches, but they refused to let go. As he began to reach toward them with his other hand, Bridget grabbed it instead.

"You can't just tear at them and hurt the trees," she reprimanded him.

"Well then, how to you propose we get it?" he retorted.

"This way," I said, taking Bridget's other hand. "All together."

And then with my free hand, I, too, reached toward the cup. As soon as my fingers touched it, the branches began to loosen their grip.

My fingers intertwined with Dylan's as we wrapped them around the chalice. My eyes met his. Warmth flowed through me, engulfing me as surely as if I had sunk into a bath of joy and happiness.

A small smile played on his lips as he looked at me. His hair stirred with the warm breeze of the good feelings I was sending to him.

We were sharing something very special, very...intimate.

In a flash of shyness, I turned toward Bridget and pulled her into our warmth. "This is the way it should be. With the three of us. Together."

Bridget's brilliant smile burst onto her face with all of her fire sparking from her eyes. "Absolutely. It takes all three of us," she said, turning to Dylan and even sharing her smile with him.

He nodded his head in acknowledgment. "Yes, the three of us, together."

And when I turned back to look at the chalice again, it was Dylan, Bridget, and I who were holding it. The branches had completely fallen away.

I followed Dylan back to the beach as he climbed through the branches, holding the chalice triumphantly.

Sir Dagonet jumped up from where he was sitting in the sand. "You did it! You got it!"

Dylan stopped. With a broad grin on his face, he turned to Bridget, "No, sir. *We* got it. It took all of us." He handed the chalice to Bridget. "Not one of us could have done it alone, right, Bridget?"

Her eyes flashed with fire as she took the cup from his hands and her mouth fell open a little in wonder. I could hardly believe my strong, brave, and bold sister was awed by this cup. But then a slow smile grew on Bridget's face, and she turned back to Dylan. "That's right. It needed the three of us."

"Not like taking on three knights at once, eh? Anyone can do that, wot?" Sir Dagonet said, hovering close to the chalice.

The warm glow that had been wafting through me intensified. I smiled at Dylan, who gave a little laugh. "Well, I don't know that just anyone could take on three knights as you do, sir. Not everyone is so strong or brave."

"Or stupid," Sir Dagonet added, laughing. He turned back to Bridget. "Mind?" he asked, indicating the cup.

"What? Oh, yes, go right ahead." Bridget handed it over.

"Huh, not quite as impress..." and there he stopped, his eyes widening as he looked at the cup in his hands. He handed it right back to me and began to shake out his hands as if he had been holding onto something too hot.

We all looked at him, laughing.

He joined in after a moment saying, "Fingers tingling, don't you know?"

"It is powerful, isn't it?" Bridget said, rubbing her own hands together.

"So what do we do now?" I asked, voicing the one nagging little thought that had been plaguing me ever since we'd come out from the trees.

"What do you do now?" Sir Dagonet repeated in shocked tones. "What do you mean?"

I got the distinct feeling that he didn't know either,

which was why he was just repeating my question back to me. I smiled, holding back my laughter.

"We're supposed to kill Lady Nimuë, isn't that right, sir? This will give us the power to do so," Dylan said.

"What? I'm not going to kill anyone!" Bridget burst out.

"But Bridget..." Dylan began.

Bridget turned on him. "I am a healer, Dylan. I do not kill."

"Not even someone like Lady Nimuë who would kill you in a heartbeat? Who, in fact, just tried to do that not a quarter of an hour ago?"

She turned away from him and took a step closer to the water. "I just want to go home," she said, so quietly that I almost didn't hear her above the sound of the waves and the wind that had picked up.

Was the wind because of me? I didn't think I'd done anything. I looked up at the sky and then out toward the sea. The others did the same.

But Bridget repeated herself, just a little more loudly. "I want to go home."

"Home," a voice repeated. It was a soft, gentle voice that came in on the wind.

"What was that?" Dylan asked, looking around. "Did you hear..."

"It was the wind," I said. That was what it sounded like to me.

"But it said home," Bridget said.

The wind whipped a little harder, but it wasn't an ordinary cold autumn wind. It was a warm breeze, filled with sweet scents of ripe fruit trees and grain freshly harvested.

"Come home, my children. Come home."

Another gust of wind suddenly came up from behind us, almost pushing us into the water that lapped out toward us, touching our toes with its icy fingers before receding once again. It was as if it was calling to us. Drawing us in.

Bridget looked toward me, curiosity covering her face. She wasn't scared, but rather concerned, as anyone would be who heard voices in the wind. Oddly enough, though, what would have terrified me just a few months ago only intrigued me now. Magic and anything related to it had become a part of my life, a part of me, and I accepted it—even when I didn't completely understand it.

"Well, I suppose that's what we ought to do, then, wot?" Sir Dagonet said with his usual cheerfulness.

"What?"

"You heard her. She wants you to go home," he said, nodding out to the sea.

"See, I told you, we should go back to Gloucester," Bridget said, brightening right up.

Dylan laughed. "I don't think that she meant that home, Bridget."

She frowned for a moment. "Then what home do you think?"

"Avalon," I answered for him. "That was Lady Morgan's voice. I remember it from my dream. She wants us to go to Avalon."

There was silence for a moment as we all looked out to sea and toward the island that lay through the mist, just out of sight.

Sir Dagonet started, "Right! Going to Avalon, for which we'll need a boat, don't you know?" He strode over to his horse as if everything was settled and we knew just what to do and where to go.

I had no idea where we could get a boat, and I didn't know whether Bridget would willingly travel on. She seemed to be pretty homesick. But neither Dylan nor I said anything. We all just followed Sir Dagonet.

Dylan took the chalice from me and wrapped it safely among the clothes in his bag before mounting his own horse.

We rode the rest of the day, following the beach south, then east around the inlet, then once again to the west following the land around the water. As usual, Bridget and I rode together.

"Don't you want to go home, Scai?" Bridget asked me quietly as we were riding.

I didn't know. I wasn't even certain where home was any more. "I don't know, Bridget. I don't know if Tallent is my home or if Gloucester is. I miss Father Llewellyn and Aron very much. I would love to go there to see them again," I said, thinking aloud.

"I didn't mean that. I meant home to Gloucester. That is where our family lives," Bridget said.

"Our family?" I turned and gave my sister a smile. "Right now *you* are my family. I was very happy to meet my brothers, but I don't know that they are the family I was searching for. You, Dylan, and Sir Dagonet are my true family."

"Wot? Wot?" Sir Dagonet said, hearing his name being spoken.

I turned to him as he rode up next to me. "I was just saying to Bridget that you, she, and Dylan are my family now."

"Oh!" He smiled at that thought. "Like a father to you, am I? Well, I am honored, honored, I say, wot?"

I laughed. "Well, I was thinking more along the lines of a grandfather, but yes, something like that, sir."

We all laughed at that, Sir Dagonet the loudest.

"Bridget is truly your sister," Sir Dagonet said, "and Dylan is like a brother, eh?"

My face became warm. I didn't think of Dylan like a brother. Not at all like a brother!

Bridget must have seen me, for she burst out laughing again. "I don't know that Scai thinks of Dylan in that way, sir."

"Oh?" He looked over at me and then at Dylan. He, too, had turned surprisingly red. "Er, no I don't suppose you do, wot?"

I was blushing furiously now, I could feel it. But I knew that Dylan and I shared something special. Even though we couldn't act upon it just now, there would be a time when we would.

Dylan cleared his throat awkwardly but gave me a smile I felt right down to my toes. "However it is, I'm also proud to be a part of your family, Scai."

"Thank you," I said, nodding my head in acknowledgment.

"You've been searching for your family for a long time," he said. "I'm glad you finally feel as if you've found it."

I turned to him and returned his smile. "I have." I then

looked over at Sir Dagonet and back to Bridget. "I truly have. I suppose I needed to find my real family in order to realize that one didn't need to be related by blood to be true family."

"I have a true family, I always have," Bridget said. "And I miss them terribly, but I think I know how you feel. Even if it means gaining another brother," she added, looking over at Dylan.

He just laughed and reached out his hand to grab hers. "Well, I've never had a sister, but judging from the way I get along with you...well, I have a feeling it's not going to be easy."

He said this with such a warm smile on his face that Bridget didn't take any offense to it at all. In fact, she laughed and said, "Oh, you should talk to my real brothers. They'll tell you—with no hesitations—how difficult I am."

"I'm certain they would!" Dylan laughed.

Sir Dagonet just shook his head and chuckled.

The cool air caressed my skin as we rode on, reminding me of all the wonderful things and people that now made up my life—Bridget and Sir Dagonet, my magic, and, of course, Dylan, whom I was certain would continue to make my life much more interesting and exciting. Yes, I realized with a start, now I was whole. I had my family, we had the chalice, and we were going home—to Avalon.

It was late into the night when we reached the inn of the little fishing village on the sea.

"This is it," Sir Dagonet said, dismounting stiffly. "We'll get some rest and then, first thing in the morning, we'll find a boat for hire."

"And go to Avalon?" Bridget asked.

"Yes. Then you'll get to meet Lady Morgan in the flesh." He paused and stared off into the sea for a moment. "A wonderful lady she is. Truly a wonderful lady, wot?" he said, obviously picturing her in his mind.

"I look forward to meeting her," I said, putting my hand into his large warm one.

Dylan took my other hand, then Bridget's. "So do we all."

"And we'll do so together," Bridget added.

"Just as we will meet Lady Nimuë, all together," Dylan added.

That was something I was not looking forward to, but it was inevitable, I supposed. But as long as I had my family around me, I would be able to face anything.

Next in the
Children of Avalon Trilogy

Coming out April 16th, 2014
Water: Excalibur's Return

Dylan has never been good enough. Neither his foster-brother nor his father have ever thought so. But now, finally, Dylan has a chance to demonstrate what he can do in the most difficult of situations. Dylan is the only descendent of the great Merlin and a member of a magical race known as the Vallen. One of the Children of Avalon, he knows he is strong enough to defeat Lady Nimuë. But when Dylan thinks he can take her on on his own, he is quickly shown otherwise.

When not even the love of a beautiful and powerful woman is enough, what will it take for Dylan to prove that he is worthy of taking on the greatest threat Britain has ever faced?

Coming out May 12th, 2014
Fire: Nimuë's Destiny

Bridget isn't sure she has what it takes to be a leader, but she's about to find out. The witch hunts are getting worse by the day. But when Lady Nimuë kidnaps Bridget's own family things get personal. Only Bridget, the brilliant Scai and powerful Dylan—the prophesied Children of Avalon—have the power to defeat Lady Nimuë. The question is, does Bridget have the strength of will to lead them through to the end?

When Scai's childhood friend, Aron the blacksmith, joins their group, Bridget is suddenly faced with a new challenge—this one from her heart. Will her love for Aron get in the way of defeating Nimuë, or will it give her the confidence she'll need?

About the Author

Meredith Bond is an award–winning author of a series of traditionally published Regency romances and indie–published paranormal romances. Known for her characters "who slip readily into one's heart", Meredith's heart belongs to her husband and two children. Her paranormal romances include Magic In The Storm, Storm on the Horizon, and the short story "In A Beginning". Her traditional Regencies include The Merry Men Quartet of which An Exotic Heir and A Dandy In Disguise have recently been republished. Meredith teaches writing at her local community college. If you want a taste of her class in book form, Chapter One is available at your favorite e–retailer.

Want to know more? Come visit Meredith at her website, www.meredithbond.com or chat with her on Facebook at "Meredithbondauthor" or Twitter @merrybond. If you'd like to be one of the first to know of Meredith's new releases and get a free vignette four times a year sign up for Meredith's newsletter.

If you enjoyed *Air* please write a review, lend it, and recommend it to a friend.

Made in the USA
Charleston, SC
10 March 2014